Praise for
## The Last Bridge

"The debut novel of the year."  —*Huntington News*

"*The Last Bridge* is Teri Coyne's debut novel, and it's a winner. Cat is a richly compelling character. . . . Readers will laugh at her sarcasm and share the pain of her horrific past, all the while hoping that she finds a way to move forward and learn to live again."
—*The Free Lance–Star*

"Thrumming with a desperate, malevolent intensity, Coyne's debut novel is a psychological tour de force, a disturbing yet ultimately redemptive tale of the burden of secrets and the tenacity of love."
—*Booklist*

"[A] compelling debut . . . Coyne's prose effortlessly carries the reader through a thorny history and into possible redemption."
—*Publishers Weekly*

"Teri Coyne grabbed me from the first page and never let me go. I read through the night until I came to the last lovely chapter. *The Last Bridge* is a whirlwind of a book."
—Amanda Eyre W͏          ͏or of *Forgive Me*

"Cat is an unforgettable cha          ͏          *ge* is at once searing and authentic          ͏          elling mystery, a family dram          ͏          e first page and you won't be able t͏          
—Masha          ͏          of *The Camel Bookmobile*
and *The Distance Between Us*

# THE LAST BRIDGE

# THE LAST BRIDGE

A NOVEL

Teri Coyne

BALLANTINE BOOKS TRADE PAPERBACKS

NEW YORK

2010 Ballantine Books Trade Paperback Edition

Copyright © 2009 by Teri Coyne
Reading group guide copyright © 2010 by Random House, Inc.

Published in the United States by Ballantine Books, an imprint of The Random House Publishing Group, a division of Random House, Inc., New York.

BALLANTINE and colophon are registered trademarks of Random House, Inc.
RANDOM HOUSE READER'S CIRCLE & Design is a registered trademark of Random House, Inc.

Originally published in hardcover in the United States by Ballantine Books, an imprint of The Random House Publishing Group, a division of Random House, Inc., in 2009.

LIBRARY OF CONGRESS CATALOGING-IN-PUBLICATION DATA
Coyne, Teri.
The last bridge: a novel / Teri Coyne.
p.  cm.
ISBN 978-0-345-50732-7
eBook ISBN 978-0-345-51705-0
1. Mothers and daughters—Fiction.  2. Suicide victims—Fiction.
3. Domestic fiction.  4. Psychological fiction.  I. Title.
PS3603.O975L37 2009
813'.6—dc22    2009020278

Printed in the United States of America

www.randomhousereaderscircle.com

2 4 6 8 9 7 5 3 1

Book design by Julie Schroeder

For my father

What would happen if one woman told
the truth about her life?
The world would split open.

—MURIEL RUKEYSER

# THE LAST BRIDGE

# ONE

Two days after my father had a massive stroke my mother shot herself in the head. Her suicide was a shock—not the fact that she killed herself but the way in which she did it. It was odd that my mother chose such a violent end to her own violent life. For someone who had endured years of torture at my father's hand, I thought she would choose a more quiet way of leaving. Perhaps she would take pills and put herself to bed in a silk nightgown, or she'd walk naked into the ocean at sunset. Instead, she cleaned the house, changed the linens, stuffed the freezer full of food, and blew her head off with my father's shotgun.

Ruth Igby, the ugly neighbor down the road, passed the farm several times that weekend and noticed the garage door swinging open. Ruth assumed my mother was at the hospital taking care of my father and took it upon herself to close it. As she got closer to the house she noticed a light was on in the kitchen and thought my mother was home. There was a strong glare coming off the snow that had accumulated into large boulderlike masses against the sides of the house. Ruth couldn't see anything until she shielded her eyes with her left hand and pressed her face against the side window. What she saw made her fall into the screen door and tear it loose from the top hinge. She grabbed the mesh for balance and ripped it from its frame, leaving it flapping in the wind.

I didn't ask Ruth how she got my number or if she had called the others. I listened to her sedated slur, compliments of the town doctor, Joshua Kramer. "Not your Dr. Kramer," she said. "His son. Remember Joshy?"

I didn't answer.

"Even in the end your mother didn't want to make a mess. She taped garbage bags to the walls of the kitchen and covered the stove with a drop cloth. She was always thinking about you kids."

"Right," I said.

I can't imagine what my mother was thinking that Thursday afternoon in February as she pulled open the utility drawer and searched for the masking tape. Was she humming or listening to the radio? Was she thinking about Paris? Or heaven? Or her kids? Did she perform her final act the same way she washed the dishes or mashed potatoes? Was it part of her weekly to do's? Did she scratch "Kill yourself" off the list, between "Call about furnace" and "Buy toilet paper"?

When I was a little girl I asked my mother what she saw before she fell asleep. I asked in the hope she would say she saw me. She said, "I don't see anything. I'm too tired." She was always so goddamned tired. She moved through the chores of her life like she was sleepwalking. It's no wonder she chose to end her life. What didn't make sense was the timing. Why would she do it now that she was so close to being released from her life sentence with my father? Maybe that was the problem. Maybe she couldn't imagine a life without torment.

I wish I could ask her what she saw before she pulled the trigger. I don't need her to say she saw me. I want to know she saw something. That she felt something. And that it felt like freedom. And then, if I could, I would ask her what that felt like.

I drove through the night, stopping only to pee or to replenish my stash. I had been driving for ten long hours before I started seeing signs for Wilton. The illuminated exits rolled by like months being torn from my life's calendar. Ten years had passed since I had seen or spoken to my mother. I only wished it had been that long since I had thought about my life here. I felt the craving again, like hunger but more urgent. I reached under the passenger seat and grabbed the bottle of bourbon I hid for emergencies. I took a long hot swig and pulled off the highway and onto County Road 48.

I found the farm easily. I could find our house of horrors in the middle of a blinding snowstorm.

I turned left onto the dirt path that led to our driveway and saw the big white house standing on top of a rounded hill skirted by snow-covered fields. A few of the green shutters had fallen from their hinges, and in spite of what looked like a new paint job, the place was daunting, like a man standing with his arms on his hips daring you to knock him over.

Hal White, the local sheriff, was leaning against his patrol car sipping a jumbo cup of 7-Eleven coffee and chomping on a dough-nut when I pulled up. I had called ahead as Ruth had instructed and asked him to meet me. I got out of the car and lost my balance from too much sitting and drinking. I steadied myself and popped a Tic Tac in my mouth. Hal tossed what was left of his coffee into my mother's prized geranium bed and headed toward me. I hadn't seen him since he tried to feel me up at a high school football game the year everything ended. I thought of his callused hands grabbing at my bra as he wiped his sugarcoated fingers across his regulation starched sheriff's pants.

"Hey, Cat," he said, walking with a policeman's swagger, as if the gun were between his legs and not at his side. "Sorry about your mom." He took his hat off and tossed it in his hands. He was as wide as he was tall and had a pebble-colored beard that clung to the edge of his jaw like gravel on the side of the highway.

"Thanks," I said. Cat is my nickname. It's short for Alley Cat. My real name is Alexandra but my family used to call me Ally. Then my sister, Wendy, called me Alley Cat and then just Cat. After a while, I was known in Wilton as Cat.

"Listen, why don't we do the coroner first, then you'll have time alone in the house. I'll drive." He climbed into his car and pushed a pile of folders and crumpled-up paper from the passenger seat to the floor. He leaned across the seat and opened the passenger door. "Sorry about the mess. This is the only place I get to live like a bachelor!" He smiled, revealing a gold cap on one of his inner teeth. I leaned into the car and tried my best to focus on Hal and not the crap he was trying to make disappear.

"I'll be right with you. I have to use the bathroom." I started for the house. The screen door was leaning off to the side with torn mesh waffling in the breeze.

"No!" Hal shouted, running after me. I stopped and felt the crunch of ice under my feet. For the first time since I got out of the car I realized I was not dressed for the harshness of the weather. After I got the call I threw on a ratty old sweater and a pair of dirty jeans and slid on my cowboy boots. My feet were so cold I wondered if I had remembered socks. The air against my cheeks felt like small brittle twigs scratching me. I wrapped my arms around myself and felt colder. Hal ran up in front of me, blocking my way to the door.

"Don't do this alone," he said, dangling the keys in front of me as I tried the door.

I stepped aside. Hal tried a series of keys until he found the one that fit. The door still stuck and required a shove before opening. A rush of heat carried the ghost smells of coffee and cinnamon cake.

"I guess Ruth told you there wasn't a lot of cleanup. Your mother made it easy." I was waiting for him to say that he wished all suicide victims were as considerate, but he didn't.

I stepped into the tiny mudroom facing the kitchen. Hal walked in and dropped the keys on the table that was covered with the same rooster-patterned oilcloth that had been there when I was a kid.

The room was alive. The clock above the pantry ticked, the radiator on the back wall hissed, and the floorboards creaked. Water dripping from the faucet into the sink clopped like horses walking on pavement. The sounds pressed against me like one heart resting on another, syncopating.

The morning sun poured through the window over the sink, highlighting the spot where the yellow linoleum was worn thin from all the hours my mother stood washing dishes and looking out onto the fields. White flecks of dust swirled in the light. My mother called them fairies.

"Let's go," I said. I stepped into the kitchen to wave him out. My need to leave overshadowed my need to pee. I was calculating how much bourbon I would need to come back later and stay. I wondered if there would ever be enough.

"She left this." Hal reached across the table and picked up a piece of lilac-colored stationery inside a ziplock bag and walked toward me with his hand out.

"I don't want to touch it if it's evidence."

"Your mother did that to . . . keep the blood from getting on the note."

"Jesus Christ," I said as I shook my head. "She put her suicide note in a ziplock bag?"

"Pretty considerate, huh?" Hal said.

"I was thinking along the lines of pretty sick," I replied, pulling the zip open, leaving one side yellow and the other blue. I thought of the commercials challenging the many uses of the special "green" seal and wondered if Glad would get a chuckle out of this one. "Yes, folks, if you were going to blow your brains out, which bag would you choose for your suicide note?"

"I'll give you a moment," Hal said, quietly brushing past me for the door.

I looked up at the empty room, and then at the letter safely ensconced in its protective coating, and thought that a trip to the coroner would be easier. "Let's go," I said, dropping the bag onto the table while taking as few steps into the room as possible.

I offered to follow Hal to the morgue in my car but he insisted on driving. "This way we can catch up," he said, flashing a gold-tinted smile. This was the first time he actually acknowledged that we knew each other.

"Great," I said, wishing I had put a small bottle of something in my purse.

"You're never going to guess who I married." We pulled off the dirt road that led to our farm and the Igbys'. "Do you want a hint?" he said, turning onto the main road of town. Murphy's Five and Dime was now a Kmart Express. Benny's coffee shop was a Dunkin' Donuts, and the sidewalks that used to be so wide you could ride a bike down the middle without knocking anyone over had been turned into parking spaces. Main Street had turned into the main strip. Outside the 7-Eleven, which used to be Sammy's Stop-n-Sip, kids in clown-sized pants rocked back and forth on skateboards, bummed cigarettes from one another, and coerced strangers to buy them beer. Some things don't change.

"Ginger LaCooke," he said, and then looked at me like the name was supposed to mean something. I shook my head.

"Don't you remember Ginger LaCooke?"

"Nope," I said, staring at the boarded-up Tastee Freez, where my sister, Wendy, had her first French kiss and I had my first French custard.

"Ginger LaCooke was on the cheering squad. She wore the mascot uniform for football games, remember?"

"Yeah," I said, resisting the memory. "Are we almost there?"

"It's ahead," he said, pointing to a squat cinder-block building in the distance. "I'm sorry, here I am going on and here you are—"

"She was one of the Purple Possums."

"Huh?" He pulled into the parking lot of the county coroner's office.

"She was the Head Possum, the one with the powder puff on her ass."

"Oh, right. Yeah," he chuckled. "Good for you, you remember!"

"Yeah, good for me," I said, getting out of the car. I sighed, imagining what ten years and a shotgun had done to change the look of my mother.

I was cold despite the wall of heat bearing down on me as we entered the county morgue. Hal had called ahead to tell the coroner we were coming. He was waiting at the door and introduced himself as Andrew Reilly, County Coroner, like he was auditioning for the role. He didn't shake my hand so much as cradle it. I guess that was meant to comfort me but, like his introduction, it seemed like something he read you were supposed to do. The only thing comforting about him was his voice. He had an even, relaxed tone that could lull you to sleep.

"She's down this way," he said as our footsteps echoed in the gray hall. Hal was trailing a few paces behind, as the corridor wasn't wide enough for three people and his hat. "I know this must be difficult. What I usually tell people in these circumstances is to . . ." Andrew Reilly, County Coroner, rattled on about what one could expect, as if one can be prepared. He was tall and flush with the orange color of a winter tan, not in the least bit crusty and bald, like I figured someone who hung out with corpses would be. Hal followed us so closely I was afraid he would slide up my ass if I stopped suddenly.

The end of the hall was punctuated by two silver metal doors. We stopped together as Andrew stepped forward and pushed a button that opened them. He led Hal and me into a small puce room filled with empty metal tables. "Your mother's over here," he said. I followed the movement of his arm as it arched toward her table as if he were a maître d' uniting me with my dinner partner.

For a moment, hearing someone say, "Your mother's over here," I thought she was waiting for me in a chair, with her purse resting on her lap.

"Hey, Mom," I would say, and smile the smile I saved for her and my school picture.

"Miss Rucker, over here," the coroner whispered to me, guiding me gently by the elbow.

She was in a bag.

As I looked at the zippered closure I thought about how much she would approve of the container. Instead of "Ashes to ashes," the preacher should say "Ziplock to ziplock."

"As soon as you can identify her, let us know," the coroner whispered as he unzipped the bag and pulled down the sides. "Your impulse is to look at her face, but try not to. It's in bad shape."

In bad shape? The woman put a shotgun in her mouth and express-mailed her brains to heaven. I think her face is in worse shape than bad. Christ, he made it sound like all she needed was a little powder and lipstick.

I didn't have to look at her face to know it was my mother. I didn't even have to look any farther than her left hand that was dangling off the metal table. I nodded and turned away.

"That's her," I said.

"How do you know?" the coroner asked.

"The wedding band," Hal answered, looking at me for confirmation.

"The tip of her ring finger," I said.

Both men looked closely. "Ah," they said in unison as they noticed my mother's finger was missing the first joint and nail bed.

"Was that a birth defect?" Hal said.

"No . . . marriage," I replied, searching my bag for a cigarette. "My mother tried to leave my father once. He found her, brought her home, and cut the tip of her finger off. He told her if she ever tried to leave again, he would cut her hand off. Needless to say, she never left after that. Anybody have a light?"

# Two

I T WAS LUNCHTIME when I got back to the farm. The sky was overcast, making it feel later than it was. I pulled my car into the garage and closed the swinging door that had alerted Ruth Igby to my mother's end. I came into the kitchen through the mudroom.

I was rarely alone in our house. My mother was always there, cooking, scrubbing, dusting, or doing laundry. It was hard to know where she ended and the house began. To me the two were inseparable; her smell filled the house, or was it that the smell of the house filled her? I could never tell. Both smelled like oranges and cloves and, during the holidays, pine needles and cinnamon. When she hugged me, her dresses smelled like my sheets and when I slept my sheets smelled like her.

Out of habit I headed for the refrigerator and opened it. As a child I checked the contents of the refrigerator to make sure that life would go on. If there was milk there was hope. An empty refrigerator meant my mother had given up. Food was the barometer by which I measured her commitment to staying. Although she only tried to leave once, I worried she would do it again. I was more afraid of what her leaving would do to me than to her.

The refrigerator was well stocked. On the top shelf was a jug of homemade lemonade and a stack of bologna and cheese sandwiches, my favorite lunch. She knew I would come.

I went to the sink and threw up.

I sat at the table with a damp towel in one hand and the note in the ziplock bag in the other. Before I opened it, I brought the towel to my face and took in the scent of the lavender water she used in the laundry.

I woke up a few hours later with my face stuck to the bag and a banging in my head that felt like a frying pan smacking against my temple. The kitchen was dark, except for the eerie orange glow from the light I forgot to turn off in the garage. All Ruth Igby needed was to find another Rucker facedown on the kitchen table. I got up slowly, working out the kinks in my neck and shoulders from sleeping hunched over. I turned on the light and filled the kettle with water and found my way up to the bathroom. The house had not changed. The floorboards on the third and fifth stair still creaked under the pressure of my feet, and even though I was the only one there, I locked the bathroom door behind me.

The white subway tile on the walls was the same, as was the black-and-white octagonal floor. The porcelain of the basin had been scrubbed way past polish, and although it was clean, there were small nicks showing the black cast iron underneath. The claw-foot tub, with its deep wide bottom and shower curtain that wrapped around like a hoop skirt, was the only welcoming sight. As a child I soaked for hours with the curtain pulled tight and my head immersed halfway into the water. I would stare at the ceiling, soothed by the slow-drip faucet, and imagine how my life would be away from the farm. I never heard my sister screaming or my brother calling, or the pounding of my father's fists on the door. I only heard the sound of the water and of my own heart beating in anticipation of places far away.

The shrill of the kettle whistling jolted me. I ran to the kitchen, turned off the burner, and searched for a tea bag. I hit the jackpot when I found a vodka bottle behind the coffee in the pantry. My mother had probably hidden it from my father during one of his bad spells. I filled my mother's rose china cup and forgot about the tea, grabbed a bologna and cheese from the fridge, and sat next to my mother's note.

The letter was facedown and written on a small sheet of lilac stationery that looked as if it had been torn in half. I flipped it over and took a swig of vodka and felt a warm surge of relief flow to the tips of my fingers.

Through the plastic I recognized the careful script resulting from my mother's Catholic school education. Whenever I marveled at it, she laughed and said, "Anyone can write nicely if they have the time." Judging from the penmanship, this was a note my mother had taken her whole life to write.

> *February 23rd.*
> *Cat,*
> *He isn't who you think he is.*
> *Mom xxxooo*

My hands shook as I slid the note out of the bag and held it to the light, not sure of what I hoped to find—a hidden message or a hologram of her smiling as if to say, "Gotcha!"

*He isn't who you think he is. . . .*

I counted the words including the hugs and kisses. Ten, minus the date—one for every year I had been gone.

I worked the note into the bag and tried to press the seal together but could not make it stick. Every time I thought I was on track, I let go and saw the bag creeping open. My fingers became slick and less steady with every attempt to get it back in.

But there was no getting back.

I pushed myself from the table, tasting the acid backwash of vodka as I rushed the stairs. Halfway up I stopped, feeling the pull of the bag on the table, imagining it opening and closing, breathing in the air from the kitchen.

I crept back downstairs and hovered over the table as if I were checking on a sleeping baby. I wiped my palms against my back pockets and reached over and sealed the bag in one swift motion, then grabbed the bottle off the counter and cut the light.

I finished off the vodka as I waited for sleep. After tossing in my bed for hours, I tried every other bed in the house until I fell asleep in the tub several hours later.

"Are you going to stay like this forever?" White light punctuated the cool baritone of Jared's voice as I struggled to keep my eyes open.

"Turn it off." I pulled myself up from the semifetal position I had been dreaming in as the room faded back to the blue-gray of morning. "How long—?" I started to speak, but winced at the pain that shot through every miserable muscle in my body.

"Just got here," he said as he leaned in and wrapped his massive arms around me and lifted me out of the tub in one swift motion.

"Christ, Cat . . . you're skin and bones." He hugged me hard, pressing my ribs against his. My cheek brushed the soft cotton of his pressed shirt as I took in his familiar smell of baby powder and sweat. In spite of everything, my body remembered his.

I pushed away. Jared stepped back and raised his hands in surrender. I caught my reflection in the medicine cabinet mirror and saw what he had seen: dark puffy circles under bloodshot eyes, unwashed hair waving in clumps away from my face, and pale cheeks with hollow indents where dimples used to be. It was hard to believe there weren't two corpses my brother had come to bury.

"You alone?" I asked, as I rinsed my mouth with icy water.

"Yeah," he said. "You?"

I nodded. I wiped my mouth with a hand towel cross-stitched with a snowman and then looked over at him. Jared had morphed from a sweatsuited linebacker into a Wall Street banker with starched khakis and a long-sleeved navy polo shirt neatly tucked in and pressed. His chestnut hair was cut short and hugged the sleek curve of his neck. The bow of his front teeth was gone, replaced by flat porcelain white caps. His new smile revealed the teeth he used to hide. His milk chocolate eyes were all that remained unchanged.

It had been seven years since the night in the motel when he walked away. The rain pounded around him as he pulled a Penn State windbreaker over his head and climbed into his fiancée's Jag. I watched from the doorway of the room I had been holed up in for three days feeling the ricochet of the raindrops crackle against my face and neck. Jared had tracked me down and had almost convinced me he cared until he explained why he came. I threw him out and made a solemn vow to drink until I forgot. I was still trying.

"Coffee?" he asked, as I followed him to the kitchen.

I didn't want coffee.

Downstairs, a pot was brewing and a box of Krispy Kreme doughnuts was on the table next to the note he had taken out of the bag.

The room felt small with Jared, me, and the elephant of our shared history wedged between us. Drinking quieted the elephant.

"Did you see the bologna and cheese?" I asked, as he pulled the milk from the fridge without looking, just as he did every morning growing up. I was expecting him to take a swig from the carton but he didn't.

"Creepy," he said, shaking his head, checking the milk label. "Whole milk; you'd think she would have bumped down to low-fat at some point."

Outside the wind whipped the screen door open and shut. Inside, the coffee bubbled in the percolator on the stove, releasing its throaty aroma.

Jared poured the coffee, holding the handle and the lid with pot holders, the way my mother did. In the light of the kitchen I saw how much like her he was, from the almond shape of his mouth to the hesitant way he pulled the cup toward him, blew, and then licked his lips before sipping gently. He even closed his eyes and tilted his head back, savoring the rush of caffeine like she did. Jared and I sat quietly, sneaking looks at each other, assessing the impact of time.

His hair was a salt-and-pepper mix of dark brown and gray. His complexion was smooth and worn, like the leather on the underside of my purse. He was handsome with my mother's plain oval features and my father's strong bones and hands. As a child I spent hours lying in the grass studying his face. Whenever Dad got rough Jared would take me to the flat patch of field behind the barn and make up stories from the shapes of the clouds. "My hero," I'd exclaim when he'd slay the dragon in his cloud tales. Sometimes I'd trace shapes on his cheeks with a blade of grass. I knew the geography of his face better than I knew my own.

"I never thought I'd see you again," he said, breaking the silence. His fingers circled the rim of his cup. "I miss you."

I got up and poured myself a cup of coffee and looked out the window. "When is Wendy coming?"

"Cat?" he said.

"Wendy?"

"This afternoon." I could feel his stare as he waited for me to turn around so he could give me another imploring look. I refused to turn around.

"Who called her?"

"I did."

"You talk?"

"Sometimes."

"Mom?"

"Sometimes."

I nodded. So everyone kept in touch. My leaving hadn't changed anything for them. Good to know. Jared tapped his fingers against his mug. I imagined myself running in the fields barefoot and numb.

"Why did you come?" Jared said.

"Mom left me the note."

"So?" he said.

"She knew where I was; she gave Ruth my number."

When I got the call, it took a while for me to place the voice. I had been sleeping off a binge and had the cloudy half-awake sense that I was dreaming the conversation. Her words were strong: *shotgun, blood,* and *stroke.* A note addressed to me. It wasn't until I was on the George Washington Bridge that I realized I was going back.

"I gave Ruth your number," he said.

"I thought Mom—" I gripped the edge of the counter.

"No."

I dropped my cup in the sink as tears filled my eyes. The idea that she knew where I was had gotten me here. I should have known better. What kind of mother lets her daughter go and never looks for her?

"I'm tired. I'm going to take a bath," I said.

"That's all you have to say?" he said.

I turned from the stairs and looked at Jared, who had moved to the sink and was looking at me. His expression was a replica of one my mother had mastered, with pleading eyes, open mouth, and desperate restraint. "Forgive me," it seemed to say.

"Call me when Wendy gets here," I said, taking the steps two at a time.

Wendy arrived as I was drying my hair. I heard a car door slam and looked out the window. She was standing by the open trunk of a car barking orders at an old bald guy as she loaded him down with suitcases and bags. "Get this. Your hands aren't full yet. Where are you going? There's more stuff to carry!"

"Has anyone called the hospital to see if Dad is all right?" Wendy asked as I came down the stairs. Jared sat staring into space, wincing at the piercing tone of her voice as his leg twitched a mile a minute under the table. Wendy eyed me up and down, taking me in as if I were a contestant in a beauty pageant she was judging. Wendy works with what she has and thinks everyone is obligated to make themselves as attractive as possible. I could tell by the way she pursed her lips that I was not obliging my looks. She was right.

I had lost the habit of caring for myself. Like Jared's, my hair was filled with streaks of gray that looked like fine flecks of white paint. The shape was vaguely reminiscent of a haircut I had more than a year ago, with bangs that had grown past my nose. Even with makeup, which I didn't bother with much, my eyes had permanent dark puffy circles under them. I was underweight by about ten pounds, which was unusual, as I tended to be fat. My clothes hung on me. Heavy drinking was my diet of choice; it shed the pounds and numbed the senses; all in all, not a bad program.

"Cat!" Wendy came toward me and hooked her hand in the crook of my elbow.

"This is Willard." She walked me to him and whispered, "Be nice."

I put out my hand. He smiled and nodded as if he didn't understand the gesture. I looked at Wendy.

"He's hard of hearing. You have to speak up." She raised her voice to demonstrate. "Not circumcised either," she whispered in my ear. Willard looked like I was about to punish him. He was painfully bald. The kind that makes you wonder if the guy ever had any hair. His glasses were Coke-bottle thick with frames that covered most of his face. His blank expression evoked the name Dullard.

"Has anyone seen Dad?"

Wendy's nonchalance caught me off guard. It hadn't occurred to me until that moment that Dad would be a subject anyone would bring up around me. The mention of his name and the nearness of Jared and Wendy brought it all back. My body's memory betrayed me first. The muscles in my thighs gave way, causing me to lose my balance. I grabbed the back of a chair.

"We were focusing on the arrangements for Mom," Jared said. "Cat identified her and filled out the paperwork. I'm planning the service."

"I'd like to know where Dad is."

I went to the pantry and found a copy of last year's Yellow Pages and handed it to her.

"You don't even know what hospital he's in?"

"No. The only person who knew was Mom, and she blew her head off before we could ask. Besides, there are only two hospitals, Mercy and Our Lady of Perpetual Sorrow. Pick one."

"Don't be so dramatic." She rolled her eyes and passed the directory to Willard and shouted, in what I presumed was his good ear, "Look for hospital . . . HOS-PEE-TALL . . . H-O-S . . . here." She opened her fake Chanel bag and took out a pen and grabbed the lilac stationery off the table. Jared pulled it out of her hands.

"What?"

"That's Mom's suicide note," Jared said.

"Oh . . . sorry," she said, as if we had told her she was stepping on a dog's tail. "Do you have something else?"

"Here," I said. I ripped a loose piece of wallpaper off the wall and handed it to her.

Wendy and Willard left for the hospital later that afternoon. Wendy had been able to ascertain from the nurse on duty that my father was still in a coma. The nurse said that it didn't look too promising.

I was relieved. Although he had been dead to me for years, part of me knew he was still alive and haunting the lives of anyone who cared about him. It was a bitter irony that he survived my mother, especially since no one thought he would live as long as he did. He was a heavyset man with a weakness for drinking and smoking. That combination, along with his lethal temper, made many people think he was living on borrowed time. Not me. I believed he would outlive all of us. Monsters always do.

Wendy was Dad's favorite. He called her his princess and showered her with gifts whenever he went to town. She forgave his outbursts and quickly forgot how afraid she was of him when presented with a new dress or pair of shoes. I suppose Wendy understood Dad in a way the rest of us didn't. Or perhaps it was Dad who understood that giving to Wendy bought her acceptance.

I wasn't sure if there was anything Dad could do to turn Wendy away. Even after he cut off the tip of my mother's finger, she defended his right to be angry. (I'm guessing the charm bracelet he bought her didn't hurt either.) The night he did it we lay in bed while she told me I could never understand how hard it had been for someone of Dad's intelligence to end up on this farm. She said he was like the lion that had the thorn in his paw in the story my mother used to tell us. She said he just needed someone to take it out and he wouldn't be so angry anymore. I asked her why she didn't do it. She said it was up to Mom to keep him happy. A lion with a thorn in its paw—he was a lot more than that.

While Wendy and Willard visited my father, Jared went out to make last-minute preparations for the service. He picked up deli platters and beer in case people stopped by afterward. He asked me to go with him, as he was planning on taking a drive around town to see how much it had changed. I told him I needed to rest. I put on my coat, grabbed a pack of cigarettes, and headed down toward the lake.

We called the huge pond on our property "the lake." I think we did it because it irritated Dad and Wendy so much. "It's not a lake," they'd shout. We knew it wasn't a lake; in fact, it was barely a pond. As far as I could tell nothing ever lived in it. There were no ducks, no fish, no beavers, just algae and cloudy water. During the hot days of summer, Jared and my mother would go in to cool off. I never waded in; I didn't like the feel of the mud squishing between my toes. I also didn't know how to swim and was deathly afraid of drowning. I did like to sit at the edge and stare out onto the vast horizon of our property.

Now, looking out, I was struck by how familiar everything felt. Like the house, the yard was an extension of my mother. It was filled with her touches, from the long clothesline that ran the width of the driveway to the carefully pruned rosebushes along the back of the house. This mother, the one who gardened and tended and threw outdoor parties for us when we were kids, was the one I wanted to remember. This was the twenty-six-year-old woman who wore capri pants with a matching halter top that she copied from a picture she saw in a magazine. "I made this for your party," she said days before I celebrated my fifth birthday in high Rucker style. "We'll invite everyone from your class, so no one feels left out," she said from behind her sewing machine. And we did. When the day arrived, she moved around the yard giving out prizes to all of my friends from school. "This one is for you." She squatted down to be eye level with my playmates. "Thank you, Mrs. Rucker," they replied as my mother smiled a beautiful, brilliant, happy-to-be-alive smile that made everyone giggle. She made everything for that party, from the decorations down to the cake we decorated together. We covered it with strawberries and good wishes for me. She even made me a crown so I could be a princess for the day. At the end of the party, we stood together on the front porch holding hands and waving good-bye to everyone. She lifted me into her arms and hugged me. I could feel her warm breath on my neck tickling me. She smelled of coffee and cigarettes and White Shoulders perfume. "I love you," I whispered in her ear. It was the last time I said it. We laughed as she sang, "You smell like a monkey, and you act like one too," into my ear. She was my good mother. She was not the woman who closed the bedroom door when my father went roaming. Not the one who let me go and never tried to find me. Not the one lying half-faced and naked on a metal slab.

*He isn't who you think he is. . . .*

It was getting dark and a cold wind was rolling up the hill. I could see the lights in the house come on and Willard's car in the drive. I got up and brushed the cold mud from my pants, feeling the chill and desperately craving a drink.

I snuck to my car without getting their attention. I saw Wendy through the kitchen window as I pulled out of the driveway. Her hands were covered in Mom's Playtex Living gloves as she scrubbed down the windowsill while Willard pulled masking tape off the cupboards. Apparently the cleanup that was done did not meet with her approval.

I headed out Connor's Road to Walt's Tavern. I figured it was far enough out of town that I wouldn't run into anyone I used to know. Just to be safe, though, I took a booth in the back and sat with my back to the door. After several beers I was beginning to feel the numbness I had been longing for all day.

"So . . . what brings you to these parts?" a ratty-haired fool of a man asked, as he leaned his stinking face into mine.

"Get the fuck away from me," I said, loudly but slow enough for him to understand.

"Cripes . . . can't a guy buy a lady a drink?"

"Get lost."

The jukebox was playing some sappy half-country half-rock song with lyrics like "I'm gonna love you forever." Yeah, right. There was a couple snuggling up on the dance floor groping each other as they moved back and forth to some alien rhythm. The girl couldn't have been more than eighteen while the guy must have been in his forties. In spite of the age difference, they both looked old. In fact, everybody in the bar looked old and tired, including me. The only difference between them and the rest of us was that they looked old and tired and happy. Maybe their happiness had something to do with the fact that she had her hand on his dick.

"That pitcher for sharing?"

I looked up at the man who was blocking my view of the hand-on-dick dancers. The face was familiar but not recognizable until I saw the silver pen in his shirt pocket. I signed my mother's papers with it. It was Andrew Reilly, County Coroner.

"Hands that touch dead bodies do not come near my beer," I said.

He smiled a car salesman kind of smile and laughed awkwardly. "You're joking, right?" he said as he sat down on the bench across from me.

"No," I responded, looking back at the dancers. The guy's fly was unzipped and her hand was lost in his pants. He was looking younger every second. The coroner ordered a beer from the wait-ress.

"So, uh . . . Hal tells me you guys went to school together."

"Yup," I said, not diverting my attention from the impromptu peep show on the dance floor. He looked over at the dancers and then back at me watching them and smiled.

"That's some dance move," he said.

I stared at him and tried to figure out if he was trying to be funny. I decided I needed more beer.

We sat in silence as I watched chunks of frost slide slowly off the handle of his beer mug. I felt his eyes on me. I didn't remember anything about him except his voice and that pen. I tried to remem-ber what he looked like, not for any other reason than to be able to describe him in detail in case something happened to me. It was a little trick I picked up along the way.

"I don't think I know your real name," he said, finally breaking a silence I was prepared to endure for much longer.

Was he joking? He didn't look like he was. "You didn't notice my name on any of the paperwork? What about next of kin, what—"

"Is your point?" he interrupted.

"The point is you know my name is Alex . . . Alex Rucker. So why are you playing this stupid game with me?"

He sat there stunned, shaking his head. "I wasn't sure if you were Wendy or Alex. It was busy today; I didn't check the paper-work that closely. I had to process the body."

I lifted my mug. "Well, here's to processing."

He took a reluctant sip while I finished what was left of my beer and poured the last of the pitcher. "People call me Cat."

"Well, Alex," he said as he finished his beer, "I'm sorry about your mother. She was a wonderful woman." He stood up and put on his coat.

"You knew her?" I said.

"Yeah . . . we used to run into each other at the park after church. She would go there on Sundays to watch her grandson. I would go to read and to get some sun on my face. You know, being in my business . . ."

"I'm sorry, but did you say her grandson?"

"Yeah . . ."

"My mother has no grandchildren. You must be thinking of someone else."

"Oh . . ." He hesitated and thought for a moment.

I felt dizzy but tried to concentrate.

"On Sundays she watched the kids climb that twisted apple tree with such interest that I assumed—"

"Nope. No grandchildren." That wasn't completely true. I didn't know for sure that Jared or Wendy had no kids. I reached into my pocket and threw a couple of singles on the table and struggled out of the booth. I felt a wave of nausea pass through me and lost my balance. The coroner put his arm out to steady me and out of instinct I flinched.

"Thanks," I said, more embarrassed at flinching than at almost passing out. He locked his arm under mine and helped me to the door.

"Are you okay getting home?"

I pulled away and grabbed the keys out of my pocket. "I'm fine," I said, walking toward my car.

"I'll follow. Just to make sure."

"That's not necessary." I was perfectly prepared to lecture him on my infamous capacity for drinking and driving.

"I'm afraid it is. . . . I don't need the business."

He pulled behind me and waved when I looked in the rearview mirror.

I pushed in the car lighter and for a moment considered smoking two cigarettes at the same time.

# THREE

THE ALARM WENT off at seven in my old bedroom. Wendy shouted at Willard to turn it off. I was asleep in my father's La-Z-Boy by the window in my parents' bedroom. I wasn't picky about where I slept as long as I'd had enough to drink to pass out.

Jared was rustling in the kitchen. I could hear his sure-to-be-polished dress shoes traversing the floorboards as he put coffee on and prepared for the service. The white winter sun was warm on my face. Dust fairies danced around the orange-and-green afghan at the foot of the bed.

*Did she know she was making her bed for the last time?*

I pushed the footrest down on the chair and rolled to a stand. My legs, as usual, felt hollow and unsure of whether or not they wanted to carry me for the day. My head soon followed; why stay upright when you could be resting on a pillow? I battled my body on a daily basis. Most days it won, and I crawled back to wherever I came from—the bed, the floor. Today I rallied the troops: I asked the legs to stand, the head to focus, and the heart to stay hidden.

I dressed slowly, putting on an old black cocktail dress I bought a couple of years ago to impress a club owner who could not be impressed. I forgot I had it until Ruth called. The dress was plain and fell above my knee, with a scoop neck and short sleeves. When I last wore it, the fit was snug against my body, showing off my "assets," as my stripper friends call them. Now the dress was loose in all the places it should be tight, and communicated "wasting away" more than "come fuck me."

I hatched my panty hose from their egg-shaped home. Off-black—do the makers of cheap stockings have something against solid black? Even people who buy panty hose at Wal-Mart like real black. A line called "Funeral Black" resting in a plastic coffin would do just fine.

I bent over, hooking my foot into the toe of the panty hose. My fingers couldn't pull with authority. I was overwhelmed with the image of my own death. The thought sent me toppling onto the bed. Who would come to bury me? What would my note say? "He was everything I thought he was."

"Coming?" Jared yelled from the bottom of the stairs.

"In a minute," I answered, giving my panty hose a final tug.

I slipped on the matching black pumps and went to my mother's jewelry drawer in her dresser for earrings and a purse. I found the beaded bag she bought on her honeymoon in Atlantic City and stuffed my cigarettes, a lighter, and an airplane-size bottle of bourbon into its tiny opening. I would need a liquor store at some point, but that would get me through the service at least.

I sat on Mom's pink satin bench rifling through the stacks of brittle cardboard boxes filled with costume jewelry and found the rhinestone earrings I had given her before I left. She had admired them every time we passed Jacob's Jewelry in town, so I bought them with my babysitting money and left them on her pillow with a note that said, "From your secret admirer." She never said anything. I wondered if she knew who gave them to her. Now they sat in a Jacob's box that said "Jacob's Jewelry, Jewels Fit for a Queen!" and were wrapped in the original tissue paper and never worn.

At the bottom of the box there was an old receipt from Abe's Dairy folded in half. It was yellowed and crisp. On the front was an order for two gallons of whole milk, a large cottage cheese, and a quart of buttermilk with a notation that said "Weekly—Saturdays are preferable." I almost threw it out until I saw a neatly written scribble on the back:

*7lbs 8ozs—20 inches.*
*name ???????*

The word *name* was underlined five or six times. The blue script was hers, delicate and lovely. I looked up to see if anyone was watching me and caught my reflection the way you do when you walk down a crowded street and think you recognize the stranger in the store window. You look closer and realize it's you.

I folded the paper and returned it. I put on the earrings and stood up. With my black and rhinestones, I looked like I was attending a memorial service for a cabaret diva instead of a funeral in Bumfuck, Nowhere.

"Cat, can I pull this off?" Wendy was standing in the doorway wearing a sleeveless black knit dress that was a size too small. Her stockings were true black, as were her gloves, which coiled up her arms like fashionable garden snakes. She wore a pillbox hat that cast dark netting over her face. She looked like the widow of a mafioso.

"You look fine," I lied. I headed for the kitchen.

She shuffled behind me, hovering as I stumbled on the stairs, not used to walking in heels.

"Are you sure I look okay? As the youngest, I thought I should look, well, you know . . ." She struggled for the right adjective.

"Sadder?" I said sarcastically.

"Yes!" she answered. She held my shoulder as we came down the stairs.

I turned around and looked at her. "You look blacker."

"I guess that will have to do."

Jared and Willard sat together drinking big mugs of coffee in their black suits. Willard looked old enough to be a father taking his grown-up children to mass. God, I wanted a drink. I felt my purse for the shape of the bottle and felt calmer.

Jared and I had stayed up the night before setting up the living room and bringing down the folding chairs from the attic. The deli platters were in the fridge, the beer was on ice, and we had cleared an entire table just for the Bundt cakes. As long as we were talking about the service, we were okay.

After deciding whose car we would take, we left for the church. Our Lady of Grace was anything but graceful. Looking at the façade, you had to wonder where all those dollars in the collection basket went—certainly not to capital improvements. The parking lot was almost as large as a football field—a callback to the days when going to mass was more than a birth/death thing, and as much a part of life as marriage and Saturday night sex. My mother's faith was old-fashioned. She believed the church took care of you, and in return, she took care of it. She had tea and potlucks with her fellow parishioners and never told anyone about the monster living in her house.

The parking lot was filling quickly with mourners. I was not surprised. My mother was well loved, and even though my father tried to keep her to himself, she had managed at one time or another to bestow her kindness on almost everyone.

It was a brittle day. The branches on the trees creaked like the bones on a skeleton waving in the wind. Nothing green would come this way until April. I would be long gone by then.

Jared and Wendy blessed themselves with holy water as we entered the chapel. I passed them and ended up walking down the aisle alone, like a bride who has been jilted and doesn't know it yet.

The church was warm and had the faint smell of fireplace ash mixed with lemon furniture polish. High behind me "Amazing Grace" boomed from a bulbous organ that was made for a better place.

The front pews were full of families and couples while stragglers and loners punctuated the back rows. As I made my way to the altar, I felt the eyes of the town watching me, hoping to see if they could find something in my manner that might reveal what had happened to me.

"She took off. No one ever heard from her again."

"Poor Maureen, all alone with that man."

As we passed Ruth Igby, I looked at her and she turned quickly away, as did most of the women when I attempted to make eye contact. I reached back and took Jared's arm, needing something to steady myself even if it was him. "You okay?" he whispered in my ear, brushing my hair off my forehead.

I nodded, feeling worse for needing him.

No one from the family spoke. We agreed my mother would have wanted the priest to handle everything. The service was long and filled with lots of standing, sitting, kneeling, hymns, bowed heads, and moments for reflection. As a little girl I would sing "Mary Had a Little Lamb" quietly to myself whenever we had to recite a prayer or sing. My mother would squeeze my shoulder and shake her head in disapproval. I didn't care; I thought God would appreciate hearing something a little different.

We piled out of the church and stood at the entrance and thanked everyone for coming and invited them back to the house. I slipped away and found the ladies' room and my airplane-size bottle of courage in the basement. I needed more to drink but was too far from a liquor store. I thought about stealing wine from the rectory but thought better of it.

The wait at the grave site was unendurable. My mother had planned every detail, down to the coffin, the hymns at the service, and where she would be buried. She had left that information with our parish priest, who had made most of the arrangements as a personal favor to her. Rather than helping her with her funeral, I wondered why he didn't consider keeping her from killing herself.

Mom was buried in Calvary Cemetery next to her parents on the top of the windiest hill in the windiest section of town. There was an empty space next to her reserved for my father. No plots had been purchased for the kiddies—we'd be as alone in death as we were in life.

"The views are great here, aren't they?" Father O'Malley said to Jared and me when he took us to meet with the cemetery administrator yesterday. "Your mother will be happy here."

"I'm so glad," I lied. I was dying to ask him if Mom was really going to go to heaven: I thought suicide was a sin. I'm guessing my mother took care of that already. She probably dropped a few extra singles in the basket, made two stews for potluck night, and, of course, had a last confession.

Most of the mourners followed us to the grave site. The air was so cold and dry, it felt as if it were slashing my face as it tore up and over the mound that was to be my mother's final resting place. The priest recited a few prayers and some crap in Latin and asked us if we wanted to say anything. None of us did. Wendy cried as Willard held her and chewed on a toothpick. Jared stood as still as a soldier on guard duty. I felt an intense pressure on the balls of my feet from wearing high heels in the mud. My legs felt chapped and exposed. My body had cooperated: legs were standing, head was focused, and my heart remained hidden. My buzz was wearing off.

I counted twelve Bundt cakes. This was part of Wilton tradition: a Bundt cake for a death, a blanket for a birth, a casserole for a heart attack. The cakes were stacking up on the card table; there were three lemon with yellow drip icing, four chocolate with coconut centers, two cinnamon swirl with coffee-cake-crunch topping, and three chocolate mousse, which were made from my mother's favorite recipe. She invented the chocolate mousse Bundt cake after her thirtieth or fortieth funeral. She decided there had to be a different kind a woman could bring to a wake, so she came up with her own. It never occurred to her that she could have brought something else, like a ham or a salad; she knew that Bundt was the tradition and she worked within her limits. Her chocolate mousse cake became so popular that we suspected some people looked forward to the next death just so they could have a piece. Today no one touched any of them, not even the mousse ones.

I tried to be polite to our guests. Many offered their condolences and all of them knew better than to wish my father a speedy recovery. Although the circumstances surrounding my departure remained a mystery, it was no secret that it might have had something to do with my father, and out of respect, no one mentioned his name all evening. It was clear from the way people checked out the place that it had been a while since my parents had company. Although the house looked the same to me, I was aware that everything had aged, but it still gave me the feeling of stepping back in time.

Andrew Reilly, County Coroner, stopped by and paid his respects. He had been at the service as well. He introduced himself to Jared and Wendy and made a point of telling them how brave I had been at the morgue.

"Cat?" Wendy snorted. "She runs from everything."

Andrew smiled politely and looked at me. "I don't see her running now," he said and then excused himself. As he left the room he put his hand on my shoulder and squeezed it.

I managed to get away from the crowd and found a spot in the kitchen. I opened the back door and faced the driveway as I smoked a butt and gulped Iron City beer and stared at the fat moon hanging in the winter sky.

*He isn't who you think he is. . . .*

Jared stood next to me and took in a few breaths of the crisp air. It was more refreshing than the moist, yeasty, moth-ball-scented atmosphere in the house.

In the living room I could hear Wendy ogling over the Smythsons' granddaughter. "She's so beautiful! Willard?" She wandered through the crowd looking for Willard, who was in the dining room skimming my mother's collection of the Reader's Digest Condensed versions of the classics.

The doorbell rang.

"Your turn," Jared said.

"I got the last one," I lied. He went to the door as I walked to the refrigerator and pulled out another bottle of the good beer I had stashed and drank it like it was bottled water. I left the back door open, but latched the screen door to keep it from banging.

Since returning from the service there had been a steady flow of mourners coming through the front door. Although I was forced to do a few meet-and-greets, I managed to stay in the kitchen for most of the evening. It was the safest place, as everyone who wasn't family (or Ruth Igby) came to the front door when they visited. The rest of us used the back door.

I sat at the kitchen table and stared at the containers of food stacked in towers on the counters. Death sure makes people hungry. It makes me thirsty. I went for another beer. I was feeling light-headed.

There was a shuffling at the back stoop like someone was shaking snow off their shoes.

"Hello?" a man's voice sounded through the screen door. The tone made the hair on the back of my neck bristle.

"Alex, can you get me two Cokes?" Jared yelled from the living room.

"Hello?" I shivered as I moved unsteadily toward the sound.

"Alex?" Jared's voice was getting closer.

The screen door shook; he was trying to get in. I stepped into view. "Hello?" he said as he placed his hand to his forehead and pressed his face against the screen to get a look at who was standing before him.

The voice matched the body: smooth, tall, and copper-colored at the top. Snow swirled in a halo around the outside light as he stepped back.

"Holy shit!" Jared's voice cracked in surprise. He had come into the kitchen in search of the Cokes and found me standing glacier-still in front of the door. There was no slow-motion revelation. There was nothing except the cold, hard drop of fear—the feeling you get when you look down from the top of the Empire State Building and suddenly know exactly what it feels like to fall a great distance.

Jared unlatched the door and pushed it open. As one foot, then the other, stepped into the kitchen, I could feel the door of my past straining to open like the screen door.

The walls of the room began to slip away, leaving nothing but the feeling of a free fall into a huge divide. I reached for the table, hoping for something to hold on to, but it was too late. I missed and fell hard on the floor. Everything went soft and dreamy. For one brief, happy moment, I thought I was dead.

I woke up next to a pile of coats on my mother's bed. The only light in the room came from the hallway and bled through the crack in the door. It felt like midnight, but I checked the clock on the nightstand and discovered it was only nine-thirty. I could hear the rustle of company downstairs, glasses clanging together, forks scraping against plates, and loud, very loud, talking. The sounds, although distant, made me feel as if I were still lying in the kitchen, all soft and dreamy and desperate to be gone. I tried to sit up and felt my head drop back onto the pillow as if it were part of some magnetic force field. "Oh . . ." I grumbled.

"You're lucky you didn't barf," a voice spoke from behind me as the silhouette of a man cast a shadow on the wall I was facing. I tried to pretend I was sleeping. The shadow lingered and then disappeared. I pulled myself up to my elbows and tried to focus. The falling feeling was gone, replaced by a sharp pounding under my eyes that felt as if someone were punching me in the face from inside my skull. I felt the urge to flee. I put my hands on the side of the bed and swung my legs over and slowly tried to stand.

"I wouldn't do that if I were you," the voice replied, coming from the direction of my mother's bureau. His body may have been across the room but his voice resonated inside me, deep down, way past the well of liquor, beyond the granite resolve and the cold clench of denial. In spite of my best efforts to kill it, his voice still lived in me.

My hands trembled as I felt my stomach push against my chest.

I searched for breath, taking in whatever air I could in short, help-less gasps. Wild memories fluttered through my mind like summer kites. I clenched my fists and felt my toes curling.

*Get in there. Get back.*

Before I knew what was happening, I was on the floor with my head in my hands, consumed by an overwhelming desire to cry. I took a breath and felt a rush of tears for the first time in many years.

He was in the room. I heard the click of his lighter and the flash of flame as he lit a cigarette, and then I saw the burning ember flick-ering near his face like a firefly trying to catch him. I imagined him leaning against the bureau watching me cry, and feeling nothing, not even pity.

"I should have told you we moved back," he said, coming closer to either me or the door. I hoped it was the door. "I lost track of you."

"I'm in New York now," I said, wondering how I was going to manage all of the snot that was coming out of my nose. I sniffled and tried to make him out in the dark. "You came alone?"

"Of course," he said, as I felt him closing in. I looked up at his shadow and shielded my eyes from the glare of the open door. From what I could make of his face, he appeared to be half smiling. "Sorry about your mom," he said as he headed for the doorway, stopping to give me a Kleenex. His hand was still covered in freck-les.

"Yeah," I said, hiccuping from the force of my crying. I reluc-tantly took the Kleenex and turned away.

"Please," I begged, but could not finish, unsure of what I would ask for. Please leave me alone, please don't speak, please go.

"I don't suppose you'd . . ." he said with his back to me.

"No . . . I'm leaving as soon as everything's settled."

"Suit yourself," he whispered, as he left quietly through the door.

# Four

IT WAS THE FIRST warm day after a brutal winter. I was coming up the long dirt driveway after my best friend, Nell, dropped me off from school. She had turned sixteen earlier that year and was the only one at our high school who had her own car.

Coming home was the worst part of the day. I dreaded the thought of walking into the house and seeing my father stretched out on the couch in a drunken haze. My mother was often at the store, where she spent an increasing amount of time shopping the sales. What had started as a weekly chore had turned into a daily ritual, with my mother scouring the three grocery stores within a twenty-mile radius looking for the best deals. She was proud of getting something for nothing. She made making do an art form.

Wendy usually stayed after school for orchestra practice. She was first-chair clarinet and the fund-raising captain, and took her responsibilities to the ensemble seriously. She had broken the school record by raising more than four hundred dollars in candy sales for the trip to the state finals in the fall, which was no small feat considering my mother refused to buy any. "Why would I spend $2.50 on a chocolate bar when I could get a whole sack at Kroger for $1.99?"

Although she loved the discipline of classical music, Wendy had the style of a band slut. At recitals, she wore her long black skirt as tight and as short as the regulation would allow. Mom said we should be grateful orchestra season didn't go into the summer or Wendy would wear a white tube top instead of a blouse.

Jared was the jock of the family and found a sport to excel in for every season. Early spring meant the end of basketball and the beginning of baseball season. Jared was seldom home before dinner, and regularly barreled through the door dragging his equipment bag just as we were sitting down to eat. It was hard to tell what bothered my father more about Jared—his athleticism or the way he never seemed to care if he was holding up dinner. Whatever it was, it made for many tense meals.

Jared had grown immune to Dad and ignored his harsh words. He was heading into his last semester of high school and counting the days before he would be released from my father's fury. Jared's dedication to sports had paid off. He was heading to Penn State on a football scholarship in the fall.

My extracurricular activity was avoiding Dad at all costs. One didn't go out for this sport as much as get drafted for it. Dad didn't do much in the way of work; he farmed the small parcel of land we didn't lease, collected rent, and occasionally got odd jobs repairing farm equipment. He was good with his hands. Whatever he touched bended to his will: crops grew, dead machines turned over, skin bruised.

Every day as I came up the drive I looked for signs as to what I could expect. Was his truck in the garage? Were the barn doors open? Were there tractors in the yard with their hoods up? These were indications that he might be working and sober. If everything was closed up, then the drinking had started. Then the question was, when? Early in the day usually meant he would be passed out on the couch. If he had started at lunch he would be hungry for company.

And that could mean so many things.

I waved good-bye to Nell and started for the house. The sun was sitting high in the sky and there was a cool, soothing breeze coming off the fields tickling the hairs on the back of my neck. It had been a good day. In school I had gotten an A on an art project, and on the way home, Nell told me she got her father to agree to give me driving lessons that weekend. I was about to turn seventeen and didn't want to wait any longer. The thought of getting my license made me giddy, like hearing the first three numbers on your lottery ticket announced during the daily drawing. With a license, all I needed were keys and I could get out of Wilton, forever.

As I slowly walked toward the house, lingering by my mother's flower beds budding with crocuses, I saw my father and another man sitting on the porch gliding on the swing, drinking beer, and talking. My father waved me over.

"Cat, you remember Addison, Jared Watkins's son." They stood together as the swing bumped the backs of their knees on its return ride. They laughed and stepped toward the railing and me.

Jared Watkins was my mother and father's oldest friend. Jared and my dad were boyhood friends who grew up next door to each other. A couple of years before I was born, Jared moved to California, where he married his wife, Barbara, and had a son, Addison. Every year until I was eleven, the Watkins family came to visit Jared's mother, who still lived in his childhood home. I saw Addison on their last visit five years ago.

I looked up, shielding my eyes from the afternoon sun, and shrugged.

My father slapped Addison on the back. "She was young the last time she saw you. Don't take it personal."

He had changed.

This was not the greasy redhead with hair that hung in clumps around his pimply face who chased me around the yard shouting, "Fatty, fatty two by four can't get through the bathroom door." I was eleven and fat, which Addison pointed out every chance he could. He claimed I deserved it because I had told him his driving sucked. He had just gotten a license and had insisted on taking Jared, Wendy, and me for a ride in his dad's Caddy. We didn't get off the property before he swerved into a ditch and had to get Dad to pull us out.

Dad loved having the chance to tow Jared's big-ass car with his 1969 red Ford pickup. He seized any opportunity to show Jared up.

"Well, look who's pulling who out of the ditch now," Dad said, beaming proudly.

When confronted with what happened, Addison looked at me and said it was because he was carrying too big of a load in the car.

"The only load you're carrying is the pus in that pimple face of yours," I said.

That's when the chasing started.

We didn't see the Watkins family again after that visit. Something happened that no one talked about. I didn't care enough to find out more. No more Addison meant one less annoying person in my life, and that was fine by me.

Addison the pimply faced teenager had morphed into a broad-shouldered man with wavy rust-colored hair. He was as tall as my six-foot-three-inch father, but leaner. He wore a faded denim shirt over a thermal undershirt with the sleeves pushed up to reveal deeply tanned muscular arms. His jeans hung loosely around his slim waist, and in spite of the chill, he wore no jacket or gloves. What he did wear was a smile so inviting it made me want to smile back. Every time.

"I hope your driving has gotten better," I said, struggling not to make eye contact. I could feel the heat of his smile.

"You might be happy to know both my driving and manners have improved."

He remembered.

"How nice for you," I said, as I walked up the porch stairs and grabbed the screen door. I tried to subtly catch a glimpse of him but he caught my eye and smiled that goddamned smile again. I felt a rush of blood to my cheeks and darted for the stairs to my bedroom.

Wendy was in our room as I jumped from the doorway to my bed against the wall. She was fussing in the closet, pulling out clothes and throwing them in outfit combinations on her bed.

"Did you see him?"

"Yeah, how long is he staying?"

"How about forever!" She threw herself on my bed and hugged my leg dramatically.

"Christ, you act like you've never seen a guy before!" I pushed her off me.

"Oh, I've seen guys, but this is a man."

We laughed. "Is that all you think about?"

She looked up at the ceiling and thought for a moment. "Yup—that's pretty much it. That and orchestra. So help me figure out what I should wear!"

"For what?"

"Dinner. I want to look like this is something I usually wear but still be sexy."

"Wendy, you're fourteen; sexy should not be your main objective. Try for cute."

I pulled off my school uniform and slid on a ratty pair of jeans and a ripped flannel shirt that used to belong to Jared.

"What are you going for—farmhand?"

"Not going for anything, Wendy. I'm not doing anything that would keep me in Wilton."

"Addison's not from here," she said.

"He came back, didn't he?"

Wendy slipped on a tight black V-necked sweater that used to be Mom's before she accidentally shrunk it. She found it tight in all the right places as she ogled herself in the mirror. Wendy had developed early and had Mom's build, with long shapely legs and full round breasts that defied gravity. I was more like Dad, with stockier limbs and a broader chest. Wendy's hair was darker than my chestnut color and thicker, with a natural curl. She wore it long and layered, while mine was shoulder length and blunt.

"So did you get his story?" I asked, as she slipped on a pair of blue jeans with the knees fashionably cut and frayed.

"Dad says his father sent him to fix up his grandma's place.

Since she died the house has been rented and gotten run-down. How do I look?"

"How old is he?"

"Mom said twenty-one. Cat, the outfit?" She snapped her fingers in my face as if waking me from a trance. The pants were so tight I could almost see the outline of the beauty mark she had on her left cheek.

"Where did you get those jeans?"

"Daddy bought them for me."

"Has Mom seen them?"

"She will soon."

"She's going to hate that outfit."

"Yeah, well, what's she going to do about it?"

She had a point. My mother had no jurisdiction over Wendy. Dad favored her so intensely that people often commented that Wendy was more like his wife than my mother was. As for me, aside from the fact that I didn't have the figure or the desire to dress like Wendy, I was certain one disapproving word or look from my mother would result in an immediate beating from my father.

At dinner Wendy took my regular spot, which was next to Addison, who was sitting where Jared usually sat. Jared had called and said he would be late and not to hold dinner. Rather than ask Wendy to move, Mom had me sit in her seat, which ended up being directly across from Addison. Dad was in good spirits, regaling everyone with his favorite stories of his youth and charming us with kind words and affectionate looks. No one could be nicer than Dad when he wanted to be.

"Everything was different then. We had a lot of plans. Did your dad ever tell you I was his partner in the driving school? The one he sold for a fortune?" Dad looked at some fixed point above Addison's head as he chewed, his face relaxed into a distant memory— whether it was a good or bad one was hard to tell.

"Remember, don't let business get in the way of friendship. And don't let anything get in the way of business." He spoke finally as he looked at my mother, whose head remained down and focused on her food.

"We had big dreams," he said, shaking his head and laughing to himself. "We actually thought we could do better than this. That we could see the world. Well, your dad did. He got out and I got . . ." He looked at Mom, who was pushing her potatoes from one side of the plate to the other. "Poor Moo. I was her consolation prize. Your father meant the world to her." He exaggerated the word *world*. My mother dropped her fork and bristled at hearing my father call her Moo.

Moo was my mother's family's nickname for her; it was short for Moonbeam, which was what her daddy used to call her. Aside from my father, who usually called her Moo before he hit her, the only other person I ever heard call her that was Addison's father, Jared.

Everyone froze at the sudden change in my father's voice. The sunny tone was replaced by the brooding baritone of bad weather. After a few moments of my father staring intently at my mother as if he were measuring her for a coffin, the storm passed. "Eat up, girls," he said, reaching over and touching my hair and face. "Isn't she beautiful?" he said to Addison.

"Yes," Addison replied, looking at me.

"No!" Dad said. "I'm talking about Wendy."

Addison nodded. I waited for my father to take his hands off me.

I looked up once during the rest of the dinner to pass the potatoes and met Addison's eyes. He winked.

After supper my father retired to the living room, where he passed out in his La-Z-Boy immediately following *Jeopardy!* He usually managed to stay awake for it, as he took great pride in shouting out the answers at the top of his lungs. "I am one smart motherfucker!" he would bellow into the kitchen whenever he got an answer right.

"*Mayor of Casterbridge?*"

"Marshall Plan?"

"Theory of Relativity?"

My father ignored the rules of the game. "I don't give a good goddamn what the rules are," he said to me once when I tried to correct him. "Alex fucking Trebek can suck my dick before I'll answer in the form of a question."

Mom and I cleared the table and did the dishes while Wendy graciously offered to take Addison on a little tour of the property. "Don't wait up," she jokingly whispered in my ear as she walked out behind Addison, who winked at me again.

"What's with all the fucking winking?" I said to my mother as she washed and I dried. My mother shrugged, no longer shocked at my use of the *F* word. She was lost in her own thoughts as she handed me another plate. "He looks like Jared."

"Addison?"

Mom wiped the same dish over and over again, not hearing the squeaking sound it was making as if it were begging to be released, like one of her memories.

"Are we talking about Addison?"

She handed me the plate.

"It looks like rain."

It's hard to say what happened on their little tour. To hear Wendy tell it, Addison ravaged her by the lake, fondled her on the tree swing, and grabbed her by the gladiolus. At a minimum she said there was a whole lot of flirting going on. Although she was two years younger than me, Wendy prided herself on being more popular with boys. She loved to brag about her conquests and made no bones about the fact she was looking for attention in whatever form it took.

"I bet Addison is a great kisser," she said as we lay in bed that night waiting for sleep to overtake us.

"I don't trust him," I said. "He winks."

"So do I," she said.

"Exactly . . ."


"Addison is going to stay with us awhile," Dad announced one night at dinner. "As far as I'm concerned, he's part of this family and will be treated as such."

Addison moved his duffel into the apartment above the garage that had been empty since my mom's parents had died a few years back. He worked hard to form bonds with everyone in the family. He was a good influence on Dad. He helped him with the equipment repairs, trailed him on errands, and showed more interest in learning about farm life than any of us ever had. He was kind to my mother and often helped her with the dishes or household chores when he wasn't working with Dad. He complimented her on her cooking, took an interest in her quilting, and loved to play guitar and sing with her after dinner. He was an avid sports fan and played catch with Jared in the yard on the weekends or would go to the school and shoot hoops with him. On Sundays he sat in the living room with Jared and my father and watched all of the games. He gave Jared advice on women (which I was beginning to suspect Addison knew a lot about), and loved to hear Jared and his friends talk about the girls at school. As for Wendy, Addison treated her in a brotherly fashion. He spent hours teaching her how to play guitar and helped her understand the basics of music composition. Addison was good at many things. He was a first-rate carpenter, and had a beautiful singing voice and athletic ability. I couldn't imagine what someone with all that talent was doing living above our garage.

Addison worked so hard to cultivate relationships with everyone that it felt as if he were auditioning to be part of our family. As if this were a family worth getting into.

I stuck to my promise that I had no intention of getting involved with someone who could distract me from my goal of getting out. And so, while the others circled around Addison for attention, I went about my business doing homework, pursuing my driver's license, and drawing.

"You spend a lot of time with your head in that book." Addison stood in the doorway of my room watching me draw one afternoon.

"So?"

"What are you drawing?"

He settled his shoulder against the doorjamb with the confidence of a man who knew the value of waiting.

"It's none of your business," I said. "Move along."

He laughed. "You don't like me, do you?"

"I would have to care about you not to like you."

The truth was, he fascinated me. When it was safe, I would watch him work in the garden from my window and wonder what twist of events had led him to our door. Everything about him reminded me that there was something beyond the farm and family. His manner, the stories he told, the things he knew, made me feel hopeful. I didn't want to be with him as much as I wanted to be him.

In the evenings, when the weather was warm, I walked around the farm and talked to myself about all of my "big plans" as I watched the sun go down. Those evenings were my favorite part of the day as I was free to imagine all of the wonderful and exciting things I would experience away from Wilton. I never shared my plans with anyone, which wasn't hard considering no one asked me what I wanted to do with my life. If they had, I would have lied and said I didn't know.

Sometimes I wanted to tell Jared that I was going to leave too, just so he knew he wasn't going to be the only one, but he was obsessed with his plans for college and graduation and didn't seem interested in the ideas of his younger sister. The only things that mattered to Jared were sports and comic books. He loved football and baseball and came alive when a ball was in his hands. Even at night in his room, I'd walk by and he'd be tossing a football or baseball up and down and acting out a great catch or save. He was never embarrassed to find me watching him; in fact, he performed all the better with an audience.

"I'm not sure anyone could ever love you as much as you love yourself," I said to him one afternoon after catching him flexing his muscles in the mirror. He had come out of the shower and was wrapped in a towel.

"You'd be surprised how much the chicks dig me," he said. He flexed again. "Check out these pecs—ever seen anything like them?"

I rolled my eyes.

"I could kick anybody's ass with these fists," he said, boxing in front of the mirror. "Name the guy and I'll take care of him for you, Cat." As he jabbed harder his towel fell off. He grabbed it before I could see anything, but not before his face flushed as red as Mom's heirloom tomatoes.

Jared couldn't interest me in sports, but we bonded over comics. He followed most of the Marvel superheroes and taught me their stories, the comic book structures, and the production schedules of the serials. On Saturdays he would often let me ride my bike with him to Goldstein's Drugs and Sundries to pick up the new releases. A new release usually meant Jared would share the old one with me, and so although I was always a month behind, I was as drawn to the stories as I was to sharing something special with my big brother.

In the last couple of years, as he focused more on college, his love of comic books waned while mine grew. Jared had an extensive collection that he lent me freely. With no one to share the stories with, I studied the books more closely and secretly began drawing and writing my own comic, called "Kat's Eye." It was the story of a girl named Kitty Kat who was banished from her hometown of "Niceville" (I saw that town on a map of Florida once) by her nemesis, "the Hand." The stories were about Kitty Kat's attempts to fight the Hand (and his fellow evildoers, "the Monster" and "the Hard Heart") and get back to Niceville.

It was stupid.

My sketches were rigid and the stories were lame, but I loved doing it. I hid the drawings from everyone, even Jared, as I was sure he would laugh.

When Jared wasn't at sports practice or studying, he was pacifying my mother. It seemed the worse my father got, the more she depended on Jared. At times she treated him like he was her surrogate husband: cooking special meals for him, leaving presents under his pillow, and massaging him after his games. I was embarrassed at the attention she showered on him, and avoided them whenever they were together. I could tell it made Jared uncomfortable, but he put up with it. He said he was all Mom had.

Between my father and Wendy and my mother and Jared, there were moments in my life when the bonds between them seemed so strong that I wondered if I had a place anywhere. But there were nights when I was feeling particularly good that being alienated from them didn't matter. I would sneak out after dinner, go to my favorite tree stump in the woods, and pull out the large sketchbook I kept hidden in a hole next to the gnarly root I rested my foot on. This was the third book I had filled. Each page was covered with my hand-drawn frames and carefully lettered exposition. I sketched my ideas on small pieces of paper: sometimes I laid out the whole frame, other times I wrote an idea for a story or character, and quite often I worked on sketches, always trying to perfect my technique. Once I felt ready, I would draw the whole story into my big black sketchbook.

After I finished a book, I would take the snippets of paper and put them in a ziplock bag. I kept the whole bundle of my work in a watertight case I had purchased with birthday money. When the weather got cold, I moved everything to a special spot I had in the barn.

My current book was about half-filled but it was already bursting from all the scraps I stuffed into it.

Some nights I imagined I was a famous cartoonist who was being interviewed on *The Late Show.* I had only seen David Letterman a couple of times, mostly from the kitchen when my mother sent me down to wake my father after he passed out in front of the TV. I hated to do it, as I was never sure what kind of mood he'd be in, so I stood in the doorway and got lost in the glow of late-night television.

Addison followed me out to the woods one night after he arrived. Dad was passed out drunk and everyone else was asleep or settled into bed. I don't know how long he was there or what he heard. I only know that I was standing up and reading aloud from a story I wrote about Kat's adventures fighting the evil Hand. As I read on about the Hand's attempt to steal the treasure Kat carried in a secret compartment on her belt, I felt a hand around my waist and was lifted into the air. My stories went flying everywhere.

"Gotcha!" he shouted.

Without thinking, I elbowed him with a force that sent him tumbling into the pricker bush, and before I realized who it was, I kicked him in the ass several times.

Addison rolled over and sat on his knees. I caught my breath. "What the fuck is your problem?" I shouted as tears sprang from my eyes. I couldn't tell which upset me more, getting caught or being ambushed.

"I'm sorry," he said, as he stood up and pulled the prickers from his pants.

I wiped my nose with the back of my sleeve. He handed me a bandanna from his back pocket. I slapped it away as I turned and gathered all the loose sheets of paper I could see in the glow of the moonlight.

"I didn't mean to make you cry."

"I'm not crying—I'm mad." I searched the ground for more scraps.

"Listen," he said, walking toward me.

"Don't!" I put my hand up to stop him. I picked up a Tastee Freez napkin with the name Freidkan Walker written on it. He served me a root beer float. I thought his name was funny so I wrote it down.

I left Addison pulling prickers from his pants. I had no choice but to take my box with me. I couldn't leave it under the stump for him to discover. I rushed through the woods toward the house, feeling the sting of tears streaming down my cheeks. Brittle branches snapped beneath my feet as I propelled myself forward. I had been caught feeling free. Now I would have to find somewhere new to hide. I was running out of places.

The next morning I left for school without seeing him. On the bus I made a list of all of the ways I would avoid Addison. I hid the box in the barn but took Book III with me in the hope that I could assess whether I had lost any ideas. It felt as full as I had remembered. To be sure, though, I was going back that night with a flashlight.

By the time I got to school I felt good about my plan. If I stuck to it, I could avoid Addison and get back to the woods to recover anything that had been lost.

I remembered too late that Nell had left early for a doctor's appointment and I tried to catch the last bus home. As the doors closed without me, I saw Addison leaning against the statue of Grover Cleveland, holding a large shopping bag. He was wearing red cowboy boots and loose jeans that hung off his waist and a T-shirt that said STINKY'S BAR AND GRILL. THE ONLY THING THAT STINKS AT STINKY'S IS NOT HAVING YOU HERE. His rust-colored hair was damp and combed off his face. He looked as if he had just showered.

The bus pulled away.

"Shit."

"I have the truck," Addison said, coming so close I could smell the orange scent of his shampoo. "Let me give you a—"

I put my hand up to silence him and began the long walk home. He went away.

After a few moments, I felt the rumbling of his engine as he followed slowly behind me in his truck. He pulled up beside me and coasted as he held a shopping bag out the window.

"Here," he said, shaking the bag.

I looked at the package. It was lilac and covered with white polka dots and looked fancy, like the kind you buy at Hallmark for a special gift.

"Don't make me drive into a ditch again," he said, as he swerved off the road a little.

The bag flew out of his hand and into the air. Before I knew what I was doing, I ran to catch it. There was tissue paper inside that matched the lilac and white of the bag.

Addison stopped the truck and hung his head out the window. "Open it!"

I looked at him and then back at that beautiful bag and the wrapping. It was lovely enough to be a gift on its own.

"Please."

There was something heavy and hard resting at the bottom. I had never gotten a gift out of the blue. We weren't big on gifts in my family, except when Dad bought stuff for Wendy. We got practical stuff for Christmas and birthdays—new socks, underwear, or sometimes a few dollars shoved in an envelope—but never anything nice and never with special wrapping.

I should have handed it back and kept walking.

Instead I reached in and pulled out a square object and slid the bag's handle over my hand. It was wrapped in tissue paper with a long curly ribbon dripping off it like spun sugar.

I slid the ribbon off the edges and slowly tore the tissue, which revealed gilt-edged pages. The wrapping floated away, uncovering a larger version of my black sketchbook only covered in red leather with gold-embossed leaves on each corner. Inside the cover was red wavy satin, and each page was smooth, cool, and white, with the faint edge of gold. On the first blank page, Addison had written:

*Kat's Eye*
*The Amazng Adventures of Kitty Kat*

He knew.

I wanted to die.

"There's more." He pointed at the bag.

I took a deep breath and rummaged through the bag and found a bundle of pens, just like the one I dropped when he picked me up.

"I know you have your own book but I thought this was—"

"Beautiful," I said. My voice cracked. I willed my body to stay still as my insides collapsed and expanded in rushes of opposite emotion, like an umbrella opening and closing inside me.

He smiled. "You like it?"

I nodded. I knew I should say something. A thank-you, at least, but I was afraid. My hands shook as I held the book and the pens and felt the bag brushing against my leg. I should have given it back. As lovely as it was, it was one more thing I would have to hide. I should have said, "Thanks, but no thanks," but I didn't. I stood stone silent and hugged it to my chest.

Addison put the truck in gear and threw the parking brake. He opened the passenger door and patted the seat.

"I won't bite. I promise."

I climbed in slowly, afraid I might lose my footing and fall away forever.

"Don't even think of giving it back," he said. "I don't want you to feel . . ."

I looked at him.

"Obligated," he said, as if he were reading my mind.

I closed my eyes and felt the smooth cover of the book in my hands.

"Think of it as an investment in your future."

"My future?" I said.

"You're an artist."

I laughed. "It's a stupid comic."

"Not stupid at all." He reached across my lap, opened the glove compartment, and pulled out a pile of scrap paper. "I went back to the woods this morning to make sure I got everything." He handed it all to me. There were half-pages of panels, detailed sketches of the Hand. There was even one notebook page titled "The Secret Treasure—What Is It?"

"You read all of these?"

He didn't have to answer. Of course he had—the book, the pens—he had read every word. He saw something I would have never shared with him or anyone.

"Please . . ." I said, pleading for what I don't know.

Addison leaned toward me as if he were going to kiss me and reached his hand across my chest to grab the door handle.

"It sticks if you don't slam it." He opened and closed my door as his cheek brushed my shoulder. I flinched.

"I don't like to be touched," I blurted before I could censor myself.

"That's too bad," he said, as he sat back in his seat. "Touching can be nice."

We sat in silence for a few moments. I felt that rush of shame again as I tried to stay in the moment, tried to feel the vibration of the motor rumbling under my thighs, the pull of his eyes on me, the smoothness of the sketchbook in my lap, and the sharp edges of my scraps he had rescued in the woods. I tried to stay in the moment, to not escape to someplace in my head where this was not happening and I was safe and alone.

"I wouldn't have read them if I had known how you felt."

I hung my head, wishing I could fold into myself and slip into the glove compartment.

"You have nothing to be ashamed of. Your sketches are . . ."

I bowed my head and began to cry. Addison handed me his yellow bandanna from his back pocket. This time I took it.

"It's okay," he said, as he put his hand on top of mine, which were folded in my lap. His palm was dry and warm and covered my fingers like a blanket. We sat like that until the setting sun glowed through the windshield, blinding us. Addison released the parking brake and shifted gears.

He took the long way through town and around the duck pond. In the few weeks he had been with us, spring had announced its arrival with cool days that were slowly wearing away the memory of another harsh Ohio winter. We cracked the windows to get some of the sweet air.

"Tell me about 'Kat's Eye,'" he said, as if he were asking me about the weather.

Maybe it was the light or the sketchbook, but I felt a small shift inside me. The memory of his hand lingered, along with a general feeling of unease at being so near him. This was not fear, though I knew the discomfort of that; this was different. Instead of fighting the urge to turn away, I was resisting the desire to slide as close to him as possible.

"Jared shared his comics with me," I said, my voice sounding queer, like I was speaking in a different language. I had never heard myself tell this story. "Before I learned about comics, I drew picture books when I was little. My mom says she saved them."

"Kitty Kat—is she you?"

"Me? No. She's beautiful and brave."

"But she has your name."

"She spells it with a *K*."

"Anything else is just coincidence?" he said as he turned in to the Sally's Sweet Shoppe parking lot.

"Yup," I said, smiling as I felt my toes wiggling, signaling a laugh was on its way.

"You like root beer floats?"

I nodded.

Addison slid out of the car and glided into the shop as the welcome bell signaled another customer. He chatted with Sally and made her laugh so hard she reached over the counter and playfully slapped him.

He came out a few minutes later with huge bubbling floats. I took a sip and put my head back and closed my eyes. The dark molasses flavor mixed with the sweet vanilla coolness was delicious.

I opened my eyes. Addison was studying my face. "You're lovely when you're smiling," he said, as I felt that warm rush again and turned away.

"Let's drive to the duck pond and finish these."

We parked and got out of the truck. Addison jumped up on the hood while I held our floats. He took them as I climbed up next to him, slipping and spilling the drinks in his lap. He slid off the hood and pulled me with him as we both fell to the ground laughing.

"Oh my God, are you all right?" I said, helping him up. He had root beer all over him, and without thinking, I started blotting it off with my napkins. I accidentally grazed his crotch with my hand and felt a wave of panic so strong I was sure I would go into cardiac arrest.

"I'm so sorry," I said. We looked at each other in unison and started laughing again. "Want to try again?" I said, pointing to the hood.

"Nah. I'm not sure I'm capable of falling for you twice."

"That's funny," I replied, "I'm not going to fall for you even once."

"We'll see," he said.

We got back in the car and sat quietly, watching the sun go down across the field behind the pond.

"You're okay," he said, nudging me, "not half as snotty as I thought."

"Thanks," I said, "I wish I could say the same about you."

He threw his head back and laughed so hard I thought it would echo. The skin around his eyes and mouth wrinkled like a nicely worn trail.

"Will you show me more?" He pointed to the bag where I had put the sketchbook and scraps.

"I don't know," I said, shrugging.

"I think you will."

"Maybe."

"Don't make me tickle you," he said, waving his fingers in front of me.

"Okay, okay, just don't touch me!" I said as he reached over and tickled me until I got hiccups.

## FIVE

"Cat."

Jared stood in the doorway where Addison had been a few hours before. I was still on the floor with my knees to my chest and my head buried in my hands. My mouth was dry with no lingering taste of beer. My throbbing head would soon evolve into a massive hangover. My cheeks were crusty from crying.

I don't know how long I had been lost in memory. The coats on the bed were gone.

"Have you returned to the land of the living?" Jared's thin frame was backlit against the pale rose-print wallpaper that lined the upstairs hall. He leaned casually against the doorway, wiping his hands with a dish towel.

"Mom's dead," I said as I reawakened to reality.

Jared turned on the lamp on the side table and sat on the bed next to me. His calf brushed against my shoulder. I felt the heat of him and wanted to rest against his leg for a few moments. It wouldn't mean I needed him. It would feel so nice.

His leg began to twitch, repelling the possibility. I pulled away.

I had gone too far back in my memory to the days when I knew he would protect me. It made me thirsty.

"You okay?"

"Fine," I said as I squinted from the glare of light. "What time is it?"

"Midnight."

Jared stood up. On his left hand I noticed a gold wedding band and wondered why I hadn't seen it before. I guess he married the woman in the Jag—what was her name? It was a street in New York. Broadway, no, Madison.

"Everybody gone?"

*Did they have any kids?*

"Just about. Andrew and Hal said to say good-bye. Andrew said to call if you need anything. He seems to think you're friends."

"Why?"

"Maybe it's your charm. You have a tendency to be overly warm to people." Jared made a pistol from his index finger and thumb and pointed it at me, punctuating his sarcasm.

"I used to be nice," I said.

"And that would have been . . . when?"

"Funny, Jared. Ever think of taking your act on the road?"

Jared swept his arm across the bedspread, feeling for something. He lifted the pillows and patted them. I wondered if he was going to strip the sheets.

"What are you looking for?" I said, scooting away from the bed. Sooner or later I would have to try to stand up. I was holding off as long as I could.

"Addison called. He left his lighter. Said he's pretty sure he left it in here."

There it was, his name, spoken aloud. The sound of it as something other than a voice in my head made me feel that rush again. I had to get up. I pushed myself to a crawling position. I couldn't have Jared, the memory of Addison, and myself in the same room at the same time with no escape. I reached for the bed to steady myself.

"You do this every night?" Jared said.

"What?"

"Drink till you pass out?"

"I didn't pass out."

"Tell that to Addison."

"What does that mean?" I eased myself down on the bed and experimented with keeping my head up.

"He's the one who carried you upstairs."

"When?"

"You dropped your beer and hit the floor. Wendy and I told everyone you were tired and hadn't eaten."

"I was tired, and I haven't eaten."

"Whatever," he said. He was looking under the bed. "Addison carried you up here and put you on the bed. As usual I cleaned up the mess."

I resisted the urge to say, "What's that supposed to mean?" His fixation on the bed was starting to annoy me. Addison told him he left his lighter in my parents' bedroom, and Jared assumed he left it in the bed.

"Try the dresser. Christ, what do you think we were doing?"

"When it comes to you and Addison, it's hard to say." He walked over to the dresser and found the lighter. He tossed it in the air as he headed for the door.

"So you haven't kept in touch with him?" he said; the edge had left his voice.

I shook my head.

"Were you happy to see him?"

We locked eyes for a moment. I shrugged. If I had the rest of my life, I'm not sure I could find an adequate answer.

"Were you happy to see me?" His voice cracked with exposure.

"Define *happy*."

"Jared!" Wendy called from downstairs. Jared's eyes fixed on me as if I were a map he was trying to decipher.

"I don't drink that much," I said.

"He's living at his grandma's place." Jared answered as if I had asked. "He's been back awhile."

I reached for my cigarettes that were on my mother's nightstand.

"Jared!" Wendy called again. I searched for a match.

"Just a sec," he shouted back as he glided toward me, flipping open Addison's Zippo lighter. He tripped the flame as I guided his hand toward the cigarette. I felt the smooth ridges of his knuckles and the bump of a vein that could be traced all the way to his heart.

"He's got a kid." His tone was cool, like the drag of menthol filling my lungs. I let go of his hand as I pulled on the cigarette and thanked the god of lung cancer for giving me something to steady myself.

"I know," I said.

# Six

ADDISON STARTED meeting me after school a couple of times a week. He introduced himself to Nell and charmed her in a way that made her blush every time he said hello. She gave up her time with me easily on the condition I told her everything.

Until Addison, I was not interested in boys. In fact, I had never been on a date. Nell had more luck and went out with anyone who asked. Unfortunately, the boys who liked her were not the ones she liked. Still, she said, a girl couldn't be too picky and attention was attention.

I didn't think I was missing anything. Nell often told me about the guys she went out with and their roaming hands and slippery kisses. It sounded clinical to me, like she was getting a medical procedure rather than having fun.

It would be a lie to say I had never been touched by a man. But the truth would be worse. So I found a place to live between a lie and the truth. Until Addison, I got along just fine.

In a short time I had gone from living deep within myself to seeking the company of another person. I wanted to hear his voice before he spoke, feel his hand on my arm before we touched. I wanted to be with him all the time. When I saw his truck in front of the school, I knew what it felt like to be happy.

Those days were like a long, slow drunk.

———

One night toward the end of spring semester, Addison didn't show up after school as he had promised. When I got home Mom was making dinner and Dad sat in the family room shouting at the television and drinking.

"Cat's home," Mom called to Dad. I looked at her with a why-did-you-do-that face. She shrugged her shoulders and whispered, "He was asking for you." Even though Mom was more than happy to turn Dad over to me, she didn't understand why I was angry with her all the time.

"Cat!" Dad yelled. I swallowed hard and went to him. He looked me over like I was a toy he was thinking of ordering from a catalog. I instinctively crossed my arms and pushed down the fear.

"You want something?" I asked as his eyes roamed over my legs.

"Your ass is getting fat," he said, smacking it hard. "Get me some ice."

I shook off the sting of his slap and brought him a tumbler stuffed with fresh cubes. He patted the armrest of his La-Z-Boy. Over the years I learned the code of his gestures and expressions. I studied it like a language, not for meaning but for warning. If I could read him I could stay ahead of him or at least try to anticipate what was coming and prepare myself.

I balanced as little of my body as I could on the edge of the armrest. He filled the tumbler with the bourbon he kept nearby and took a long cold pull as his left hand wandered up my skirt.

The sandpaper scruffiness of his fingers kneaded my thigh. It wasn't a squeeze so much as a grip, as if I were a chicken and my leg was the drumstick he would tear off and devour. It was warm that day so I wore kneesocks instead of tights. Tights were better for encounters with Dad.

As his hand sought more of me, I thought of Kitty Kat and the battle she would fight against the Hand. I would draw it tonight. I would make her body a weapon, rage would be her arsenal, and her reward would be a life in Niceville. Wherever the hell that was; sometimes even Kitty forgot.

"Where's Addison?" Dad asked as he stumbled to his chair. I had been released from sitting with him to help set the table.

"He's visiting a friend and won't be home until later," Mom answered as she served Dad steaming spoonfuls of baked macaroni.

Dad tried to pick fights with all of us during dinner. All except Wendy. He started with Mom about the dinner, saying macaroni was slop for pigs. He threw the plate at her, and after dodging it, she fixed him a ham sandwich and sat back down and pushed a clump of bread crumbs around her plate.

Jared was next.

"So how's that pussy team of yours doing this season?"

"Fine," Jared responded, staring blankly into space.

"How many girls are on the team, besides you?"

Jared didn't flinch. "There are none, sir. No girls on the team."

"If you ask me, all boys are girls nowadays. When I played ball, you had to be a mean motherfucker to survive out there. You had to have hate in you." Dad pointed his thick index finger at Jared. "You had to have the desire to kill a man with your bare hands." He took a long swig of his liquid ammunition. "You have that in you, boy?"

Jared's focus shifted from a fixed point on the wall. "Yes, sir," he answered as he locked eyes with Dad. Jared clenched his butter knife.

We finished the last few moments of dinner in a silent standoff. After years of mealtime conflict, we had perfected the quick eat. From start to finish, we could get the meal on and off the table and dishes washed in fifteen minutes.

"What's for dessert?" Dad asked. He had a thing about sweets; he said he didn't like them, but at least three or four times a week he asked for dessert.

As Mom cut pieces of apple pie Mrs. Igby had dropped by earlier, Dad said, "Don't give Cat any. She doesn't need it." My mother looked at me and then at my father and nodded.

"Keep chubbing up like that and no man will have you," Dad said. Wendy giggled. "And don't even think of sneaking a piece up to her room." He pointed at Mom when she looked my way.

"I don't want any!" I said before I could calculate the consequence.

Dad put his fork down and slid what was left of his pie over to me. Before I knew what was happening, he grabbed my neck with his hand and pushed my face down into the plate. "There—eat your pie, piggy."

I felt shards of light smashing against my eyelids as I quickly tried to assess what had happened and what he might do next. Before I could get my bearings, he lifted my head from the plate by my neck and tried to stuff the crust in my face as I swung my arms in front of me to stop him. My nose and mouth were throbbing. My eyes were tearing. The force of his hand caused my chair to tilt onto the back legs. I flailed my arms out like a baby bird trying to fly. I heard Jared's chair fall behind him as he jumped up and pulled Dad off me.

I fell forward and tried to keep my head up. I sat in a daze staring at the roosters on my mother's plastic tablecloth.

*Count the roosters. One, two . . . Don't cry. . . . Count the roosters.*

My nose was bleeding onto the orange-and-brown feathers of the roosters and I let it. My father grabbed the car keys and stormed out of the house.

"Cat, if he says no dessert just say no," Wendy said.

"Eat shit, Wendy," I said. "I hope he dies."

"You don't mean that, Cat." Mom held my head back and cleared the crumbs and blood off the table.

As soon as the room stopped spinning, I left the house for the woods.

I sat alone on the stump for a while before Jared came out with a washcloth and a bag of ice. "I thought you might have a bit of a shiner." I nodded. He knelt next to me and dabbed the dried blood off my face. "There, that's better," he said. I rolled my eyes and felt tears flowing down my cheeks. "You know Dad's mean to you because you're so much smarter and prettier than Wendy or Mom."

"I'd settle for being dumb and ugly if it meant he'd keep his paws off me."

We stared at the stars that appeared through a small clearing of trees. The wind rustled the leaves, making them sound like skirts swirling at a dance.

"Thanks for getting him off me."

"No problem," he said, taking my hand.

After a few minutes he got up. "So how about coming back to the house with me and we'll have some pie." I looked at him and smiled.

"I've got some on my sleeve here," I said.

"And a little on your blouse." He kissed the top of my head and walked back.

I kept the ice on my eye until my fingers grew numb, then tossed the cubes on the ground in front of me and told myself I would go back when the last one melted. I pulled out my black book and tried to sketch the fight I had mapped out in my mind, but my eye throbbed too much for me to concentrate. Some nights I couldn't draw my way out.

It was around midnight when I headed back. As I made my way out of the woods, I saw the headlights of a truck pull around the barn toward the garage and figured it was Dad. I waited some time before going in to make sure he had a chance to pass out in bed or in front of the TV.

I heard talking by the barn and thought maybe it was Addison and my father, until I caught the crackle of a giggle. I followed the driveway that led to the garage away from the house and saw Addison against his truck with a tall blond woman wearing a loose peasant skirt and a white sheer cotton top that was lifted up over her breasts.

"Let's go upstairs," she said as Addison buried his head in her neck as his hands inched her skirt up her thighs. I stepped into the shadow between the pools of light from the garage and the side porch.

"No one can see us," he moaned, without looking to see if that were true.

She looked around as he whispered something in her ear that made her tip her head back and sigh, responding to his touch.

Addison's hands worked her skirt up and pulled her underwear down. His focus was absolute, his mission clear. The woman reached for his pants and unbuttoned his fly.

I had seen animals doing it before and watched in fascination at the quick and awkward way a male and a female came together. I had imagined sex between people to be different, less frantic. This did not appear to be the case, at least with Addison. His intensity was no different than that of a bull.

Their sounds were more guttural than tender. She grunted as Addison banged his hips against her. Their rhythm increased rapidly as she gripped his back. Addison grabbed the truck like he was afraid his thrusts were going to topple it over.

I watched them in full view. All Addison had to do was look up and he would have seen me standing there, hands clenched into fists and feet apart as if I were ready to fight. What I was fighting for was painfully unclear.

I watched until a final grunt signaled the finish. Addison moved away and buttoned his pants.

"I'll take you home," he said.

She pulled her blouse down and fluffed her skirt as if they had finished searching for something she had lost. "You promised me that drink," she said as she reached under the truck and picked up her panties and shook the dirt off.

"One drink. I have to get up early," he said, as he walked up the stairs to the apartment without checking to see if she was following.

I felt my hands uncurl from fists and my body go limp like a boxer down for the count.

# SEVEN

THE SOUND OF the phone ringing reverberated inside my head. I shot up in bed and looked frantically around the strange room. Amnesia was a by-product of the black edge of sleep I drank myself into most nights. My mother's dressing table, the four bed-posts—I was in my parents' room and my mother was still dead. The clock said 9:00 A.M., but outside it was rainy and dismal and looked like it could have been evening. My head ached, my chest was tight from too much smoking, and my feet were sore from wearing pumps all day. I was wrapped in my mother's bedspread and still wearing the black dress and stockings but had managed to take my mom's earrings off and put them on the nightstand.

I slid to standing and groped my way to the mirror. My face was pale and sallow. I had finally mastered the perfect marriage of emaciated and bloated. My mascara had raccooned my eyes and left tiny polka dots along the edge of my lower eyelids. My hair was as smooth and silky as the head of a mop.

I should have crawled into the casket with her.

I shuffled to the bathroom and restarted my bladder and kidneys through intense concentration and focus, then brushed my teeth and spilled cold water on my face. I left tracks of black mascara on my mother's crisp white guest towels.

The upstairs was empty, with open doors revealing made beds and packed bags.

I made my way down the creaky back stairs. The harvest-gold telephone cord stretched past the landing. Jared was mumbling into the receiver as I limboed under and faced the blinding fluorescent light of the kitchen.

"Yes, I understand." His back was to me as he tried to untwist the long phone cord.

He caught my eye and waved. "Madison," he mouthed, as if I had asked.

There was a fresh pot of coffee on the stove. No Mr. Coffee for my mom. We were a farm family and that meant fresh coffee from a percolator all day for whomever stopped by. Farmers drink coffee like teenagers drink Coke.

Jared pointed to the store-bought muffins and juice on the table. A fresh pack of cigarettes sat on top of my car keys.

I checked the driveway for cars; Wendy's was missing.

I poured a tumbler of coffee, grabbed a muffin and my cigs, and headed to the stairs en route to a bath.

Jared poked me and then held his finger out as if to say, "One second."

"Yes, I know. I'm going to speak to her about it. Maybe tomorrow. I love you too."

Jared finally said good-bye and untangled himself as he hung up the phone.

"You'd think she would have gotten a new cord," he said.

"Why? It went everywhere she needed." I lit up a cigarette.

"Wendy went to see Dad before they head back."

"They're leaving?"

He nodded.

"Doesn't she have to take care of stuff?"

I assumed Wendy would stay to deal with whatever it is one does when your mother kills herself and your father is practically dead in the hospital.

"She's got to get back. Willard's got work and she's got treatments."

"What's wrong?"

"She and Willard are trying to get pregnant."

"I thought you and Wendy didn't talk that often." I walked to the sink and flicked my ashes in the drain.

"We talked last night—after you passed out."

"Fell asleep."

"Whatever. They've been trying for years."

"I didn't realize people actually tried to have children," I said as I took a long drag. Nothing like the first nicotine rush of the day.

"Some people try to get over their problems," Jared said, with just enough edge to his voice to make my skin crawl. He had taken a seat at the table and was picking at a muffin.

"Are we talking about Wendy or me?"

"I'm talking about all of us. Don't you think it's time?" He took a deep breath that looked as if it were more effort to hold in his words than to let them out. "Look, you've been MIA for how many years? Eight, nine?"

"I'm coming up on my tenth anniversary. What's that—rock, paper, or scissors? I get them confused."

"How long are you going to do this?" he said as he threw his muffin in the garbage like he was tossing a fastball.

"Do what?"

"Hold me responsible. I am NOT responsible." He came toward me and I flinched. "I did not ruin your life."

I put my cigarette out in the sink and stared him down.

"If my life is a mess, it is my own. I take responsibility, Jared."

"Glad to hear it."

"And your mess is yours. You live with what you did."

"I didn't do anything, Cat. I helped you. I saved you." Jared was shouting with an intensity that mirrored my father's when he was angry.

"You saved me?" My voice and my resolve cracked. I gripped the counter to steady my shaking hands. It was drink time.

"I wouldn't have let him kill you," he said.

"You should have. It would have been easier."

"Christ, I said I was sorry." He threw his mug into the sink with a force that made it shatter. I couldn't catch my breath or focus. I had a feeling that the floor beneath me would open up at any moment and swallow me whole. Outside a car horn honked. Jared walked to the window. "It's Wendy, she's got groceries." He stopped fishing for broken pieces and went out to help.

Wendy came in carrying a clear plastic cup filled with a pinkish liquid. "It's a smoothie. Can't have caffeine. Do you mind putting that out?" I had lit another cigarette in a lame attempt to steady myself. It wasn't working; I was crying.

I turned away and wiped my tears with my sleeve. "I'm going to take a bath."

"Help me with this stuff," she said, as she buzzed around the kitchen, wiping the counters and scraping the plates from breakfast. "Willard is going to make a big Italian feast for our last dinner together. We also got staples for you." She handed me stuff from the bags to put away. "No caffeine or nicotine, though. You're on your own there."

"Sounds like you and Jared have everything figured out. Remind me not to fall asleep on you again," I said.

"You didn't fall asleep. You passed out. All you have to do is get the bills and stuff in order. We have to wait to see what happens to Dad. I'm sure Mom took care of most of it ahead of time." Wendy shoved cans and boxes into all the right places. She had Mom's arms and had taken to wearing her apron. From behind, it was like watching Mom return from the store. "Besides, we figured you could use a break." She stopped to think about what she thought I needed to get away from.

"For all you know I could have a fabulous life in New York," I said, heading toward the stairs.

Wendy grabbed my arm and turned me toward her. "Do you?" she asked, with a tenderness that caught me off guard.

# EIGHT

I WENT TO SCHOOL the next day with a black eye. No one suspected anything was wrong; cuts and bruises were a regular part of being a Rucker kid. People assumed we played hard.

I told Nell that I would walk home. I wanted to be by myself and wasn't in a big hurry to get back. I thought a lot about leaving for good that day and I toyed with the idea of getting a bus ticket for New York and just taking off. The more I thought about it, the happier it made me. There was no reason to stay. Going home would mean facing my father, who would act like it was my fault for getting between him and his pie, and Addison, who would . . . God, what was I thinking?

Addison was weeding my mother's flower beds when I came up the drive. He had made good on his warning to get up early. His truck was gone by the time I woke up. On the days he worked at his grandma's he was usually home by late afternoon.

"Where's the fire?" He sat back on his heels and waved his small garden shovel at me as I hurried past.

I went through the side door and up the stairs to my room. The house was empty. There was a note on my bed from my mother.

*Cat,*
*Went to supper with Dad and Wendy. Jared is at football*
*practice. There's leftover macaroni in the fridge.*
*Mom xxxooo*

So I get a black eye and Wendy and Mom get steak? Great. As if things weren't bad enough she leaves me with him. I started thinking about my plan again. I opened my backpack and pulled out some sketches I had been doing for Kitty's big fight with the Hand.

Addison rapped on the doorway. I ignored him.

"How about I take you to dinner?" Addison took a bandanna out of his back pocket and wiped his hands. He wore a Pittsburgh Pirates baseball hat and baggy overalls.

"I have homework," I said, putting away my sketchbook.

"Is something wrong?"

"I'm busy." I gave him a fake smile. His cheeks were flush, like they were after he finished fucking her.

"What happened to your eye?" I touched my face. I had forgotten.

"Nothing."

"It's black and blue," he said, coming toward me.

I put my hand up to stop him.

He stepped back into the doorway.

"There's macaroni in the fridge; help yourself."

"Was it an accident?"

I ignored him.

"Did you put some ice on it?"

I pulled out my homework and laid it on the bed.

"Are you angry with me?"

I opened my *World Cultures* book and found the chapter I was supposed to review for the test tomorrow and pretended to study. But no matter how hard I tried to concentrate on reading, I could feel him in the doorway.

Outside the wind made the screen door bang open and closed. The room was filled with the honey glow of the setting sun. In a few minutes it would be dark. I would have to get up and hit the switch by the doorway—by Addison.

The space between us filled with shadow.

"I saw you last night . . . at the truck."

"Were you spying on me?"

I laughed. "Yeah, Addison, I'm obsessed with you. Can you go now? I've got work to do."

He crossed his arms. "I'm sorry if what you saw upset you. I didn't think anyone was around. I wouldn't have done it if I had known you were—"

"If I was what? Alive?"

"Alex, you're young, you don't—"

"I understand what was going on. What I don't understand is why you need to be here now."

"I thought we were friends," he said.

"Please go."

"Besides, that girl doesn't mean anything."

I was done listening. If he wasn't going to leave, I would. I started for the door with the intent to blow past him before he knew I was coming. But he sensed my movement before I could react and threw his body in the doorway to block my exit. I jumped back and looked up, giving him a full view of my black eye.

"Who did this to you?" His hands were on my shoulders holding me in place. He had the sweet iron smell of my mother's flower beds mixed with that orange shampoo. I could feel his breath on my neck and the pressure from each of his fingers pushing into my shoulders.

My mind raced with snappy retorts. I wanted to say something that would prove I didn't care about him or who he slept with or who hit me. His lips were inches from mine, smooth and pink and glistening. The same mouth that whispered in that woman's ear and made her giggle. What were the words? Would they make me laugh?

"My face collided with a piece of pie," I said.

He reached into my room and switched on the light. I tried to squirm away but he held me steady. "Stand still," he whispered gently.

"God, you act like you've never had a black eye," I said as he inspected me.

"And you act like it's normal." He touched the swollen crescent lightly with his cool fingers.

"Stop," I said, but he didn't.

"Did someone hurt you?" He traced the outline of the bruise and brushed the hair off my face. I reached for the wall to steady myself.

"You are," I said, pushing away.

"I didn't mean to," he said. He fixed his gaze on me, and although he appeared to be listening, he studied me as if I were an object he wanted to possess.

"You do this to everyone, don't you?" I said as I struggled to regain my footing. Before I could stop him, his hands enveloped my face and his thumbs held the corners of my mouth as his fingers reached toward my neck and lifted me toward him. Before I felt his lips, I felt his warm breath on my eyebrow and his chest brush against mine, and then, when I thought my legs would give out, he kissed me lightly on the lid of my black eye.

We went to the Omega diner out past the airport for dinner. I didn't have to look at the menu to know what I wanted. The Omega had the best chocolate milkshakes and onion rings in the world—well, at least in my world. After I ordered, Addison didn't say anything grown-up, like, "Is that all you're having?" or, "Maybe you should have a salad"; he smiled and said, "Good choice; I'll have the same."

"Stop trying to get me to like you. It's not going to work." We didn't say much after the doorway. He asked me to go with him to eat and I found myself following.

"Come on, are you really immune to my charm?"

"Is having sex on my driveway part of your charm?"

"I guess that depends on who you ask."

"Does your girlfriend think so?"

"She's not my girlfriend. She's a woman I met at Walt's—no biggie."

The waitress brought our food. I lifted the long metal tumbler to my mouth and began to drink. I closed my eyes and felt the chocolaty smoothness coat my throat as I bent my head back and smiled in milkshake ecstasy.

"You look like a little girl when you drink." Addison was giving me that look that made me feel like he was touching me.

"I was never a little girl, Addison. Just a smaller version of this." I pointed to my eye.

"I bet you were sweet." He tried to touch my hand but I pulled away.

"You said we were friends."

"So?"

"So friends don't do this." I imitated him trying to touch me. He laughed.

"You're right. I'll try to control myself."

"It shouldn't be that difficult."

He laughed. "It's harder than you think."

We ate the onion rings in silence.

After a few minutes he looked at his watch and said, "I have to make a call." He slid out of the booth and looked around for the phone as he searched his pockets for change.

I waited for him as I watched the straw wrapper unwind in the sweat from the water glass. The scrunched-up paper blossomed from contact with the water, unfurling and opening, only to flatten and dissolve into a wet paste that fell apart if you tried to hold it.

He slid back into the booth.

"So what's your story?" I said. He raised an eyebrow.

"You tell me yours and I'll tell you mine," he said.

"I'm sixteen, you're twenty-one—you have a better one, I'm sure."

"I'd like to know what happened to your eye."

"You're changing the subject," I said.

He had a way of looking at me that made me feel like he saw who I was and it didn't scare him.

"Let's start with the woman. Is that who you called?" Addison shifted in his seat and picked up the knife and tapped it against the table. I took the knife out of his hand and put it down.

"Okay." He took a deep breath. "The woman from last night— it was . . . a . . . quickie—hell, I didn't even remember her name until I found her number in my pants this morning. And yes—that was who I called."

"Is that all there is?"

"With her? Yeah."

I nodded and looked away.

"Hey, I'm not ready to settle down, and I'm not the looking-to-fall-in-love type. I've seen what a mess it makes of people's lives."

"Whose lives?"

He was slipping away again. He drummed on the table with the knife and checked his watch.

"Whose lives?"

"Everyone's." He thought for a moment and then reconsidered. "No that's not true. Your family's life doesn't seem ruined by it. Not like my parents. Man, talk about a train wreck."

I wondered how bad a mess his parents' life must be for him to think mine had it better.

"That's why I came here to work on Grandma's house. I needed to get away from all that . . .." He looked out the window and lost his train of thought.

The check came and as he paid he said, "Listen, you're young. You probably have all these romantic notions about love. You're expecting some guy to come and sweep you off your feet and everything will be all right. Maybe that will happen, but as you get older you'll see that there are two kinds of sex: sex for love and sex for sex, and both are great."

I laughed.

"Why are you laughing?"

"There are more kinds of sex than that."

———

In the truck, on the way home, I started to drift off. I tried to rest the side of my head against the door, but every bump banged my black eye. Addison pulled me toward him, placing my head on his shoulder. I sat up.

"You want to tell me what happened?"

"It was an accident."

"I told you my story, so cough it up."

"My father did it."

"Not on purpose?"

Now it was my turn to avoid the question. I looked out the window.

"It was an accident, right?"

"Define *accident*."

Addison pulled over and turned toward me, putting his arm on the back of the seat. "Tell me what happened."

"He didn't want me to have pie. He said my ass was getting too fat. I said I didn't want any. He shoved my face in the plate. My head hit the table. My eye got black."

Through my open window I could hear the gentle snapping of twigs. We sat quietly for a few moments.

"I'm sure he didn't mean it," he said finally.

This was his big assessment?

This was why I didn't tell people. They never believed me. Deep down they wanted to think it wasn't as awful as it seemed. Instead of feeling bad for me, they'd rather act like I was doing something to deserve the treatment. When I was in fifth grade I told my homeroom teacher how I got the bruises on my wrists (my father had grabbed me too hard when he was punishing me for sneaking out to the woods); she called the principal, who called my parents. Dad rewarded my honesty with a broken wrist and a warning to keep my mouth shut. When the teacher asked me the next day why I was wearing a cast, I told her I fell.

"He's always been so good to me," Addison muttered.

"Let's go," I said.

"Do you want me to talk to your dad? See if he'll apologize?" he asked as we pulled off the main road to our farm.

He was delusional. "If you speak to my dad about what happened, I swear I will never talk to you again. I will leave and never come back and you will be the one I blame."

It wasn't very much, but that was all I could threaten him with.

"Okay."

"Okay what?"

"I won't say a thing on one condition."

"Addison, you're pushing your luck."

"Let me kiss you good night."

"Oh, please," I said, feeling a rush in my throat.

He banged the steering wheel in frustration. "It's just a kiss, Alex. . . . It doesn't—"

"I know, it doesn't mean anything."

"You should loosen up," he said as he climbed out of the truck and came around to my door and opened it. He took my arm and helped me out, trying to seize an opportunity to get close to me. I pushed him away. He threw his hands up in defeat and walked me to the door.

Upstairs, the light was on in my parents' bedroom. The sheer curtains were closed but I could see the shadow of my father standing at the window watching us through the filter of the fabric.

# NINE

I VOLUNTEERED TO RETURN the chafing dishes and deli platters to Sal's to get our deposit back. Aside from having the opportunity to get away from the madness brewing in the kitchen, it gave me a chance to hit the liquor store and replenish my stash. Willard put Wendy and Jared to work chopping and shredding. One night of planning my future had made fast friends of Jared and Wendy.

The truth was, I had nowhere to go. The months leading up to my mother's suicide had not been good. I was working as a cocktail waitress in a strip club (gentlemen's club, titty bar, call it what you will) and had failed out of my last semester of school, postponing my dream of finishing college before I was dead or thirty, whichever came first. If that wasn't enough, the rent for my tiny Brooklyn apartment had just doubled.

My life had become one long drink service—either I was pouring one for myself or serving them to the miscreants who came looking for T and A in the bowels of the meatpacking district. In spite of my great charm and wit, not to mention my decent legs, I was getting fewer and fewer shifts at work due to an issue the owner called my "inability to come to work in a sober state." He had a bug up his ass because I wouldn't blow him.

In the year of my tenth anniversary away from home, I had stopped paying my rent, lost my job, and formed a close bond with a man named Jack Daniel's. In this stupor of impending doom, I got the call that Mom had checked out.

Ten years of stuff from twenty jobs, five apartments, a bunch of crappy relationships, and three and a half years of college fit into three boxes. I packed them along with two lawn-and-leaf bags filled with clothes into the trunk of my twenty-year-old powder-blue Honda, which I had bought with stolen money. For the second time in my life I left a place I called home and never looked back.

I spent the deposit money on booze and bought a bottle of wine to say that's where it went. I drove to the 7-Eleven to buy smokes and sat in the parking lot and drank while I watched women in sweat-pants coming out with milk and Wonder bread. I wondered if their homes were worth returning to.

There was a brown Ford Bronco in the driveway when I pulled up. I drank half a bottle of bourbon on the way and was feeling more prepared for a last supper with my siblings.

"So we need to find those papers," Wendy said as I came through the door, stumbling on the uneven top step.

"Oh, God," Jared mumbled as I caught the wine before it slipped out of my hands. Wendy liberated the bottle from me.

"Cat, you've been . . ."

"Hey, there." Andrew Reilly, County Coroner, stood up from the table and came toward me.

"What is he doing here?"

"I ran into Andrew at the hospital. We got to talking about Dad and he had some good advice so I invited him to dinner," Wendy said.

"I want to help," Andrew said as he put his hands in his pockets and shrugged his shoulders.

"Yeah, I get that. What I don't get is why." I stumbled over to the sink and poured myself a glass of water.

Willard was standing over the stove stirring tomato sauce. To his left, on the back burner, was a cauldron of sputtering steam. "Spaghetti Bolognese," he said. "It will put some meat on you."

Willard's thick black glasses steamed over from the pasta, giving him the look of Sherman from the Peabody cartoons we used to watch on Sunday mornings when Mom and Dad slept in. He was so short he almost needed a step stool to reach the stove. Everything about Willard screamed harmless, from his small quick hands to his quiet voice. He was so innocuous it was hard to tell he was even there.

Behind me, Jared, Wendy, and Andrew talked about the house and Dad. I fought the urge to lie down on the floor and sleep and joined them at the table.

"So if they decide to move him to a nursing home, you'll have to use his assets first before the state will pay for anything."

"What if he doesn't have any assets?" Wendy asked, passing up Jared's offer of wine. He moved on to Andrew and then to Willard, ignoring my empty glass.

"If the house and land are in both your parents' names—it's all his now. Do you know where the deed is?"

Jared and Wendy shook their heads and looked at me. "I don't even know where the sugar is," I said.

"That's your first assignment," Wendy said. "Find the deed so we can figure out how to take care of Dad."

"Pulling the plug would be the best way to take care of Dad." Jared smiled.

"Cat! Pull it together; this is important."

"If we can figure out where they kept their important papers, we may be able to find out what your father's feelings were about being left in this state."

"What's the 'we' thing?" I said.

"Be nice," Wendy said.

"It's okay. I understand," Andrew answered.

"You do? How big of you."

"Would it matter if I told you I promised your mother I would help?"

"She talked to you about this?"

Andrew nodded.

*He isn't who you think he is. . . .*

# Ten

SPRING CAME AND went, along with the final days of my junior year. I celebrated my seventeenth birthday quietly at the end of May with chocolate cake and no bruises.

After that night at the Omega diner, Addison and I kept our distance. If I had learned anything, I knew when it was safe to be around a man. The events of that night and everything that led up to it convinced me it was best to stay away.

It wasn't as hard as I thought. I suspected Addison had drawn the same conclusion. I was pretty sure my father had seen me getting out of Addison's truck and had warned him off me.

Addison was busy putting the final touches on the renovations to his grandma's house and was planning on heading back to California in a few weeks. My father had pitched in to help and together they had managed to get the work done without spending any money on labor. Dad and Addison took pride in their accomplishment and I suspected both were excited at the prospect of pleasing Addison's father, Jared, who was coming for a visit.

Dad was so focused on getting ready for Jared, he neglected his real job of being the family terror and drunk.

The news of Jared's arrival made everyone come alive. My mother embarked on a serious cleaning campaign that forced Wendy and me to dust behind our beds, dressers, and wardrobes, and sweep and polish the floors. Mom was on a mission to eliminate all dirt from our lives; but no matter how hard she tried, the dirt beneath the surface could not be buffed away.

With the windows open and adorned with freshly starched white curtains, it was hard to think of the dark days we had endured. My mother's smile was a welcome treat at breakfast, as were my father's kind words for her efforts. Even the lines on Dad's weatherworn face softened in anticipation of the praise he would get from the only man he had ever admired.

I was happy to clean, scrub, sew, haul, toss, or do whatever was necessary to bring some polish to our lives. And like my parents and Addison, Wendy, Jared, and I looked forward to Jared's arrival with joyous expectation. I was dying to be in the company of the man who elicited such devotion from the people I cared about.

Jared was to arrive on Flag Day, June fourteenth, and in honor of both, my father hung a new American flag from our front porch. My mother baked fresh bread, made strawberry preserves and apple pie (all Jared's favorites), and laundered and pressed our Sunday best.

According to Addison and Dad's calculations, Jared would arrive from the airport (which was a two-hour drive) by lunchtime. We were washed, dressed, and sitting on the porch by ten A.M.

We waited in silence, interrupted by occasional bouts of "Get your feet off the furniture," "No food until Jared arrives," and speculative talk about how he would look and what he would say. Our Jared fell asleep on the porch swing. He had been up with Dad and Addison hanging molding until three A.M. Addison had the lethargic posture that comes from being too tired, but his eyes were alert and gleamed with a look I understood to be the love he had been saving for his dad.

By four Mom broke down and let us have a slice of bread with butter and preserves. By six, Dad started drinking and Addison said he would be in his apartment if anyone needed him. At seven the phone rang with word that Jared wasn't coming. Mom took the call, twirling in the phone cord like she was wrapping herself in someone's arms. Her fingers fluttered as she gesticulated and blushed her way through his disappointing news. She kept the conversation going as long as possible, savoring second best.

After hanging up, she adjusted her dress, smoothed back her hair, and exhaled, letting go of whatever dream she had of Jared's visit. She walked to the living room and told my father he had urgent business and was sorry he couldn't come.

"I wonder what her name is," Dad said as he turned the volume up and swallowed his disappointment in long burning pulls of bourbon. Mom retreated to the laundry room, where she spent the evening meticulously ironing my father's work shirts.

"Tell Addison," Mom said. "Take him some pie." Wendy offered, but Mom, in a surprising bout of strength, told Wendy to go to her room and mind her own business.

I walked barefoot to Addison's apartment. The hem from my best summer dress tickled the back of my calf. My mother made it as a birthday present. It was cotton, with a pattern of wild strawberries in honor of my favorite fruit, and had a scooped-neck bodice with a full skirt that fell below my knee. I felt the cool grass between my toes as day eased its way into evening.

The kitchen light was on as I climbed the wooden stairs. The apartment also had a screen door that did not stay shut. It clapped against the jamb. I knocked. All I needed were pearls and a cardigan and I'd look like a lady from the church welcome wagon.

"Addison?"

No answer. I looked over the landing and saw his truck. If he had gone for a walk, I would leave the pie and a note. I went into the kitchen.

It had been years since I had been in the apartment. As a girl I spent many afternoons here with my grandma watching TV and hiding from my father. After Grandpa died, Grandma took to her bed and stayed there for almost ten years before my mother found her asleep for good. The apartment was left as is after that. Mom said she didn't see the reason to change anything.

The kitchen was sparse; an empty jelly-jar glass sat on a small round table next to a crumpled paper napkin. The white linoleum counter that bridged the small stove and half-refrigerator was bare and yellowed from too many bleaches. The porcelain sink had a thin rust stain that snaked from the edge of the faucet to the drain. In the second of the two rooms, the glow from a mute television illuminated a chair covered with discarded clothes and the dulled footboard of the brass bed my grandparents got as a wedding present more than half a century ago.

"Hello?"

I put the pie on the table next to the glass and walked into the main room. Addison was lying on the bed. His arms were crossed in front of his eyes, blocking the late afternoon sun that lit his half of the bed. His good khaki pants and starched white shirt were abandoned to the chair in favor of torn jeans and his "Stinky's" T-shirt. His feet were bare and pale.

"Addison?" I waited. He didn't move. I tiptoed to the television and looked for the power switch.

"Leave it," he said, his voice muffled by his arms.

I looked out the window and followed the line of the road that should have brought Addison's father to him. In the distance you could see the hint of cars passing on their way to somewhere better.

"I brought pie," I said, turning to him.

Addison rolled on his side toward the wall and curled into a fetal ball. Dust fairies danced in the final burst of sunlight that cut across his waist.

"Your father called." I spoke slowly, infusing each word with as much care as possible. I believed the right words would make it better. "He's sorry he couldn't come." I made that part up. I didn't know if he was sorry or not; he should have been and that was all that mattered.

"Go away," he said, enunciating each word slowly.

"He doesn't know what he's missing," I said.

Addison laughed. "Run along, Alex."

The voice that spoke was not the one I associated with Addison. This sound had a harder edge and resonated from somewhere back behind his heart. I felt the sting but waited for an apology or shift of some kind, but he just lay there, appearing smaller and smaller.

After a few minutes, I gave up and started for the door.

"Go ahead and leave. Everyone does eventually." His voice softened.

"Is that how it works? You drive them away and then cry when they go?"

Addison sat up and pointed to the door. "I said go away!" His hair and eyes glowed a gold-red color. His body was so tense I was afraid it would spring forward and attack me.

I stepped back toward the door.

"This is me." He pointed hard at his chest. "Man who doesn't finish anything. Who is still waiting for a father who will not come." He moved closer to the foot of the bed toward me with each word as if he wanted to shake me.

I knew he wouldn't hurt me; I recognized his rage—it was similar to my own. I understood what he needed and, if it was possible, what I could do for him.

I did not move.

"Please go!" He fell back on the bed with his arms and legs out as if he were asking God instead of me.

I moved closer.

" 'Three colleges and five different majors,' " he said, imitating the sound of his father's voice. " 'What do you want, Addison?' " I sat on the edge of the bed. "I want to be someone else!" He answered himself and then rolled closer to me. "Do you understand that?" I nodded and put my hand out to him as if to pull him to shore. He didn't take it.

"He cheats on her," he said, pounding the bed. He fell back.

His left hand was inches from mine. I reached for it and placed it between my own. His palms were dry and cold. I rubbed my hands against them, trying to bring life back.

"He lies to his business partners. Cooks the books."

As I held his hand the rawness of his voice began to thaw and the familiar, gentler tone slowly returned.

"It's okay," I said calmly.

"I'm poison," he said, pulling his hand away. "Stay away."

I resisted the urge to laugh, not because it was funny but because it was absurd. If Addison was poison, he was not lethal like my father. Most of what I knew about men was dangerous, but this one thing I trusted. If Addison was poison, I might be his antidote.

The sun had set. Grandma's lace curtains floated in the air, buoyed by the warm evening breeze. Addison had turned away and rolled back into a ball facing the wall. I thought about doing what he asked and leaving, but I also thought about doing what he needed.

I eased down next to him with our backs touching and closed my eyes, hoping this was all I had to do. Addison didn't move.

After a few minutes, I rolled slowly around and fit my body over his. I put my arm around his waist and found his hand trembling and laced my fingers in it. "Turn around," I whispered.

He rolled slowly toward me. The tear-streaked bristles of his beard brushed my cheek like wet sandpaper. I smiled. "See," I said, "I'm not afraid of you." I wiped the tears off his cheeks.

His hands moved to my face and traced the soft spot between my chin and ear. I felt a coil of heat deep beneath my pelvis as his fingers traveled back toward my neck and up into my hair and then pulled me to him.

My eyes closed first and then there was the warm rush of his mouth and the overwhelming sensation of being engulfed. Instead of pushing away, I moved toward the feeling and was shocked by the urgent groan that came from my throat.

For all that he had failed at, Addison had mastered kissing, and although I did not have anything to compare it to, I sensed that few experiences in my life would ever measure up to the intensity of that moment.

He rolled on top of me, and for a moment, I imagined how nice it would be to spend the rest of my life kissing him, until I felt his hand on my thigh moving toward my underwear. I pushed him off me and jumped up.

Addison sat up. "I'm sorry, I . . ."

I adjusted the skirt of my dress, pushing the memory of his hand away with my own shaking hands.

"I don't know what I was doing," I said, looking toward the window, which faced the house.

"What happened?" He came toward me with arms outstretched. I left him.

The house was silent when I came through the back door. Mom had put away the pie and bread and left a set of dirty dishes in the sink. Dad was passed out on the chair with an empty bourbon bottle next to him. Wendy and Jared were in their rooms.

At four I rolled out of bed and slipped into the bathroom, careful not to creak the floorboards. I was unable to sleep. It wasn't my mind that kept me awake; it was my body. In the short time I had been with Addison, my senses had recorded every detail of the kiss, from his orangey-musk smell to the wet cinnamon taste of his mouth to his smooth hands on my neck and face. The moments replayed over and over, rendering me more awake than I had ever been.

I avoided the bathroom at all costs on most nights. If I could help it, I would hold it until I heard my father go downstairs for his morning coffee. Some nights I couldn't wait, and I'd make my visit as short as possible. It wasn't the bathroom that was dangerous; it was passing my parents' bedroom.

Once I was in the bathroom, I'd put my ear to the door to listen for any movement. After a count of one hundred, I'd relax, throw the lock, and pee in peace. If I was especially concerned about night rustling (that's what I called Dad's evening wanderings), I would avoid flushing the toilet or washing my hands, as the water pipes often burped.

I was careless that night and didn't do the count or check the hallway before I flushed. I ran the water to wash my hands and even wondered how my hair might look pulled off my face. I took a rubber band from the medicine cabinet and made a short ponytail, thinking I might try it that way for the summer dance that was in a couple of days.

My father was standing naked in front of the door when I opened it.

"I'll get out of your way," I said quietly.

"What did you do to your hair?" he said, his voice a steel tone of danger. He grabbed my ponytail, found the rubber band, and tugged it until it snapped. I winced. "You do that for some boy?"

"No, sir," I said as I reached for the door to steady myself. He grabbed a clump of my hair and pulled me into the bathroom with him. I tried not to make eye contact. I learned at an early age that looking into his eyes was the biggest mistake I could make. I imagined there were worse punishments he could bestow on me if I did.

"What are you looking at?"

"Dad, please," I said, as calmly as I could. My focus was blurred. All I could see was the gleaming white of the floor and wall tiles we had polished so hopefully. The room smelled like a pool from all the bleach we used.

"Please what? Leave you alone so you can run off with some punk?"

"I'm not going anywhere."

My hand was on his forearm trying to pry it off my neck but it kept slipping as my palms were sweating. I was losing my footing as he pulled me over to the toilet. He dropped the seat cover and sat down as he pushed me to my knees in front of him. Most times he did stuff to me, but sometimes it was me who had to do it to him. I felt the cold sharp edge of the octagonal floor tiles imprinting their shape on my skin as he forced my head closer to his crotch. My mouth went dry.

"We're going to have a little conversation about who is the boss of you," he said. Sometimes when we were alone he sounded like he was talking to someone other than me. I didn't understand what he was saying or what weird thing he was seeing in his mind; I only knew that the monster was out and I was in its throes.

The sound of a door creaking open and footsteps in the hallway brought me back into my body and into the bathroom. Someone going or coming?

*Let it be Jared, it's Jared, it's Jared, it's Jared.*

"James?" It was my mother.

My father looked toward the door and slightly loosened his grip. I pulled myself up from the hunched position and clawed my father in the face and pushed him with all of my might. He fell toward the tub and screamed, "You cunt!" as I barreled down the stairs and out the door. It wasn't until I had hidden myself safely in the woods that I realized I had wet myself.

I watched for lights to come on in the house, but nothing happened. The full moon cast a cool light on the night. I sat alone, shivering from cold and the memory of his grip while everyone slept. My nightgown smelled like a cat's litter box. I sat for hours, staring at the house and thinking about that cold, dark hand reaching out for me—even when he wasn't there, it was still reaching for me. I pulled my sketchbook from under the stump and began to draw furiously as tears streamed onto the page and made my bold lines soften like watercolors. "Kitty Kat makes a final stand against the Hand," I wrote as I had her slice, dice, karate-chop, and use all of her powers to defeat the Hand.

The kitchen light came on in the first rays of dawn. I walked quietly to the clearing and saw my mother at the sink washing dishes as she looked out into the yard.

I waited and hoped she would find me and take us away. I wanted her to be willing to lose another finger for me. I wanted her to be someone else.

"We all have our crosses to bear," was her answer the last time I tried to tell her what was happening.

After a while, my mother crossed over to Addison's apartment and climbed the stairs to his door. The lights came on and his shadow passed between the two windows. He opened the door and spoke to my mother, who pointed to the woods. He grabbed a jacket and followed her to the house. She went back to the kitchen window as Addison headed into the woods.

I felt my breath against my knees and a cold chill swoop under my nightgown. I shut my eyes and tried to make myself disappear. Sometimes I could do it: I would float above my body and watch as an impartial observer of my own life. I wanted to be gone by the time Addison found me. I was certain I would dissolve from the humiliation.

"Alex . . ." I heard the twig-snapping walk mixed in with his whispers. "Alex . . . it's me." Snap, shuffle, breeze, birds chirping, "Alex . . . Alex . . ."

"I'm over here," I shouted back, and startled myself at the anger in my voice. "What do you want?"

"Your mother is worried. . . ."

"Yeah, I bet," I said, still holding my knees.

"Have you been here all night?"

I nodded.

"What happened?"

He knelt down and put his hand on top of mine. "Alex?"

I pulled away, embarrassed by my own smell. I rocked back and forth, holding my knees to my chest. Finally, he stood up and took my hand, pulling me up to him.

"Come on, you need some rest," he said, as he led me toward the house.

I broke away. "I can't go back in there. He's going to kill me."

"He's passed out . . . it's fine . . . I'll walk you back."

"How do you know it's fine when you don't even know what happened?"

"Look, it can't be that bad. Did he hit you?" I shifted focus and relaxed a little.

"No. I'm fine. You can let go." As soon as he did, I ran. My bare feet pounded the cold ground littered with sharp twigs that jabbed my soles and slowed me down. In the distance was the clearing that bordered our property with the Igbys'. I would go to them and see if they would help.

Addison's steps mirrored my own but were surer in their mission. He caught me around the waist and lifted me in the air. "Stop!" he said, huffing. His grip was strong as I tried to pry his arm from my waist.

"Let me go!" I shouted so loud a gathering of sparrows fled from their nest.

"Tell me what happened!"

We struggled together, trying to catch our breath as we hunched over. I could feel the pulse of Addison's rapidly beating heart against my shoulder and imagined my own responding back in the Morse code of the body.

"Come back to my apartment. We'll go the back way."

"He'll kill you if he knows you helped me."

Addison looked at me as if I were crazy and then reconsidered as he stepped back and saw my tear-stained cheeks and wet night-gown. "I'll take the chance. Let's go."

He took my hand and led me back. Aside from my mother, there were no other signs of life at the house.

In a few hours the apartment had changed. Maybe it was the way the morning light hardened the edges of everything in the same way the dusk softened them.

"Can I take a shower?"

"Sure. There's a towel in there. I'll find you a shirt." He searched the pile of clothes on the chair.

The hot water felt good on my back. I washed my hair with his orange-ginger shampoo and used the suds to wash my body without looking at it. When I had cleaned everything once, I lathered up and did it again.

I dried myself in the shower with the curtain drawn. Addison knocked on the door and opened it.

"Here," he said, "you can sleep in this." I peeked behind the curtain and saw he was holding a faded denim shirt and a pair of sweatpants.

"Drop them," I said.

I took in his smell as I put the shirt on, musky with the sweetness of Old Spice. I pressed my face to the sleeve and felt the smoothness of the denim and pulled on the sweatpants and tied the drawstring as tight as it would go. I felt small in his clothes.

Addison was sitting at the kitchen table drinking instant coffee. His hair was rumpled from sleeping and he was wearing the clothes from the night before. His jeans had been pulled on in a rush, as the last two buttons of his fly were open. His feet were bare and bony. He jumped up when I came out.

"Better?"

I nodded. He came and led me to the bed.

"This is the plan. I'll see what's going on. If everything is okay I'll let you sleep and go do some chores. If it isn't okay, like your dad's looking for you or something, I'll find a way to warn you."

"I need clothes."

He nodded. "I'll get some."

While he was talking he gently pushed me down on the bed and pulled the covers around me. I rolled over, with my back to him as he sat on the edge of the bed.

"About last night . . ." he started.

"I don't want to talk about it," I said, beginning to drift off.

———

I don't know how long I had been sleeping when I felt a hand on my cheek. I jumped to the farthest corner of the bed.

"I didn't mean to scare you." Addison was holding a pile of clothes. "Everyone left for Rucker's Ravine to walk the plank and they won't be back tonight." He shrugged, not fully understanding what that meant.

"It's a place we go to . . . a game. It's hard to describe," I said. Addison sat next to me on the bed and put his hand on my leg as he listened. I was embarrassed by the way he was studying me. He subtly glanced down at my chest and then back up to my face. I looked down and saw that the shirt had come unbuttoned and one of my breasts was pushing its way out. I wanted to button it, but I didn't want him to know I had noticed or cared. I pulled the covers up around me and pretended I was cold.

"Did anyone—?" I said, avoiding his gaze.

"I told them you were okay."

"What about Dad . . . did he ask about me?"

"No," he said. "He didn't mention you at all. He was in a good mood. Couldn't wait to get everyone together to go."

"He didn't say anything?"

"Why do you care?"

"Tell me."

"He said he would have his time with you at the ravine later."

A shiver rushed down my spine. The kind that Mom said meant a goose walked on your grave.

"So it's just us . . ."

"He didn't ask where I was?"

Addison moved through the apartment picking up things, hanging up a towel, sidestepping himself from my question.

"Addison . . ."

He came out of the bathroom and leaned against the doorway of the bedroom. "He said, and this is quoting him directly, he didn't care if you ever came back. Are you happy now?"

"Why are you getting so mad?"

" 'Cause I don't know what you do that makes—"

"You think I'm doing something?"

"Well, it always seems like you're on his shit list. At least since I've been here. He doesn't seem to bother Wendy or Jared."

"So it's me . . . I'm causing it?"

"I didn't say that. . . . I just want to know what's with you two."

"Nothing is with us, you asshole." I jumped out of bed and peeled his sweats off as I reached for the jeans he brought and pulled them on. I was so angry I forgot I wasn't wearing any underwear. I scooped up the rest of my clothes and headed for the door.

"Where are you going?"

"Back to the house. I don't want to be with you."

"Hey . . ." He grabbed my wrists.

"Don't touch me. . . . I may be his property but I'm not yours."

Addison let go of me and I walked out into the afternoon light toward home.

I made a bologna and cheese sandwich and poured myself a glass of lemonade and sat on the swing on the front porch. My mother hadn't left a note this time. I didn't expect anyone to be back until lunchtime tomorrow. Walking the plank was always an overnight adventure.


"Are you going to ignore me all day?" Addison stood at the bottom of the porch stairs an hour or so later.

"I'm not ignoring you."

He climbed the stairs and walked tentatively over to the railing closest to the swing and looked out over the front yard toward the road.

"Want to go for a swim?"

"I can't swim," I replied.

"I could teach you," he said, not looking away from the road.

"I don't need you to teach me anything," I said, between the creaking of the swing.

"You're a hard one, Alex."

"Well, life is hard," I replied.

We stayed like that for a while. A million opposing thoughts passed through my mind; I wanted him to stay so I could tell him what happened as much as I wanted him to go.

A warm breeze brushed against my neck. Addison closed his eyes and leaned his head back.

"My father left," he said, fixing his eyes back on the yard. "My mother didn't want us telling anyone. He left about a year ago. Just walked out. Business was bad, he'd lost almost everything, except the house. Ran off with my girlfriend. One day I left for school, I was trying college again, came home and there was a note from her, we were sort of living together. She said she had gone away with someone. Took us a while to put the pieces together."

"How do you know? It could have been a coincidence."

"That's what I thought, until we got a letter that said they were together, not to go looking for them, you know, the usual."

"Did you love her?" I asked as nonchalantly as I could.

"I'm not sure I know what that is, but I liked her. She was kind—"

"Of mean," I interrupted.

He turned back to the yard. I continued to rock myself and waited for him to speak again.

"Anyway, I quit school and got a job as a carpenter. I moved in with my mom to help with expenses. I felt obligated. I was planning on staying. And then, I found out she was pregnant and they wanted the house."

"Pregnant, who, your father and his girlfriend?"

"Yeah . . ." he said, lowering his head.

"Oh, God. Why did they want the house? Wasn't it your mother's?"

"No, it was both of theirs, but my mother just gave up when he came back. She couldn't bear to fight him so she said they could move in."

"Where'd your mother go?"

"She lives in the basement. They rigged up an apartment for her."

I leaned forward. "She lives in the same house with them? Is she crazy?"

"Where is she going to go, Alex? She's never had a job. She doesn't have a high school diploma and she still depends on my father for everything. Where the hell was she going to go?" he said, yelling at me.

"I don't know," I yelled back.

We sat still for a few moments.

"My parents worked out an agreement that my mother could live off the rent on my grandma's house if I fixed it up and found a tenant.

"Why don't you sell the house so your mom can live on her own?"

"My mother thinks if they sell it, my father will leave with the money."

"So why did you want your father to come?"

He shrugged. "I don't know. I wanted him to see the work I did on his mother's house and be proud of me, I guess."

"Bad idea."

He laughed. "Frightfully bad idea."

"So where are you going after the house is rented?"

"I don't know. My mother thinks my father is going to come around eventually."

"He's not," I said as Addison turned toward me. "He's not going to come to his senses any more than my dad is."

"This isn't the same thing. Your dad isn't like my dad," Addison responded. "At least your dad stayed with the family. At least he takes care of you guys. He loves you."

I jumped off of the swing. "Do you really want a father so much that you would delude yourself into thinking that my father is actually better than yours? Have you seen anything since you got here?"

"Okay, so he drinks a little. I can see that, but—"

"Addison, he does more than drink a little."

He shook his head, refusing to hear what I was trying to tell him. "When I was five my father burned the bottoms of my feet with his cigarette because I complained that my church shoes gave me blisters. He said that would take away the pain of the blisters. When I was seven, he threw my mother down a flight of stairs and broke her arm. When I was ten, he smashed a plate over Jared's head and wouldn't take him to the hospital for stitches. Jared has a scar this thick on his head that no hair will grow on. Ask him, he'll show it to you. The first and only time my mother tried to leave him, he cut the tip of her finger off with an ax and made us watch. . . ." Addison tried to pull away from the words but I grabbed his hands and wouldn't let go. The more he resisted the louder I spoke. "You want to hear about what happened in the bathroom?" But I couldn't say it. I swallowed it down.

"Never mind," I said. "It doesn't matter."

I went back to the swing and pushed myself. The chains creaked as he studied me. His eyes took in every outward feature: my hair, eyes, hands, lips. Maybe if he looked long enough he could see right through to the heart of me. And in seeing that dark core, would he understand or would he run away?

He got off the rail and sat next to me and took my hand and wove our fingers together. We sat like that for a while, moving forward and then backward, together.

# ELEVEN

ALL THAT REMAINED of the porch swing were the grooves in the floorboards worn down from years of pushing off and landing.

Andrew found me leaning against the rail, the same spot that Addison had occupied so many years ago. My smoking had banished me from the house. Wendy said she didn't need to be exposed to anything that could keep her from getting pregnant. One look at Willard and his dull, expressionless face and you had to wonder if he fell into that category.

"Aren't you cold?" he said, hugging himself. He was wearing a starched pink oxford shirt, khaki pants with creases sharp enough to cut paper, and black Gucci loafers. He reminded me of the city college professors who came to the club for lap dances after a hard day of teaching and making passes at students. They were lousy tippers and pretended to be concerned that a smart girl like me hustled drinks in that shithole for a living. I preferred the sweat- and beer-stained convention center carpenters who told me they liked my tits as they shoved a fifty in my cleavage.

Andrew motioned for a cigarette and a light.

"I quit," he said, as he took a drag.

"Yeah, me too."

A lone pair of headlights passed along the country road. We

faced forward and said nothing. Andrew shifted his weight back and forth in an effort to keep warm.

"I can't believe you're not cold," he said finally.

"I'm freezing," I said.

"But you're perfectly still. You're not even shaking."

I dropped the butt and ground it out with my foot.

"I guess I've been cold so long I stopped trying to warm up."

He nodded. I started for the door.

"I miss her," he said to my back.

The sound of his voice made me turn. For an instant I thought I heard Jared.

"Who were you to her?"

"We went to the same church. We were acquaintances."

"Not friends?"

"No, well. Yes, I suppose it grew into that. We had things in common."

"What? A misguided belief in God?"

"No, other things."

"Are you always this vague?"

"I was her sponsor," he said finally, throwing his hands up in defeat.

"Of what?"

"AA."

"My mother didn't drink. She was too busy. She worked from sunup to sundown; she was quiet and reserved. She was . . ." I shook my head and started for the house. Andrew grabbed my arm.

"Drunk most of the time. For many years."

"That's ridiculous. I never saw the woman take a drink in her life."

"She snuck it; she took lots of little sips throughout the day. She covered it up by saying she had stomach problems."

"She did. She carried a blue Mylanta bottle around with her all day. . . ."

Andrew mimed my mother nipping at her Mylanta bottle. A cold shiver bolted through me as I fell back against the railing.

"I need a drink," I said.

"You want to go inside?" Andrew asked as the sound of laughter and music came from the living room.

"I'd ask you to join me but I guess that would be tacky."

"I don't have a problem with alcohol. Heroin was my downfall."

"Well, well, well, how did a junkie end up the coroner of Wilton County?"

"Let's just say this is the last bridge. I've burned all the others. I have nowhere else to go."

"Yeah, join the club," I said as we walked into the living room and found Wendy and Jared on the couch looking at a photo album.

"Cat, come here, look at this picture of the three of us with Georgie." Wendy waved me over. Georgie was our horse. He had a lame back leg that rendered him useless for anything except being a pet. The Igbys gave him to us when they realized he'd never amount to much. Wendy, Jared, and I adored him. They were looking at a black-and-white photo Mom took of the three of us sitting on Georgie, wearing our cowboy hats.

"Did you know Mom was a drunk?" I said. Jared and Wendy looked at each other and then at me.

"Yeah," they both said, as if everyone in the world knew but me.

"The Mylanta bottle," Jared said. Wendy nodded her head.

I sat in Dad's La-Z-Boy. "How come we never talked about it? Why didn't I know?"

"You knew," Jared said. "You did, come on."

I swallowed hard, wishing for the burn of some bourbon to replace the wave of shock that was coming over me. This wasn't the first time I had the sensation of being a stranger participating in my own life, but it was one of the worst.

"The finger thing," Jared said. That had been our code for Dad's punishment for Mom trying to leave. It was too awful to call it "the night Dad dragged us to the barn and chopped Mom's finger off," so we called it the finger thing.

"She started drinking after that," Wendy said. The album was balanced in her lap as her open palm rested on that picture of the three of us and Georgie. That night of the finger thing, Jared said he wished Georgie could run like the wind and carry us away. But Georgie stood in the barn like the rest of us and watched my father hack away another piece of my mother.

I felt sick. I put my head between my legs to keep from throwing up.

"Willard!" Wendy yelled into the kitchen. "Bring Cat a drink."

"Bourbon," she added, as I looked at her through my legs. She shrugged with the resignation of a death row warden bringing an inmate his last meal.

Willard, donned in my mother's KISS THE COOK apron, came in with a jelly glass half-filled with amber relief. I would have preferred the bottle, but I took what I could get. As I drank, Willard patted the back of my hair lightly, like a father touches his child when she wakes up from a bad dream. Andrew sat on the couch next to Wendy.

"Andrew's a junkie," I said, before I felt the medicine sear through me.

"Was a junkie, Alex, was," Andrew said.

"Once a junkie always a junkie," I said, licking my lips to get the last drop.

"Why do you have to be so mean?" Jared asked.

"The truth hurts," I said. "So I guess you both knew that Mom was hanging out with a coroner junkie."

"No," Wendy said, "Andrew told us today."

"I want to know why she stopped drinking; that's the part that has me stumped. I'd say she found Jesus, but Christ, she had Jesus all along and look what He did for her. And please don't tell me she and Dad walked the twelve steps together because then I'll really have to puke." I was feeling stronger now; the bourbon sent away the dark spirits that haunted me. I went to the kitchen for a refill.

Willard was finishing the dishes and putting away the food from the enormous feast he had prepared. Although food was not my thing, I had to admit he had a gift. He filled both the apron and the room with the same frenetic energy my mother had. He was built like her too: slim and small-boned, with fast, efficient hands. I would have thought Wendy would have gone for a linebacker, a lumberjack, someone more brooding, like my father, but she went for delicate, reserved.

"She's got you wrapped around her finger," I said loud enough so he could hear. I filled my glass twice before returning to the living room. Willard wiped the tablecloth with a rag, lots of Fantastik, and elbow grease. Those poor roosters couldn't catch a break.

"I love her," he said, without looking up.

"Well, if that's love, count me out," I said, tripping as I licked the bourbon that spilled on my hand.

"Looks like it has," he said.

"The meetings are in the church basement. Everyone loved her cakes."

"So why didn't you say something at the morgue that first day?" I leaned against the doorway.

"I didn't think it was appropriate. I told Wendy and Jared after the service. You missed all that."

"So you were close with her? Did she tell you she was going to kill herself?"

"Cat"—Jared stood up and came toward me—"enough."

"No. You don't have a suicide note addressed to you hanging over your head."

Andrew shrugged his shoulders. "The last time I saw her she said something about the deed. She said it was in the safety deposit box at Farmers Union Bank and you would know where the key was." Andrew was pointing to me.

"How would she know?" Wendy said.

"Yeah?" I said, in a rare moment of agreement with Wendy.

"She said, 'Cat will remember. She remembers everything.' "

# TWELVE

I OPENED MY EYES and discovered I was alone on the swing. Addison's hand was replaced with a note that said he was at the store and would be back to cook dinner.

I felt a throbbing in the base of my neck where my father's hands had left his mark on another part of me. The territories of my body were being seized by him at an increasingly violent and rapid pace. My body would never be my own; that much was certain. If being a woman meant you had to be possessed by a man, then I would at least have a say in who would have me first.

I took another shower and shaved my arms and legs. I used my mother's hand lotion on my feet and elbows and blew my hair dry, taking the time to curl it under in a smooth, soft line that edged my face. I brushed and flossed my teeth, plucked my eyebrows, and put on blush and a little lipstick. I chose a flowered sundress from Wendy's side of the closet that made me look as pretty as I could be. I was playing at being a girl, imagining what it was like to be someone's treasure.

I went to my mother's jewelry drawer to find her pearls. Although they were fake, she said they were "good imitations" and valued them as such. Mom kept them in a special place that she claimed only she and I knew about. She wanted me to know where just in case something happened to her. "What's in this pouch is for you," she said.

I figured I would borrow them for a few hours and get them back before Mom returned. The pearls made me feel grown up and ready to seize the future. The pouch was in the back of the drawer hidden in a worn brown paper lunch bag. I pulled the drawstring loose and turned it upside down to empty the contents. The pearls came sliding out along with an odd-shaped key. I put the pearls around my neck and tossed the key in my palm, wondering what it could possibly fit. It wasn't for a door or a car or any of the locked storage bins we kept in the barn.

I heard Addison's truck in the driveway and put the key back.

"Coming," I said when I heard him calling for me. I went to the window and watched him lifting paper grocery bags from the back cab. He followed the sound of my voice and smiled as I stood in the same spot my father had when he watched us a few nights before.

Addison was making a salad when I opened the door and came into the small kitchen. His shirtsleeves were rolled up and his feet were bare with one foot balancing on his calf like a flamingo.

"We're having steak and salad—it's pretty much all I can cook."

"Can I help?"

Addison put the knife down and turned toward the bag on the table. "Grab the potatoes and wrap them in foil. We'll stick them on the grill with the steaks."

I went to the table and felt embarrassed by my expectation that all the primping I had done had made a difference. I might as well have been standing there in a flannel shirt and jeans. I fought the urge to run.

With potatoes and foil in hand, I turned to find Addison leaning against the counter watching me.

Our eyes met, but his did not linger there; they followed the line of my cheek, the smooth curve of my chin and the long open collar of powdered skin, and trailed down to my waist and hips and legs and finally my bare, dew-wet feet. In his review of me, I felt what he saw, the way the parts of me made a body, a living, breathing equation that had been ravaged but could also be adored. And while I had vowed to never look my father in the face when he was touching me, I could not look away from Addison as his eyes seemed to reconstruct me into someone different. I could not push away from the danger of that feeling; instead, I found myself sinking into it and liking it.

I felt the sharp point of the foil box poke at my upper arm and the gritty skin of the potatoes in my hands. I smelled him from across the kitchen. His mouth opened slowly. His lips glistened as his chest rose and then fell. If a meteor crashed in the fields behind us, I would not have heard it. If my father arrived with a shotgun and blew a hole in my chest, I would not have felt it. All I sensed or knew was here, in the small space between his body and mine.

I took the first step. This would be what I would remember. I had made it happen.

He took the next ten and wrapped his arms around me so quickly I dropped the potatoes and foil to the floor and stumbled on them as he pulled me to him.

"Ow—that hurts," I said, as his mouth smashed into mine and our teeth clacked together.

"Sorry." I could feel every inch of his hands in my hair and on my head.

My mouth opened and moved to find his. I put my arms behind me as the force of his passion pushed me back toward the table. I struggled to keep my balance, to push back so we could be on equal footing, but it was useless. I was not accustomed to having to manage so many feelings at once. His hands fluttered over my body. They moved from my breasts to my back and reached between my legs and pressed hard. I gasped.

I didn't know what I was supposed to do to him. All my experience with touching had been forced so I let him guide me. I let him put my hand on his crotch and felt the block of hardness inside his pants.

There were noises too. Addison whispered my name as he pressed himself against me. I tried to suppress my own moans as I struggled to stay as close to the surface of desire as I could.

We found our way to the bed, slipping on his discarded clothes littered around the room. I cried out as I stubbed my toe when we fell together on the bed. He examined my foot like it was a diamond he was checking for flaws and took my stubbed toe in his mouth and sucked it.

I reached for him and begged him, for what I don't know, but I needed it to stop and continue all at once. Addison understood; he nodded and kissed me as he reached under my dress and pulled off my white cotton underpants. My dress was half on and half off as Addison had worked the top half down and reached inside the bodice to touch my breasts.

I pulled his shirt off him, marveling at my own boldness. Who was this girl who was courting so much pleasure? He unzipped his pants as his hands explored inside me.

This would be the only time I was ever ready for someone.

It hurt when he pushed himself inside me. I instinctively reached for his shoulders to push him off me but he grabbed my wrists and held them down. "Breathe," he said. "It's all right."

Tears welled in my eyes; this was not what I thought it was. It was too much. Did everyone feel this way or just me?

He began to move against me, his hips and abdomen banging on me. Inside I felt nothing except a repeated jabbing that felt like a piston from someone else's engine trying to work inside me.

I felt myself moving out of my body and floating above us, feeling the good part was over as I watched Addison's face contort and retreat from any connection to me. He was grunting now in that way that animals do when they're fucking. I fought the urge to throw him off me and run to Canada or Mexico or someplace where there were no men and all the trouble they bring.

He came. I finally exhaled, relieved it was over. He collapsed on top of me. His dead weight felt like a sack of pig feed.

After a few moments, he rolled over on his back and sighed. "Wow," was all he said.

I sat up and adjusted my dress.

"What are you doing?" he said in a dreamy, exhausted voice.

I looked up at the room. It was still the same. I didn't know what I was doing, but as I focused on the misty gray walls of the living room, the chair draped with clothes and a few towels, his nightstand with a copy of Ayn Rand's *The Fountainhead* open and resting on its belly with an empty beer bottle next to it, I knew what I wasn't doing. I was never having sex again with anybody.

Addison pulled me back down. I started to cry.

He rolled me toward him and wiped the tears off my face with his hands. "Shhhh," he said, "it's okay." His tenderness made me cry harder.

As his words comforted me, his hand found its way back between my legs, and although I resisted, he asked me to let him as he kissed me lightly on the cheek in all the places my tears had been. The low, even sound of his voice and sureness of what he knew his hands could do were hypnotic. I relaxed into his touch and hoped he wouldn't hurt me.

I screamed his name a few minutes later as my body buckled and then released. When he tried to pull his hand away I held it there a little bit longer, wanting him more than I had ever expected.

# Thirteen

The key was in the pouch when I went to look for it the morning Wendy and Jared left. The pearls were long gone.

Outside, Wendy, Willard, and Jared packed the cars and said their good-byes. Earlier, I feigned sleep when they called for me. I didn't see the point of a send-off. They would be back when Dad died, which I hoped would be soon.

From the window I watched Jared and Wendy hug. Whatever had been broken between them seemed mended. I wondered if that was possible or something they just wanted to believe.

I put the key in my pocket and went to the kitchen. At last I was free to smoke and drink as much as I wanted. No more of Wendy watching over me, safeguarding an unborn child that might never come, or Jared with that beaten-dog look begging for forgiveness.

I poured myself a breakfast of bourbon and lit a cigarette. "Bottoms up." I took a swig and tossed my head back. "Fuck you all."

The phone rang so loudly I thought the receiver would jump off the cradle. I grabbed it to silence it.

"Cat? Hello? It's Ruth Igby."

I balanced the receiver on my shoulder as I struggled to light a second cigarette, not realizing I had one burning in the ashtray on the table. The cigarette wasn't the only thing getting lit.

"Are you there?"

"Yes, Mrs. Igby."

"Call me Ruth." I refilled the Flintstones jelly-jar glass with the last of the bourbon and made a mental note to make a liquor store run on my way to the bank. I found a backup bottle of vodka under the sink next to my mother's Playtex Living gloves. I guess she really wasn't as sober as she pretended to be.

"Marty and I would like to know if you would come to supper tonight. I'm making pot roast."

"No, thanks."

"It's your first night alone; we thought you might like company." Little did she know I was alone every night.

"Nope, I'm fine."

"Cat, please come. Your mother would want you to."

"What the fuck does that mean?" I wiped the sting of liquor from my lips.

"Nothing. I think she would like to know you were being taken care of."

"That's funny. She didn't seem to care that much about me when she was alive."

Ruth sighed. She was close to giving up. My goal was to make sure she gave up for good.

"Cat, come for dinner."

I pulled at a piece of wallpaper that was coming loose. How hard would I have to tug to peel away this layer? And if I did, what was underneath?

I felt Ruth's desire on the phone. Her need to stuff me full of her fatty pot roast and make herself feel better for ignoring us all those years while family atrocities were being committed over hill and dale. I picked up the bottle of vodka and took a long swig of all that was left.

"At least come for a drink," she said.

"Did my mother talk to you?" I asked as I grabbed the wall for support. The floor was moving in waves beneath me.

"We were neighbors. I found her."

Why did everyone speak so cryptically? A simple yes or no would do just fine.

I smacked my hand against my forehead, a habit I had whenever someone was being obtuse. It was transference, I assumed. I hit myself to keep from punching their face in.

"Did my mother talk to you before she died?" I asked again as I stared at an old brown water spot on the ceiling that was shaped like a cartoon balloon.

Ruth put her hand over the receiver and whispered something to Marty and then shushed him.

"Mrs. Igby, I don't have time for your—"

"Dinner is at four P.M.; Marty can come for you if you're not up to driving."

Even though the Igbys were neighbors, you still had to drive to get to their house—unless you crossed the old field and waded across a small stream.

"I can drive."

"See you at four, then." She hung up before I could say no.

I woke up on the couch tangled in the lime and olive zigzag afghan my mother crocheted for my father to match the green tweed upholstery on his La-Z-Boy. The late afternoon sun insinuated itself through the venetian blinds that covered the picture window, making vertical prisonlike shadows.

I stood up and lost my balance.

The phone screamed. If this is what life was like for my mother, no wonder she killed herself. I let it ring and ring and ring.

Until it stopped.

It began ringing again and again and again.

I ripped it off the receiver.

"What?"

"Cat? It's Ruth—are you coming?" The squirrelly tone of her voice burrowed itself into my ears and reverberated through my head. If a hangover had a sound, it would be Ruth Igby's voice.

The kitchen clock read 4:20 P.M. It couldn't be right. I had just spoken to her a few minutes ago. I lay down for a bit to clear my head before I went to the liquor store and bank.

"Do you need a ride?"

"Oh, crap." I grabbed the counter to hold myself steady. "I can't come . . . I'm not . . . "

*There's nothing to drink. You need something.*

"Can Marty come and get me?"

"What can I offer you . . . coffee, soda?" Ruth asked, as I stumbled into her living room.

*Didn't she mention cocktails?*

"Wine or beer?"

*There we go.*

"Beer's fine," I replied nonchalantly.

Marty handed me a semichilled bottle of Rolling Rock with a cocktail napkin wrapped around it. I tried to sip it as I fought the temptation to guzzle it. Ruth brought out a cheese ball with saltines on a silver-toned plastic platter. She had carefully placed the cheese over a paper doily, believing everything looked better with lace.

Marty offered mixed nuts from an opened can he had resting on the TV tray next to his brown recliner with duct tape patches on the armrests. It didn't take Columbo to notice he had eaten all of the cashews and peanuts. All that were left were Brazil nuts. I politely refused and prayed there was another, colder beer waiting for me.

Shirley, the Igbys' severely overweight basset hound, waddled her way into the living room and plopped herself on top of my feet.

"You remember Cat . . . don't you, Shirley?" Ruth said. I looked at Shirley snoring on my feet and half-expected her to respond.

"I can't believe she's still alive. How old is she?"

"Fourteen," Ruth replied icily. I wished the beer was as cold as her stare. I guess I offended her. She probably thought the damn dog would live forever.

Marty turned on the television. I asked to use the bathroom and took a detour through the kitchen and checked the fridge for beer. There were five shoved on top of a bakery box. I grabbed one, stuck it in my shirt, and headed upstairs, where I at last fulfilled my desire to guzzle away the boredom of a night with the Igbys. When I was finished, I sunk the empty bottle in the toilet tank and headed back to the fun.

A couple more beers would be enough to get me to sleep through the night. Tomorrow, I'd go to the bank and liquor store and settle everything and move on.

There was a rustling in the hall as I came down the steps. Ruth was hanging up a toffee-colored barn jacket in the hall closet. She looked up and smiled for the first time all evening.

"Come down and greet our guest."

No one said anything about visitors. Christ, I was barely up for the Igbys and now I had to be nice to some yahoo they invited to keep us all from sitting in silence?

I walked into the living room prepared to take my leave and saw Addison standing with Marty, watching what sounded like a hockey game on the big-screen TV. His cheeks were rosy from the cold, his hair more rusty than I remembered and shorter, with long, tousled bangs that framed his freckled-tanned face. He was wearing a teal flannel shirt and a white turtleneck with jeans and work boots.

He looked at me and smiled sweetly, as if we were still in that apartment above the garage, trying to finish what we started.

I felt light-headed and reached for the wall to steady myself as my senses registered the moment. The booming baritone of the announcer on the television. The smell of pot roast burning in the kitchen. The dust fairies dancing around the doily-covered furniture. The faint hint of citrus coming from Addison. My mind raced, taking inventory of the moment. He's here, I'm here, she's there, he's there, pot roast is for dinner, the couch is old, Shirley should be dead.

"Hey," was all he said as he turned back to the TV.

"Hey," I answered, adding a lame wave.

I looked at Ruth, hoping for some explanation, and then at Marty and waited. Addison watched the game and glimpsed me from the corner of his eye as we all stood in a semicircle around the altar of the TV and prayed for someone to say something.

"You didn't tell me you invited other guests," I said to Ruth.

"Not guests, friends."

*Addison is a friend of the Igbys?*

"Right, okay. Listen, I think I'm feeling a little—"

"Drunk?" she said as she turned away and headed for the kitchen.

"What?" I said as I followed.

"You're a little drunk? Is that what you were trying to say?"

"No. I was going to say I'm under the weather and I'd like to go."

Ruth grabbed a potholder from a hook that was shaped like a cow's head and opened the oven and pulled out a giant hunk of black smoking meat.

"There's beer in the fridge, dear."

I walked away, determined to show her just how much I needed to drink to be friendly.

"Why don't you go back in the living room and visit with the boys?" Ruth said.

I grabbed the thigh of my jeans and scrunched a handful into a fist. God, I wanted to punch that smirk off her face. I would be god-damned if I was going to give her the satisfaction of knowing how awful this was. The coat rack was on the way to the living room—I would grab my jacket and slip out the side door. I would pack the car when I got home and leave town after I went to the bank in the morning.

"Where are you going?"

Addison had slipped behind me and was standing so close I could feel his breath on my neck.

"I can't do this," I said as I grabbed my coat.

"I came alone."

"Did you know I was going to be here?" I turned around and moved a few steps back.

He nodded. "I asked Ruth to invite you. I couldn't think of another way of seeing you."

"Did you try knocking on the door? Calling?"

"I thought it would be better with other people around."

"Did you get my mom to kill herself so I would come back?" I snapped.

"Wow, you've gotten—"

"Mean? Bitter?"

"You were never . . ." He shook his head. I guess it was hard to see that that hopeful little kitten that purred when he touched me was gone.

"That's right; you were the mean one back then."

"Not mean, stupid. There's a difference. I think you know that."

"What I know is that I should go. I don't belong here."

"Nobody really belongs at the Igbys'," he tried, smiling.

"In Wilton, Addison. I don't belong in Wilton." I reached for my coat again.

"Stay."

He put his hand on top of mine and pressed it against the hook. I pulled away but the warmth lingered.

"Dinner, kids," Ruth yelled from the kitchen.

"Come on, you're not going to make me eat with them all by myself, are you?"

"You promised you'd leave me alone," I said.

"I never said anything. You took off, remember?"

I took a breath and tried to collect myself. The only way to get any of them off me was to be far away. If my goddamned mother hadn't . . . shit. My hands were shaking. Why couldn't I go?

"You coming? Ruth's got the chow on," Marty said as he

passed through the hall to the dining room. Marty had grown to look more like Ruth every year. Even his nose had taken on her hawklike shape. Like most old married couples, they looked more like brother and sister than husband and wife.

"What's going on out there?" I heard Ruth whisper as Marty entered the dining room.

"For the love of God, Ruth, leave them alone for a minute."

"Stay. Eat. Go. I won't come after you, I promise."

"Did you really think this would work? That I'd come to the Igbys' and make small talk with all of you?"

"You came, didn't you?"

"Shut up."

I wanted to slump to the floor and put my head in my hands and cry. Just like I did the night of my mom's funeral when all he was to me was a shadow on the wall.

"Come on," he said, in a voice so sure of its desire that it was hard not to follow. He led me by the hand to the table.

The dining room was filled with so much furniture that sitting and standing had to be synchronized. God forbid you had to go to the bathroom. Ruth was a collector, all right. She had knickknacks and the furniture to hold them. Everything on the table, from the pewter candlesticks to the cut crystal butter dish, had a doily underneath it.

Ruth put Addison and me across from each other. I tried not to look at him during the meal, but occasionally he asked me to pass something and I had no choice. I was hoping that it would get easier being around him but it didn't.

The black meat wasn't pot roast at all, this much I knew. It was roast beef or some other kind of beast. The mashed potatoes were bland and starchy. I imagined I could use them to paste the loose wallpaper in our kitchen. Canned peas were the green vegetable; apparently Birds Eye technology had not invaded the Igby house.

I washed the first three forkfuls down with the last of my beer.

The only sounds were the clanking of the utensils against the two-for-one china that was given away down at the local Kroger years ago. Ruth had also gotten the matching plastic goblets, which were scratched up and dulled from years spent trying to be crystal.

Shirley Basset was lying at my feet and farting in that toxic way the near dead do. I expected the little gnome figurines would talk before anyone at the table did. Finally, Ruth spoke, with her butter knife pointed at me for emphasis.

"Why don't you tell us what you've been up to all these years?"

I looked around the table. Addison was acting casually, eating his peas, hacking away at his roast beast, while Marty shoveled food into his mouth and stared at his plate. The truth was, no one but Ruth was really interested, and the truth was not something she had an intimate relationship with, so I chose to lie.

"Oh, this and that," I said, trying to imitate the tone of someone who was nice. "I live in New York now and work as a bartender on the West Side. I'm going to school at night and trying to get a nursing degree. My dream in life is to take care of people."

I drank my water as if it were booze and looked at Addison. He rolled his eyes, releasing another small burst of all that disappointment he had been brewing for ten years.

Ruth put her utensils down and wove her hands together in front of her as if she were about to lead us in prayer.

"Whatever your path, you are welcome here."

Addison looked at Ruth and then at me, and we both laughed. Certainly he could have come up with a better way to see me again than dinner at this crazy woman's house.

"If you're going to laugh at me . . ." Ruth hung her head.

"No, no." Addison reached for her arm to pat it. He still had that effortless charm. The natural ease with women that made them bend to him.

"Good dinner, Ruth," I said, surprised at my own burst of kindness.

"Thanks," she said, as she studied me as if she were wondering how I would look on top of a doily.

The cake and coffee part was painful. Marty jumped in with sports talk. He and Addison kicked the usual set of stats back and forth as I studied the hundreds of dirt-colored Hummel figurines jammed in the breakfront behind him.

"Tell us about your little one," Ruth interrupted when the conversation lagged after Addison confirmed that he too believed the Browns had a chance for the championship next season.

"He's fine," Addison said.

"How old is he now?"

"Going on ten," Addison mumbled. He got up and tried clearing the table but he was boxed in by Marty.

If I could have jumped from my skin I would have—here it was at last—the words we had not uttered since my return. The mention of the baby who had become a boy.

"Have you met Addison's son yet? He's delightful," Ruth said to me.

"I have to go." I leaped up and realized I was boxed in by Ruth. My knees buckled as I struggled to keep myself from flipping the table over to get out.

"Everybody, stand the fuck up!" I shouted.


"Alex, wait." Addison was running after me. I was taking the hard way home—through the fields and eventually over the creek—but I didn't care. The air was bitter cold and the ground was quilted in patches of snow and muddy puddles that seeped into a small hole in one of my cowboy boots.

Behind me Addison's footsteps crunched in the same path a few paces behind.

"For God's sake, Alex, stop before I have a heart attack!"

I kept walking but turned. "You planned that. You can't leave well enough alone, can you? I don't want to see him!"

"I'm not asking you to," he shouted as he closed in on me. Christ, why did I always have to be so goddamned drunk? I could move better sober—it was the standing still that was hard. "Don't you want to know if he's happy? If he asks about—"

"Does he have a mother?" I shouted. The words rushed out before I could stop them. This was the hardest part of being back—the way my own feelings betrayed me.

And yet, in that instant it made sense to ask. Surely Addison had found a mother for him. What was the point of all that charm if he couldn't conjure a Mother and Wife?

Addison stopped and put his hands on his knees and caught his breath. He shook his head.

"I'm not married, if that's what you're asking."

"I'm not asking about you. I'm asking about him. Does he have a mother?"

God, I wanted him to say yes. To say he didn't even know about me. To say he had a wonderful mother who took care of him from birth, someone he called "Mom." Someone who couldn't tell him anything about me except this: "I don't know why your real mother left you."

Addison nodded and walked toward me with his arms up in surrender as I backed away.

"You, Alex. You are his mother."

## Fourteen

"So what is walking the plank?" Addison asked the next morning as I searched the room for my mother's pearls. He was stretched across the bed with his arms behind his head and the sheet loosely draped over his hips. He looked like he was posing for a painting.

I could feel him dripping out of me and wanted to take a shower and get back to the house before they came home.

"It's this stupid game my father makes us play." I looked under the pillow I had slept on. "Can you help me find those pearls? Mom's going to kill me if I lose them."

"Did you check under here?" he said, as he flipped the sheet off, exposing himself. I didn't want to look. I had seen one other penis in my life and it was my father's. I had no desire to compare them.

"Addison, come on." I felt the nausea of regret. What was I doing?

"So much for pillow talk." He sat up, pulled on his jeans, and made a halfhearted attempt to get me to smile, but gave up and went to the kitchen.

I followed him. "Promise me you'll look for them. I should get back." The pieces of me did not fit back together smoothly. My dress was wrinkled and half-zipped, my underpants were missing, and I couldn't remember if I had worn a slip. I had woken up in another body, a different model with controls and switches no one had warned me about.

"You're so . . ." He kissed me before I could stop him. He reached for my hand and put it on his crotch. "See what you do to me?"

I pulled away. "I have to go." I walked to the door and stopped. "At the far end of our property over by Rucker's Creek, there's a crack where the land splits. The ravine is deep and rocky and goes for about a mile. There's a rope bridge that spans the crack that's been there my whole life. My dad and your dad built it before my parents were married. You can climb across it and get to this sweet patch of wood and grass and a small hunting shack."

"I'm sorry, what?"

"Walking the plank, I'm telling you about walking the plank." I looked at him. All I saw were his flaws, the ragged way his hair fell in his eyes, the small pimples on the back of his neck, and the dirty soles of his feet. How could I have let him touch me like that?

"Dad takes us there to camp. The game is getting across. The bridge is old and there are some gaps. We draw straws; the one with the shortest straw gets blindfolded and has to cross on their own."

"That's dangerous."

"No pain, no gain," I said.

"What's the point?"

"Dad says it builds character, plus it's thrilling to watch your loved ones quiver in fear. The reward for getting across, aside from the obvious one of being alive, is that you get first dibs on searching for the treasure."

"Treasure?"

"Dad claims there's money buried somewhere but I don't believe it. Jared and Wendy have never found anything."

"What about you?"

"I've never made it across. I'm petrified. I tried once and didn't make it. Dad punished me but it was worth the bruises not to have to go. After that Jared and I worked out a system: if I pulled the short straw he would go instead of me. We only had to do it once."

"Jared doesn't mind?"

"He hates it but he said he'd rather be blindfolded than to watch someone else cross."

"Is that the only way to get over?"

"I think the land connects again on the Palmers' property—and you could navigate back to the patch but we never do. That would defeat the purpose."

"Right." He put his water glass on the counter.

I had to say something. I had to be clear how it would be. I took a breath as I faced the broad stretch of driveway that connected our house to his. "If you tell anyone what happened, I'll kill you."

I reached for the latch as I felt him moving toward me. He put his hand on my cheek and turned me back to face him. "I won't tell anyone," he whispered in my ear as his hands reached for my breasts. His mouth found mine before I could process what was happening.

We kissed for the last time.


"All clean?"

My father was standing in the doorway of my bedroom when I came out of the bathroom in my robe. I had scrubbed my skin raw trying to remove the memory of Addison. Steam billowed around me as I stood dead still in the hallway with my brush in my hand.

"You look different." He inventoried my body like a landowner surveying his property. He was most dangerous when he was intensely sober. "You missed the fun. Jared almost didn't make it." If he were an animal, he would have sniffed me, checking to see if someone else had marked his territory.

I looked down. His boots were covered with mud. Late spring rains had made the area slick. The slope to the rope bridge was slippery when it got wet. The first and only time I tried to cross, I slid and fell while blindfolded. The distance of the fall from standing to the feel of cold mud against my cheek felt longer than the sum of all the moments I was captive to my father's wandering hands. That was when I discovered there were worse things than being touched.

"Jared!" I called out, without taking my eyes off my father.

"I sent him to the store with your mother and Wendy."

I waited for him to make his move just as I had since the first time he pulled me on his lap and put my hand in his pants and said, "Touch me like this. Don't look at me while you're doing it."

I was seven.

"I hope there's hot water," he said, as he came toward me and pinched my cheek. I winced and stepped aside as he unbuckled the straps of his overalls. I fled to my room, closed the door, and lodged my desk chair under the knob.

The afternoon sun was riding full and high, beaming a white hot light into our bedroom. I looked around as if I were seeing it for the first time. Wendy's bed was neatly made, with two heart-shaped pillows resting side by side. Above it was a bulletin board where she taped pictures of models she thought she looked like and articles from magazines on how to be the best damn girl she could be.

Wendy's desk was empty except for her math book and an open issue of this month's *Mademoiselle*. Her side of the closet was full of neatly pressed dresses and coordinated skirts and blouses. Her clothes took up most of the rod, except for three hangers that held my warm-weather dress, a cold-weather one, and my dress for the summer dance that Nell gave to me. It was hers from last year.

My bed was bare except for a white flat pillow and an old red and green Christmas afghan folded at the foot for when I got cold from the drafty window above my head.

I reached under my bed and found the small duffel bag I used whenever I was allowed to sleep over at Nell's, which wasn't very often. I put it on the bed and went to the dresser Wendy and I shared. I took out my underwear and socks and as many pairs of jeans and shirts as I could fit. I left just enough room for my two sketchbooks: the crappy one I carried with me every day and the beautiful embossed book Addison gave me. The crappy one was in my schoolbag. Addison's was hidden in the barn. I would have to get it before the dance.

In the back of my closet, under a broken floorboard, I had $234 hidden. I started saving it the night he first touched me. Every chance I got, I stole what I could from him; sadly, it wasn't very much.

I stuffed the money in the side pocket of the duffel and slid it back under the bed. Tomorrow was the dance. I would get Mom to let me stay at Nell's. Dad would get drunk and pass out after they got home. This was the best chance I had. I was going to take it.

"You look . . ." Addison was sitting at the kitchen table when I came down the stairs dressed for my last night with my family. I was wearing Nell's pale lavender dress, which fell above my ankles in a sweeping bell skirt. The bodice was fitted with a scooped neck and a small bow that rested at the tip of my breastbone. My mother lent me a pair of white-heeled sandals that she said hurt her feet.

"They'll look better on you anyway. Your father hates it when I look too pretty," she'd said as she crawled around the perimeter of her bed looking for the mate. She offered to get me the pearls, but I told her they would be too much. I would be gone by daylight; now I would never have to explain what happened to them.

"Shhhh," I said, looking upstairs, where everyone else was finishing getting ready. This was the first time Addison and I had been alone since we had slept together. He had spent the afternoon with my dad working in the barn—which had precluded me from getting the book. I was hoping to get it before we left.

As the day unfolded, I thought of nothing else but how I would get out of Wilton. I had gotten permission to sleep at Nell's and was planning on sneaking out in the middle of the night and taking her car. I would leave her a note and promise to pay her back when I got settled. My plan was to drive as far as I could and lie about everything else.

Jared and Wendy came down next. Jared was wearing a suit my mother got at Goodwill. In spite of its poor fit, he looked handsome. His chestnut hair was slicked back and smooth. He winked at me when he caught me smiling.

Wendy wore a slim, straight black dress she had also bought at Goodwill but had altered to suit her figure. She wore black stockings and a pair of plain black pumps. Her hair was pulled up in a French knot. Her schooling in magazine fashion paid off, as she looked like she belonged on a runway in Paris rather than at the Wilton Jaycees' summer dance at the Elks Lodge.

Mom wore the dress she always wore for weddings, which had gotten baggy as her stomach problems had gotten worse over the years. She doused herself in the Charlie perfume Dad bought her every Christmas. Wendy tried to get her to put on some lipstick, but she wiped it off when Dad told her it made her look cheap.

In his midnight-blue funeral/wedding suit, my father looked like he was wearing someone else's clothes.

"Let's get this show on the road," he said, as he came down the stairs. He had small dabs of white tissue on his face from shaving. He was smiling and sober and happy. Every year the summer dance brought out this kinder man. And like the spell cast on Cinderella, it was beautiful while it lasted. I imagined this was the man my mother loved.

"I'm going to get a dance with each of my girls tonight," he said, as he peeled the tissue paper from his face. "You two are on your own," he said, pointing to Addison and Jared.

"Good, because I wouldn't be caught dead dancing with my sisters," Jared said in disgust.

"What about a dance with your mother?" Mom asked, with just a hint of hurt in her voice.

"What kind of a pussy do you think he is?" Dad answered.

Wendy and Jared rode with Addison. I stashed my duffel in the back of his truck and figured I would grab it on my way home with

Nell. There was no time to get the book from the barn. I squeezed in between Dad and Mom and took what I thought was my last ride in that red pickup truck.

The theme of the party was Starlight Serenade, which basically meant the ceiling was decorated with twinkling foil-covered stars cut from shirt boxes. The refreshment table was covered with silver glitter that left a trail on everything that touched it. The esteemed Wilton community spent most of the evening either dancing to songs spun by Hal White, future sheriff, or standing by the punch picking silver glitter out of their food.

I found Nell instantly. We stood together and chatted, not expecting anyone other than our fathers to ask us to dance. The evening was warm and humid with a threat of storms later. I had checked the weather earlier and was worried that my amateur driving skills would not be a good match for an Ohio downpour.

My father danced with Wendy and my mother between taking long pulls from the silver flask he kept in his breast pocket. He made periodic stops to the truck to refill it from the fifth he kept under his seat.

From the way he was stumbling I figured he had an hour left in him and then he would have to go home.

If I didn't know any better I would have sworn Addison was getting paid for dancing with every available (and not so available) woman in Wilton. He periodically looked over at me and nodded or waved; I shrugged it off.

Jared was with his jock buddies over in the corner. They stood in a clump with their arms crossed, acting like they'd rather push tackling sleds across the floor than dance with a girl.

I was anxious to leave before I lost my nerve. It was strange I would pick the only day of the year when my family seemed normal. Stranger still, I was having second thoughts as I watched Mom and Wendy dance together and saw my mother laugh for the first time since that day on the phone when she spoke to Addison's father.

Dad went out to smoke with a few of his friends. Before he left he looked at me and made the shape of a gun with his thumb and index finger and then pulled the trigger.

"So how about a dance?" Addison had slipped up next to me.

I shook my head. "Bad idea."

"He'll be gone for at least ten minutes. Come on, one dance."

"What's the matter? Did you run out of women?" I asked.

Addison took my hand and pulled me to the floor. We weaved in and out of families, couples, and the odd pairing of girlfriends dancing until he found a spot in the center of the room under the twirling disco ball.

He stopped short and I tripped into his arms. He held me there by putting his right arm around my waist and interlocking his left hand with my right. "Sometimes you just have to take the bull by the horns," he said, smiling.

"So I'm a bull?"

"A beautiful one."

I tried to pull away. "What if my dad . . . ?"

"I'm watching the door; don't worry."

"I love this song," I said, surprising myself at my own enthusiasm. Nell found the tape in her father's music cabinet. We used to lie in her bed and listen to it over and over again; we didn't know the lyrics or even the name of the song; we liked the way the sound pulled you away from yourself. We liked the message about wanting to stop the world to be alone with one person and the chorus that promised things would get better.

"Me too," he whispered, as he leaned forward and made up his own lyrics and sang them in my ear.

I laughed; it was the height of cheese to sing lyrics in someone's ear. Addison laughed too and spun me around. I opened my eyes and focused on his smile, the thin cool lips, his straight ivory teeth, and the laugh lines framing his mouth like quotation marks. He held me as if the lyrics were true.

"Let's go." My father's voice sliced through the music as his thick hand grabbed my wrist and tore me away from Addison. "You dance with me and no one else." His words sprayed spit in my ear.

The crowd parted around us, leaving Addison, my father, and me in the center of a widening circle. My heart raced as the electronic beat of the music vibrated the floor.

"I can explain," Addison said.

"You couldn't keep your hands to yourself, could you?"

My toes felt like they would snap from the pressure of all my body weight pressing down on them. Why hadn't I worn flats? How was I going to run in high heels?

My father pushed Addison.

"Dad, don't!" I said. Addison's face drained of color and his jaw slackened like he had been punched instead of pushed.

My father pulled me by the hair out of the lodge. I struggled to keep my balance as he twisted my hair in his fist. If I could have scalped myself to get away from him, I would have.

He slammed the exit door open so hard it swung back on its hinges and banged against the side of the building. It had grown dark. There was a cold wind blowing up from the north that whipped my dress above my head. Bad weather was coming.

"Get in," he said as we reached the truck. He opened my door and shoved me in. I banged my head against the gearshift. I held my temple and tried to focus as I blinked away the sting of tears. Everything was double and blurry, like waking from a dream in the dark. I reached for the door handle.

"Open it and it will be the last time you feel anything," he said as he climbed into the driver's seat and caught my sleeve in his grip. My dress ripped.

My head throbbed. I could feel a welt forming over my left eye. Outside, dark clouds swirled above us like hands waving in a funeral parade. I worked at the straps of my shoes, hoping I could get away faster in bare feet.

My father put the key in the ignition and tried to start the truck. The engine was having difficulty turning over.

I pushed the heel strap on my right foot down with my left big toe, trying to move as little as possible. I got it down but still had to get out of the other intertwining straps. One good flinch of my leg would get it off me.

I was hoping someone had followed us into the parking lot or called the police.

"You're just like your mother," Dad said as he kept trying to start the truck. He banged on the dashboard. "You couldn't keep your hands off him."

Someone had to be coming for us.

I got the other heel strap down.

I took as deep a breath as I could muster and in one swift motion kicked both my legs out and shook the shoes free as I reached for the handle and slammed my body against the door to get it open fast.

The engine turned over just as my father caught the back of my dress and pulled me back toward him.

"No, you don't," he said, as I cried out into the parking lot. He gripped my thigh and squeezed hard.

My voice was faint, like I was gurgling underwater and not screaming for help.

*So this is how you save yourself?*

Outside, the sky opened up with a squeal of thunder and a deluge of rain.

"Son of a bitch," my father shouted, as he banged the steering wheel and tried to navigate his way out of the parking lot.

The windshield wipers blinked furiously back and forth, trying to ward off the blanketing rain. Empty bottles of Jack Daniel's rolled at my bare feet.

Dad put a cigarette in his mouth and pushed in the lighter. The ashtray was overflowing with butts and the cellophane wrappers from new packs.

"You think I'm a fool, don't you?" he said as he balanced the unlit cigarette on his lower lip.

I shook my head.

"He wouldn't marry your mother. Just like Addison won't marry you."

"Who?"

"Shut the fuck up!" he exploded, with a smack that threw me against the passenger door. I felt blood trickling out of my nose. Tears burned my cheeks, and once again I could not see what was in front of me.

The lighter popped out as Dad turned the radio up louder.

Janis Joplin was begging a man to take another little piece of her heart.

The inside of the cab filled with smoke as my father took long careful drags on both his cigarette and stash of Jack. We were traveling down the main road, which could lead anywhere. I shoved my hands between my legs to warm them as the rain beat down on us with a fury matched only by my father's. If he would only slow down, I'd roll out.

"I married her. I stayed in this goddamned hellhole. And for what?"

He looked at me but it wasn't me he was seeing; it never was. The ticktock of his turn signal synchronized with the swishing of the wipers. My face was expanding. My teeth ached.

We turned off the main road just as the rain let up.

There was a rumble in the back of the truck like a log shifting.

"We built that bridge together. He was like a brother to me."

We veered left at the fork; we were heading for Rucker's Creek. I rolled my window down to get some air. Black spots like tiny crows fluttered in my peripheral vision. Droplets of rain splashed on my face. I stuck my head out the window and vomited. I tasted blood from my nose as it trickled down my throat.

Dad pulled me back in.

"Roll it up."

He turned onto the path in the woods that his truck had made from so many trips. He didn't slow down enough for me to jump out. I needed a chance to run if I was going to escape. I couldn't risk him catching me.

We pulled up to the clearing with the rope bridge that connected the ravine.

"Let's go," he said as he put the truck in gear, left the headlights on, and came in front of the truck toward me.

We were going to walk the plank.

## FIFTEEN

ADDISON'S COFFEE WAS as strong as his grip.

"Drink up," he said as I sat at our kitchen table and let Addison slide my boots off. I'd backed into the creek and twisted my ankle trying to get away from him and the words I had traveled great distances not to hear. I would have crawled home if I had been alone but I wasn't. Before I could get up I felt Addison's hands reach under my armpits and hoist me up.

"Lean on me," he said.

"Please don't." I couldn't finish the thought. The pain was blinding.

We hobbled like that the rest of the way home. Neither of us spoke except to communicate direction changes or a need to rest. He held me against him, his arm wrapped around my waist and his shoulder wedged against my own.

I was too tired to struggle and too drunk to care.

"Want me to carry you?" he said.

The last time he carried me he thought he was saving me.

How wrong he was.

We made it to the house. He found the key we left on top of the lamppost and unlocked the door. Inside, he helped me to a chair and made a pot of coffee.

"You can go," I said as he squatted down in front of me and

pulled the boot off my good foot and warmed my toes with his hands.

"God, Alex, you're frozen."

He stood up and took my mother's washbasin out from under the sink and filled it with steaming hot water and soap and brought it over.

"This is going to hurt." He carefully removed my other boot as he held my calf. He winced before I did. "Sorry," he said.

I began to cry as he slipped my wet, holey socks off and gently rolled up my jeans. He placed my feet in the hot, sudsy water and slowly rubbed feeling back into me.

## Sixteen

My father caught me by the arm about twenty feet from the car. I screamed and clawed at him with a fierceness that startled me. The sounds emanating from my throat were not human.

"Let go." I pushed away from his massive arms.

"Stop it," he said in a voice that was so calm I almost relaxed into the sureness of it. Maybe I was wrong about what was happening; maybe we were just going to talk about walking the plank.

The wind was howling. The ground beneath me was slippery and muddy as I scrambled for footing. My father released me and shoved me down on the ground so hard he knocked the wind out of me.

"You need to grow up, little girl," he said. "You need to get some balls if you're going to survive your life."

My father was haloed in the headlights from his truck. I struggled to get up but the ground was slick. The best I could manage was getting on all fours.

"Do you know what it's like to lose everything?" he said, his thick bear arms waving at the sky. "She was mine and he took her. This farm should have been mine. And you . . ." He walked to the truck and opened the passenger door.

*He's getting a gun. He's going to kill me.*

He rummaged behind the seat as I pushed myself up to a standing position. The high spindly trees lush with summer leaves waved around me like a crowd around a boxer waiting for him to hit the ground. I put my arms out. If I had to, I would feel my way out. I stumbled toward the woods.

"You think I don't know?" Each word moved closer to me. I could hear the slapping of his boots on the mud. Even in his funeral suit he wore his steel-toed work boots. He grabbed my shoulder and spun me around. The force threw me back to the ground. He leaned over and lifted my head up.

He was holding the red sketchbook Addison had given me. It was still in the big plastic bag I kept it in.

I reached for it. He snatched it away and walked to the ravine.

"You won't cross for me; maybe you'll cross for this." He threw the book out past the bridge, past the streaks of light from the car, far away from my line of vision.

"I wanted one thing to be mine. I settled for you," he said, as he walked back toward me and put his hands under my armpits and pulled me up. "Let's go."

The sky had opened up as we were halfway across the bridge. My father held me by the waist and pushed me across as I trembled and wished for death. We were soaked by the time I slipped on the step up from the bridge and almost fell into the ravine.

Sadly, my father caught me and dragged me to solid ground. I felt his weight bearing down on me, one hand pressing my head into the smooth mud and the other under my skirt . . . tearing at my underwear, and then it was inside me, but it wasn't a hand. No, it wasn't a hand at all.

He passed out on top of me. I managed to push him off and pull myself to a dry patch of ground under a pricker bush. My right leg had swollen to twice the size of my left, and judging by the snapping sound it made when my father tackled me as we made the final step on the bridge, I was certain it was broken. I had partial eyesight from the swollen slits each of my eyes had become. My lips were bleeding and swollen. My chest felt like someone had reached in and pulled my heart out with his bare hands.

My hands were strong, though, and I used them to get away.

I blacked out once I was under the bush. I felt pain everywhere, and while I had heard it called blinding, this was more vivid. This was pain that had no sound, no voice.

"Cat." I was dreaming of my father slicing me in half with his band saw when I felt a hand on my cheek and then two arms lifting me.

It was Jared.

It had stopped raining.

"What did he do to you?" he muttered, as he carried me through the slippery mud and grass away from the bridge and deeper into the clearing. I had made it to the other side, the one I had never been on. He laid me down on a cot inside a small hunting shack. It smelled like moss and dried leaves.

"I'm getting help."

"Don't leave me." I reached for him as I began to cry.

"I'll be back."

He walked to the door and came back and held my hand.

"Dad's gone. You're safe."

Jared carried me back across the bridge slung over his shoulder, like a fireman. My pelvis ached against his shoulder. I wanted to vomit but convinced myself I wouldn't as there was no way I could get my mouth open wide enough.

Addison was at the other side with his truck. They made a bed in the back for me out of sleeping bags. I threw up on Addison when he tried to wrap me in a sweater.

# Seventeen

"DOES IT STILL HURT?" Addison asked, as he massaged feeling back into my legs. His hands felt like a warm salve on my chapped skin as his fingers kneaded my muscles, willing them to respond.

I shook my head. After the bridge, my leg was fractured in three places. I wore a cast for two months and had lingering stiffness whenever it was cold or rained. It wasn't the leg that hurt.

"This ankle is larger." His index finger outlined the bone.

I pulled away.

He got up and tossed me a dish towel to dry my feet off. "I'll help you to bed."

"I'm not tired."

"I am, and I have to relieve the babysitter. I'll get you upstairs."

"I can crawl."

"I don't want you to."

I started to cry again. Addison walked to the counter by the phone and found a piece of scrap paper and a pen and wrote something down and placed the sheet in front of me on the table.

"This is our address and phone number. Come anytime. I won't tell him who you are. You can if you want."

I tried to say something but it was too late for that. Too late to say, "I have not forgotten him." Too late to tell him why.

"I wish I was different," I said. We looked at each other. He smiled.

"Put your arm around my shoulder." He reached for me. "Take it a step at a time."

I woke up and knew it was time to go. I didn't have much to pack. I'd been taking stuff out of the car as I needed it and I didn't need much.

On a long shot, I checked my hiding place in the barn to see if my red sketchbook had magically reappeared. It hadn't. Of all the things I had tried to forget, I couldn't let go of the image of my drawings flying across the ravine in the blinding rain.

My ankle was sore, but not so bad that I couldn't push through the pain. I hobbled to and from the barn and the car. The sun made a brief appearance before retreating behind a gang of nasty-looking rain clouds.

I had the safe-deposit key in my pocket. I would make my stop at the bank, get the papers, limp to the post office, and mail everything to Jared.

I was bone-tired and numb. I focused on the relief I would feel after a long pull of something 80 proof and tried not to think about Addison.

Pam Cassidy, the mousy-haired bank manager, introduced herself after offering her condolences for my loss. "Your mother said you would be coming."

"She told you she was going to kill herself?"

Pam shook her head. "She said she was moving to California and you would be handling her affairs."

"California?"

We walked to the back of the main floor, which was as empty as my stomach. Her spike heels clicked against the marble tiles. The bank, with its dark-paneled walls, big mahogany desks, and sour-faced tellers, was desperately in need of an update.

"Did she say where in California?"

Pam stopped and looked at the fluorescent light above her. She shook her head and continued leading me down the long hallway.

"In here." I entered a room filled with tightly rowed banks of drawers. Pam scanned the numbered columns, found my mother's box, slid in our keys, and took out a long tin drawer and put it on the small table in the corner.

"I'll be outside if you need me."

I opened the box, expecting it to be empty except for the deed, and found it stuffed full of documents in a big ziplock bag. I took out the bag and pulled out the documents. The deed was on top, along with a note.

*Cat,*
*Find Addison and ask him about this—he's in Wilton.*
*Mom xxxooo*

My hands began to sweat.

I opened the deed to the signatory page in the back. I didn't recognize the handwriting. I looked at the name printed in block letters beneath it:

JARED ADDISON WATKINS

Addison's father owned our farm. He had since 1979, the year my parents were married. I dropped the deed and pressed my palms against my eyes and rocked back and forth. I took a breath and put the bag into my purse and left the room.

"Jared owns our farm," I said to my Jared on the phone.

"I'm sorry, someone is in my office; what did you say?"

"Jared owns our farm."

"He gets a set of copies," Jared said, away from the receiver.

"Listen!" I shouted. Pam put her fingers to her lips to shush me. It was bad enough I asked to make a long-distance call, but screaming was not in the charter for good customer relations even if there were no other customers around.

"I'm sure there's a reason," Jared said. "Can't you sort it out?"

"There's nothing to sort out. He owns the farm; call him," I said, and slammed down the phone.

I did not go to the post office as planned. I ended up at Walt's Tavern at a table in the back with a pitcher of beer, four shots, and the pile of my mother's papers. It was hard to remember the last time food tasted good to me. I took another shot and pounded the table as I swallowed hard.

"I thought you'd be gone by now." Andrew Reilly sat on the bench across from me holding a frosty draft.

"Are you following me?" I asked.

"I saw your car in the parking lot."

"It's two o'clock; aren't there toes that need tags?" I said. I lifted my mug and chugged it.

"I need to talk to you," he said, lifting his mug in the air. "There is something I've been meaning to tell you."

Great. Bring it on. I leaned forward but Andrew said nothing. He looked at his mug and slid farther down in his seat. I surveyed the stack of papers and wondered if I had the balls to go through them. I took a shot and waited for him to speak.

"I miss her," he said, in the confessional tone of afternoon drunks at a bar. "Your mom was . . ." He hung his head and shook it back and forth. "I don't mean to make you uncomfortable."

I laughed. "You're not even in the zone."

His eyes met mine and studied my face.

"You look like her."

I struggled to steady my hands long enough to light a cigarette.

"I saw pictures of both of you when you were younger. You could have been sisters. You probably knew that."

"You sure know a lot about my family." I exhaled and felt the heat of menthol in my throat. As much as I smoked, I never got used to the initial burn.

"We got close toward the end."

The wind blew the front door open. The bartender asked one of the regulars to close it. He shielded his eyes from the light as he walked to the door. Daylight and bars don't mix; drinking is best done in the dark.

"Did she tell you she was going to kill herself?" I asked, trying to sound as nonchalant as possible.

"No. She said she was going to—"

"California?"

"Yeah."

"Did she say why?"

He shrugged. "She said she wanted to be somewhere nice. I told her it was. I grew up there."

She wanted to be somewhere nice? Since when? I wanted to puke.

One of the barflies put a dollar in the jukebox and queued up more country songs about cheating lovers and wasting time.

"I'm adopted!" Andrew leaned over and shouted over the song as it ended. The jukebox stopped; a barfly kicked it to start it up again.

"Recovering junkies aren't supposed to drink," I said as I watched him sip his beer. "It's not part of the twelve steps, is it?"

"No."

I took a pull of my own and stared at the brown paneling lining the wall behind Andrew.

"Did you hear me? I said I'm adopted."

Our eyes met. His searched mine for recognition as if he were communicating to me in code. I wasn't sure what that meant. I watched him.

"You weren't her sponsor, were you?" I said, as a picture started to form in my head.

"No."

I took another shot.

"I got transferred to Wilton on purpose."

He took a long pull on his beer. The frosty crust of his mug had long ago melted, forming a sweat that dripped on the table when he drank.

"I was looking for my father," he said, as he put the mug down. *He isn't who you think he is. . . .*

"I'm going to throw up." I tried to stand but landed back on my seat. It wasn't the drink that was making me dizzy.

"What does that have to do with me?" I said. "Oh, God, is it my father?"

"No," he said, in a way that felt more like a precursor than a resolution.

"Her," he said, after a pause.

He reached across the table and grabbed my wrist as if he were trying to stop me from spinning away. I looked at the peach complexion of his slender, delicate fingers and followed the line of his wrist to his arm and shoulder across the hollow crevice of his collarbone up to his chin and the pencil-sharp edges of his nose. The left side of his smile creased down rather than up. I scanned the small details that made a body part of one family and not another. I had missed them until that moment.

"She was my mother," he said.

# Eighteen

I WOKE UP IN A hospital bed. My eyelids were swollen, leaving just enough room to see the pale green paint peeling off the ceiling and dangling above me like tongues wagging. My room contained a bed, a nightstand, and a chair to my right that was pushed against the only part of the wall not covered by a picture-frame window. It had the cozy institutional feel of a janitor's closet.

The smell of ammonia and piss perfumed the air, one attempting to disguise the other. Beeps and intercom sounds came from the ceiling. "Dr. Kramer, Dr. Kramer, please call extension twelve." Sometimes it was clear, and other times it sounded like marbles rolling across cobblestones.

My mouth felt like it had been wiped dry with steel wool. The insides of my cheeks were scraped as if I had been gnawing at myself in my sleep. My teeth throbbed and felt confined in my gums. My upper lip was split.

*He beat the shit out of me.*

I curled my fingers into fists and felt a strain of soreness between my legs. My body felt dense from my neck to my pelvis, like I had been deboned and prepped for butchering. My hips resisted movement when I tried to shift my weight. At first I thought I was restrained, until I saw a cast covering my right leg from my toes to the middle of my thigh.

"Bad break," a voice said from the doorway. I looked toward

it, unable to lift my head more than a few inches off the pillow. "I'm Dr. Kramer," he said as he walked into the room.

"You need to dial extension twelve." The dryness of my mouth combined with my puffy lips made it sound like I said "You bead tension hell." Dr. Kramer smiled as he came into view. He was old, with dark, kind eyes couched by baggy eyelids. He looked like a basset hound with a stethoscope. His hair was silver and combed neatly off his face with what might have been the aid of VO5.

"There seems to be some discrepancy about what happened to you." His tone was friendly, as if he were asking me my favorite color. I didn't know what Addison or Jared had said when they brought me in.

"I fell," I said, making a conscious effort to speak clearly.

He reached for the bed controls and pressed a few buttons to adjust me to a sitting position. "There," he said, as he put his stethoscope in his ears and warmed the bottom with his hands. He put it into my gown and listened while staring at the wall in front of him.

"Did you fall on a fist?" he asked, as he moved the stethoscope to different places on my chest and then gently eased me forward and held me as he checked my back. I was too weary to care about anyone touching me. He lifted the sheet and looked at my leg, touching my cast. "It's almost dry. What's your name?" he said as he moved around the bed checking different parts of me. It was hard to swallow.

"Why is my throat so sore?" I said. My eyes watered from the pain of speaking.

Dr. Kramer took a mirror from the nightstand drawer and held it in front of me. "There's your trouble," he said, pointing to two hand-shaped bruises around my neck.

The mirror reflected a face I did not recognize. I gazed into my own eyes and did not feel the visual handshake that happens when you see yourself. My face had morphed into someone different. I turned away.

"Name?"

"Alex." Cat was gone. I would never see her face again when I looked in the mirror. All I would see were the dead eyes and split lips.

"Age?" Dr. Kramer lifted my hand and felt for my pulse. His fingers warmed my wrist as he counted my heartbeats to the second hand on his watch. He smelled like licorice.

"Seventeen."

He put my wrist down. "You have a strong heart," he said.

I shook my head and turned away from him. A beating heart is not necessarily a strong one.

He pulled up the chair and sat down and cradled my hand between his; maybe he was trying to heal me, but I was through being touched. Through with men trespassing on my body.

"Let me help you. You're a minor."

Dr. Kramer handed me a cup with a bendy straw and lifted me by the shoulders to get a better angle for drinking. The water was warm and wet on my lips and tasted a little like the inside of the plastic pitcher it had resided in for God knows how long. I wanted ice-cold water that sweated down the sides of a glass. I wanted lemonade with extra sugar, iced tea with mint and honey; I wanted something to burn away the flashes of memory I had been having since I opened my eyes. I wanted something to take away the taste of blood that ran down my throat as he pressed my head into the ground.

"Hello, Bug," my mother's voice rang from the doorway. She hadn't called me Bug since I was a little girl. "Can I come in?"

Dr. Kramer nodded. "Please." He stood up and motioned for her to sit as he inched out of her way. "Perhaps you can convince your daughter to tell me what happened so I can help her."

My mother looked down at the floor.

"Or maybe you can tell me," he said to her.

"I fell," I tried to say, but it sounded like "I hell."

Mom clutched her handbag as if it were stuffed with cash. Her hair was pinned back off her face the way she wore it to church. She looked peaceful, as if she knew everything was going to be all right.

Dr. Kramer hung my chart back up on the end of my bed and squeezed my good foot. "I'll be back later. Get some rest."

My mother smiled.

"I think we're going to have a mild summer."

I stared at her.

"Your father is thinking if the weather holds, he might try to paint the barn. I don't think it's been painted since I was your age. Only problem is, once you paint the barn it will make the house look shabby."

"Mommy," I said as I began to cry. I felt my stomach convulse. I needed her to hold me. I reached my hand to her as I called, "Mommy," over and over again.

She did nothing. The more I cried, the more I wanted to. I was crying for all of it, for everything they had taken from me and everything they put in its place.

Through my black eyes and tears, it was hard to make out the look on her face as she sat there. Her head was down as if she were lost in prayer, or as if, like me, she had learned how to vacate her body at will.

There wasn't a lot left. I could still feel the warmth of a human hand on mine, still wiggle my toes, and still see what was in front of me. I could also still feel something—and listening to my mother as she spun her conversation away from the truth, away from me and toward her carefully manufactured view of the world, I felt the black oil of rage bubble up inside me.

"I hope he kills you," I said in a gravelly tone.

Her body relaxed as her purse dropped to her lap. She looked above me at what I guessed was a crucifix because she blessed herself and said a prayer to herself and started to cry.

We locked eyes. I made sure with all my might she saw that cauldron boiling inside me. This is what I would need to live now.

"You can't stay here," she said evenly. "You have to leave." She stood up and stepped closer to the bed. I felt my fingers curl into fists under the sheets. She reached over and pushed my hair out of my face. "You'll die here," she said. "Just like I did."

She took a tissue from the box and wiped my eyes.

That was the last time I saw my mother.

That night I dreamed I was a boy playing baseball. I hit a home run and was floating around the bases. My body was strong and lean and powerful. I woke up feeling a cool breeze coming from the open window. Outside there was a ballpark across the parking lot of the hospital. I could hear the clonking of bats making contact with a ball but could not see anything but the floodlights turning night into day if only for a few hours.

"Dr. Kramer says she needs to stay for another day for observation." I heard voices outside my door.

"He wants to know what happened." That was Addison's voice.

"My father is going to end up killing her," Jared's voice replied.

"Not if he's arrested, he won't."

"Trust me, he'll kill her first," Jared said.

I felt them looking at me. I closed my eyes.

"She say anything to you?" Addison asked.

"No. You?"

"She slept the whole time I was with her. She looks . . ."

"Different."

Wendy came for a visit and sat next to me and cried the whole time, like it had happened to her. "I can't believe he did this to you," she said, over and over, as if she were trying to believe it as truth and not a fiction I made up to get attention.

"Promise you won't tell anyone what he did," she said. "What will people think about us?"

Jared snuck into the hospital after visiting hours and carried me out. There was no point in staying. We didn't have health insurance and no amount of nursing would change anything. Addison was waiting in the truck and drove me to his grandma's house. He and Jared had gotten an air mattress at a camping store and made up a bed for me in the dining room, which was close to the powder room.

The plan was for me to rest for a few days and then leave Wilton with Addison.

By the third day I was able to walk on crutches and the swelling in my face came down. The pain had become more localized, a twinge here, a pang there. My body had become a stranger to me; its ability to be beaten felt like a betrayal. I wondered how I could live out my life in a shell that was so easily broken.

I thought about Dad and what would happen if he found me. My feeling for him had progressed way beyond fear. There was no point in trying to get him punished. No point in speaking out; he lived in my head now, as the force of defeat. Part of me hoped he would come for me and finish what he started.

That night on the rope bridge, at the edge of the ravine, the "Amazing Adventures of Kitty Kat" came to an end.

By the second week, I felt strong enough to travel. Addison and I left together. We drove to Pittsburgh, where he had a friend he said we could stay with until we figured out what to do. There wasn't a lot to say and no one, not even Jared, managed more than a good-bye and a hug. He didn't even look me in the eye. I wondered if this was how it would be with us forever.

Jared gave me all the money he had saved for school—it came to twelve hundred dollars. He also gave me the watch he got for graduation, and although he wanted me to sell it, I couldn't. I wore it like a Saint Christopher medal—hoping it would protect me against further harm. Twelve hundred dollars seemed like a lot of money to me, enough to get lost, and for that I was grateful.

After helping me to the truck, he reached for me and tried to scoop me in his arms like he did that day at the ravine when the look of despair on his face was almost worse than the beating. I couldn't tolerate being hugged. I had developed a sensitivity to human touch. I tried to hide it whenever either of them came near me, but I didn't pull away very elegantly.

"Let me say good-bye." Jared coaxed me back into his arms. The burden was too heavy to avoid; he had rescued me and needed assurance.

I had no plans for myself. Going to Pittsburgh with Addison seemed as good an idea as driving off a bridge or smothering myself with a pillow. Jared promised he would never tell where I went. It wouldn't be hard to keep a secret from people who didn't care.

On the drive, Addison tried small talk, but I had no interest in the three rivers that converge in Pittsburgh or whether or not it was going to be hot. We drove through the night. Addison offered to get a hotel room so we could rest. He was relieved when I said I could keep going.

We pulled up to a small two-family house in Mt. Lebanon, a suburb of Pittsburgh. Addison honked his horn and a tall, slim woman with long, straight, jet-black hair came out of the house on the right. From a distance she looked like a shopworn version of Cher. Her wrists and fingers were adorned with turquoise and silver jewelry. She wore cutoff jeans that frayed mid-thigh and a loose embroidered gauze shirt. I hadn't been in Pittsburgh very long, but I sensed she was too cool for most places. As she came closer, I realized she was at least ten years older than Addison.

Addison jumped out of the car and lifted her in his arms in a big hug. Her hair flew in the air as she laughed and held on to him. He put her down as she held his face in her hands and shook her head in a "I can't believe it's you" fashion.

I was crippled and could not leave or else I would have. This was my fate, to watch others connect while I waited. I thought of the boy in my dream, the strong-in-his-body boy who floated on the bases. I wanted to be him.

They walked toward the truck holding hands. Addison was smiling for the first time since the dance.

"Diana, this is Cat." Since the "accident," as Jared and Addison started calling it, Addison had taken to calling me only Cat.

Diana put her bejeweled hand out to me and stopped as if she sensed my desire to not be touched. She nodded and waved. "Welcome to Pittsburgh and to my house."

I nodded and said nothing.

"Let's get you settled," she said. Her smile revealed a set of perfectly matched white teeth. Her slightly tan skin complemented her warm green eyes.

As Diana opened my door to help me out of the car, she leaned forward, giving me a clear view inside her shirt. Her right breast was missing. In its place was a long ropelike scar. I pulled back. She caught me staring, stood straight, and placed her hand on the empty part of her chest.

"Cancer," she said. "About three years ago."

I nodded.

"I know what it feels like to lose a part of yourself."

Diana settled me on the couch while Addison carried our stuff upstairs. Her living room was filled with mismatched furniture that individually looked out of place but in the context of the room all seemed to go together. Her walls were filled with masks, paintings, photographs, and shelves lined with tokens, dolls, plates, pitchers, bowls, and other assorted objects picked up from God-knows-where. There was more life in her living room than in all of Wilton. To the left was a fireplace with a furry pink stuffed pig sitting on the hearth. On the mantel was a photograph of Diana, standing in a doorway resting her arms above her head. She was illuminated from behind and smiling at the photographer. She was naked and stunning in the bold way she presented herself to the camera, as if she knew her own beauty.

"Addison took that before the cancer." She was standing behind me holding a glass of iced tea. "I taught photography at UCLA—he was a freshman." She handed me the glass.

"You fucked him?" I said, surprised at the anger in my tone.

She nodded. "Not the best idea I ever had. He was eighteen, a little bit older than you are. I was . . . am much older."

I started to cry. This happened a lot. For no reason I would start weeping. When it first happened in the hospital, I thought it was a by-product of my black eyes, but even after they started to heal it continued.

Diana sat on the armrest next to me and, using the sleeve of her blouse, dabbed my cheeks.

"I won't bother you," she said.

Diana stood in the doorway of my bedroom holding a breakfast tray. It had been three days since I arrived. I had slept for most of them, as I was tired all the time. Diana woke me to eat and to help me to the bathroom, but other than that she made good on her promise not to bother me.

"He's gone," she said, as she put the tray down on the end of the bed to help prop me up. "I don't think he's coming back." She put the tray in front of me and walked to the window and crossed her arms in front of her. She was wearing a red embroidered kimono and baggy white socks. Her hair was pulled up in a knot on top of her head.

"Did he leave a note?" I asked. Since we had arrived Addison and I hadn't had much contact. Between my long naps and his need to "go for walks" we managed to steer clear of each other.

Diana laughed. "Addison, leave a note? I don't think so." She opened the blinds and looked out into the yard, which was filled with the exotic flowers she spent hours cultivating.

"They're strange creatures, aren't they?" she said.

"Who?"

"Men."

"Brutal."

"Yes, they can be."

The summer was hot. Some days my cast itched so badly I thought it might be easier to saw my leg off. Other days the heat made me feel like I was in a slow cooker, waiting to be taken out and served as a not-too-tasty treat to a hungry monster.

Diana brought me food and often sat with me and watched *General Hospital* on an old black-and-white television she brought up from the basement. Channel 7 was the only one that came through clearly, and, sadly, *General Hospital* was the only show we agreed on. I didn't like game shows and she hated the news—that's about all there was before eight o'clock.

Diana taught photography at Point Park College. She had eager students who often stopped by for advice, or, as I soon discovered, to share some of their stash. Sometimes one or more of her students would wander down the hall after using her bathroom and try to engage me in conversation. I saw it as a chance to hone my talents at repelling people. I was quite good at it.

Two months after I arrived Diana took me to the hospital to get my cast taken off. She said her doctor friend would take care of me. Diana had a friend in every walk of life.

Melissa Worthy was even more exotic-looking than Diana. After an intern who didn't look much older than me removed my cast, Dr. Worthy took me into an examination room to talk while we waited for the results of my X-ray. She helped lift me onto the table.

"So I hear you had quite a fall." She looked into my eyes and my ears and even up my nose.

I nodded.

"You still have some shadowing from the bruises. Never saw rocks shaped like hands before, but hey, I've also never been to . . ." She looked at my chart. "Ohio. So what do I know?"

"I don't feel well," I said.

"Lean back." She sandwiched my shoulder with her hands and helped me lie down. She brushed my hair out of my face. I started to cry again.

"I'm going to give you an internal exam, if that's okay." She said that after she felt my abdomen. "You say you're tired?"

"Yes."

She placed my feet in the stirrups, using extra care with my bad leg. Although the cast was off, I was still compensating for the weight of it. I was shocked at how sore it was—I assumed when the bone healed I would be able to walk normally again. Not true. I would be hobbling on crutches for a while longer.

"Scoot down a little," she said. "That's good."

The air felt cold between my legs. Even though it wasn't raining in the examining room, it felt that way to me.

"Nausea?" she asked, as if she were offering me a mint. She had slipped on a glove, and as I nodded, she inserted her fingers inside me. It is one thing to be touched, another to be invaded.

I screamed and kicked her hard with my good leg.

She fell back against the guest chair, which kept her from falling. She picked up her stethoscope, which had flown off her neck, and adjusted her lab coat before walking back toward me.

"Let's talk about what happened," she said, "while I take some blood."

Diana took me out to dinner and the movies to celebrate getting my cast taken off. The doctor said I would be back on my feet within a couple of weeks.

"I could use some help getting ready for this show I'm doing on the South Side," she said, as I sipped a chocolate milkshake and tried to remember how much I liked them. "I have some grant money. I could pay you."

"You've done enough," I said. "I can help."

We sat in silence for a while, neither of us wanting to bring up the news that was hanging over us. Dr. Worthy said the blood tests would confirm what she was almost certain of.

We had to walk slowly back to the car, as I was struggling with my leg.

"You don't have to have it," Diana said.

For a moment I wondered what she was talking about—the thing growing inside me hardly felt like an "it," let alone a person.

"I don't want to think about it," I said.

"Whatever you decide, I'll help you."

"I think it would be better if I—" I began to say.

"No, it wouldn't. Let's keep walking; it's a beautiful night and the exercise will do you good. We'll take it slow."

# Nineteen

"I WANTED TO TELL YOU that first day at the morgue." He spoke in a tone so measured it felt rehearsed. Andrew's eyelashes were long and curly. My mother's were so long she couldn't wear sunglasses. I wondered how he managed.

I waved the waitress over. "Two bourbons, straight up."

The waitress came with the drinks and cleared off the shots I had emptied. "Pay her," I said to Andrew. He obediently took out his wallet and gave her a twenty. The longer I looked, the more I was able to conjure my mother. Even his hair was the same color, and there was a wave that seemed familiar, but her hair was straight.

"How old are you?" I said.

"Thirty-four."

Four years older than Jared. He laid his palms flat on the table as if he were going to shove off.

"What do you want? There's no money," I said.

"I want to know who she was. What she was like . . . what you were like . . ."

"Hold up. Slow down," I said, trying to temper his enthusiasm.

"Don't you want to know more about me? About your mother?" he said innocently.

I didn't want to know, not really. I had tapped out my capacity for understanding my mother a long time ago. So she had a kid and gave it away. There's no crime in that. What did it change?

He brushed his bangs off his face, revealing a small patch of freckles at the top of his forehead. I had a memory of connecting the dots of Addison's freckles as we lay in bed together.

Freckles and wavy hair don't make two strangers brothers.

I swigged the first of the two bourbons and lost the feeling in my knees. Outside, the sun slowly drifted behind a dark wall of clouds. From the window by the door, I saw my car and the highway that would lead me out of town.

The second bourbon dropped like a heavy stone in the pit of my stomach. I should go while I could, while the truth was blurred by my drunkenness. I could add this to the pile of fuzzy-edged memories I was collecting. I could try to do to Andrew's story what I had failed at with my own. I could forget it.

Numbness traveled up my thighs and through my waist. Even if I wanted to I would not be able to run, not without help.

Addison; Jared Sr.; Jared; Mom; Andrew. This wasn't a family tree; it was a twisted vine choking at the roots.

"How did you find her?" I asked.

Andrew's body slackened from its usual upright countenance. He looked toward the door as if the memory of his abandonment was an uninvited guest he didn't want to come in. He took a deep breath. "I thought about it since I was fourteen. After my adoptive parents died, I bounced through a bunch of foster homes and got really . . . lost." He hung his head. "At first I didn't want to know; I just wanted to be happy. School helped, and when that wasn't enough, drugs did. But all the while, I thought about her. What she was like." His tone changed whenever he spoke of her, like he was talking about an angel.

"She never looked for you?" Andrew's hands balled into fists and retreated under the table.

He shook his head. "It's hard to believe a woman who gives up a child could forget like that."

"Giving up is not forgetting."

He smiled. "That's what she said."

It was my turn to pull away. Tears welled in my eyes.

"After I finished college I jumped from state job to state job trying to locate my birth records. I wasn't sure what I would do with the information once I got it, but looking gave me purpose. I got a break a couple of years ago. A private detective I hired obtained the adoption records."

"You hired a private detective?"

"I spent my money on searching and heroin. I wasn't doing very well. I burned most of my professional bridges and was close to getting fired. Once I knew she was in Wilton, I used one of my last connections to get the appointment as coroner. We met at church, that part was true."

"You told her right away?"

He shook his head. "Once I saw her, I lost the desire to confront her. What was I going to say?"

"Tell her the truth. Make her see you."

He laughed.

"What's so funny?"

"I didn't have a chance to do anything. Once she saw me, she knew. She came to me."

"And everything was fine after that?"

"No, she drank. I used. It was great at the beginning, but after a few months the novelty wore off and I felt so angry. She didn't understand. She had a hard time seeing herself as a person who made choices."

Life just happened to my mother; it washed over her like waves reaching for the shore. She loved a man who impregnated her but left, so she let my dad decide what her next move would be. She lived in suspended animation, waiting for something better. Killing herself was the only real choice she ever made.

"Did she ever say anything about me?"

"She knew you had a son."

I felt my stomach lunge. Here it comes. I gripped the edge of the table.

"Addison would bring him over and say hello whenever we sat in the park."

"Addison?"

"Yes."

"How did he introduce him? Did he say, 'This is your grandma'?"

Andrew shook his head. "Addison told Alex your mother was an old friend."

"And what did he say about the kid's mother?"

"He told us she was dead."

"Dead, huh?" My leg twitched as if driven by an internal motor. There were thousands of potential follow-up questions, plenty of details to discover, but where would it lead me? She knew, maybe everyone did. So what? We sat in silence and drank some more.

"She said she had to think of a way to get you back. She couldn't let you make the same mistake," Andrew said after a bit.

"Which mistake was that?"

"I think she meant leaving your son."

Outside, the sky opened up and pelted rain so thick I couldn't see beyond the door. I smoked my last cigarette and felt the weight of the booze bearing down on me.

"I should leave." He took a final drink of his beer.

It was time to go.

Andrew helped me to my car and offered again to follow me home. "I'm not going home," I told him, but I didn't say where I was going. The cold rain on my face woke me up a little and I felt surprisingly capable of finding my way to the highway and heading out of town. I would pull over as soon as I got to the first rest stop and sleep it off. When I woke up with a puffy face and a mouth as dry as a good martini I would be ready to press on and put some more miles between me and the past. I rolled the window down and called out to him as he was walking away, "Did she ever tell you who your father is?"

He shook his head and turned back. "Not really, except she said he wasn't your father. I figured it out. Especially when she wanted me to go to California with her. And there was Addison and the way she always asked about his dad whenever we ran into him. I was waiting for her to tell me, though. I wanted to hear it from her. And now I won't have that chance."

I turned on the ignition. "God, to think she had a chance with someone else and blew it."

"The man who was my father left her. Your father saved her."

"Is that what she said?"

He nodded. "Your father was awful, but being alone is worse, don't you think?"

"Worse than having your finger cut off?"

"No, not that, but putting up with the meanness was better than being alone. I was so lonely growing up."

"You can be lonelier with someone else than by yourself. That kind of love, that life she made, destroyed everything. Being alone never hurt anybody."

# Twenty

"Y OU ALWAYS HAVE a choice, sweetie. If you want to have this
baby, have it, but it's also okay to have an *abortion*." She
whispered and finger-quoted the word and laughed. "God, I hate it
that the word is considered so dirty. Pro-lifers—those are the folks
who say abortion is murder, you're killing a child, blah, blah,
blah." She sipped her coffee, which had grown cold, during one of
the many mornings we sat together on her wicker glider on the
front porch and felt summer winding down and the crispness of fall
creeping in. She wore a long, flowing, faded paisley cotton caftan
that she pulled over her knees and legs as she swigged coffee and
rocked back and forth. She smelled like cinnamon in the morning,
from the incense she burned in her room to help her sleep. Her hair
was wild and peppered with gray, but it was soft and smooth when
it brushed against my shoulders as we talked.

Some days I thought just being with her would be enough.

"Being pro-choice doesn't mean you're not pro-life—it just
means you get to choose whose life is most important to you." She
touched my stomach and smiled. "This one inside you will con-
sume you. There are rewards, huge ones I would imagine, but there
is also loss; you lose yourself."

"Do you have kids?"

"Oh God, no, I was way too focused on myself to have children. I had an abortion once. Now that I'm older, I think I'm finally ready, but that's the thing about life, kiddo. . . . Sometimes you're ready at the exact moment it's too late."

I knew that day on the porch I would not have an abortion. The hard bubble that floated inside me was no more a baby than I was a mother, so it wasn't my fear of killing something that made me not do it. To be honest, I wasn't spending too much time in my body anymore. The part of me that had thoughts and occasionally feelings about it was not the same part that tried to zip up jeans that were getting too tight or fit into bras that were getting too small.

If there was a body I lived in, I guess it was Diana's, as hers seemed more resilient, more lovely than mine could ever be, and so in an odd way, it was Diana who was carrying the baby, not me.

As I grew bigger, the reality of what was inside me expanded as well. Diana was enthralled with the process and took me to every doctor's appointment and bought lots of books on childbirth. She told me she thought I would be a good mother and to make her happy I played along. We never discussed Addison, never talked about getting in touch with my family, never really spoke of what would happen after the baby came. I could tell she had a plan for us and, in a way, that made it easy for me to make my own.

One night, when I was about eight months along and feeling like a tenant in my own body slowly being evicted by its angry, kicking landlord, I tried to imagine what this thing would look like. Certainly there would be a deformity of some kind or maybe brain damage. Would there be a marker—some way to know who the father was?

I thought again of that night at the ravine on the bridge and how the rain pounded down on me in a way that almost made me forget all other details. All of them except one: the monster was in me now and it was never going to be over.

Addison was sitting on the front porch when we pulled up with a car full of groceries. Diana had gotten a commission check for photographs she sold and decided we should stock up on as much food as possible. She had insisted we stop at Atria's for lunch so I could have one of their massive cheeseburgers before I had the baby. She was counting the days and full of excitement.

Addison was leaning forward, resting his arms on his legs like he was waiting for an answer from a doctor who was performing some lifesaving operation on someone he loved.

I didn't want to get out of the car. Diana walked toward him. He stood up and smiled and put his arms out to hug her; she pushed him away and led him into the house, where they stayed for almost an hour. I dug out the Oreos, ate a row, and then threw up.

Finally she came out and leaned into the passenger window. "He wants to stay for a while. He knows about the baby. He says he won't leave until we figure it all out."

"You called him, didn't you?" I said. I wasn't able to look at her. All her talk about choice and freedom, and she needed a man as much as my mother did.

"Sweetie, he's the father."

I laughed. Little did she know.

"He has a say," she continued, but I wasn't listening. Warm water rushed out between my legs.

"Oh God, something bad is happening," I said.

Addison followed us to the hospital in his truck. I didn't want him near me. Diana drove and muttered about breathing and con- centrating and all that shit they taught us when she made us go to Lamaze. All I wanted was to rip out the thing tearing at me.

I was in labor for twelve hours. Diana stayed with me and left periodically to give Addison updates. She fed me ice chips from a cup. "Open up," she said during one of the more quiet times. She took a long cotton-tipped swab and wiped the inside of my mouth. I looked up at her. She shrugged.

"I'm going to make an offering for a happy life for you all," she said. Diana was always mixing herbs and potions. She claimed what saved her from cancer was healing, not medicine. I chalked it up to another one of her wacky beliefs.

After six hours of holding my hand, she took a break for coffee.

I knew he would come in. His hair was pushed off his face from handling it too much. His face was tan and clear except for the colony of freckles that danced on his forehead. He had the slow gait and forlorn expression of a man paying his last respects.

"Don't hate me," he said when he reached the bed. I turned away. "I didn't know. I called Diana to find out how you were. . . ."

A contraction came and I reached for him. I felt the searing burn rising from the bottom of my pelvic bone up to the top, where the wave of pain crested into a feeling of my hips snapping in half. After a count of ten, the peak slowly subsided.

"Let go," I said. Addison loosened his grip.

Addison and Diana took turns sitting with me. It felt as if they were the real parents and I was the surrogate they hired to birth them a healthy, happy baby. What they didn't know was that there was a chance this child would be neither.

When the baby came out, everyone sighed at the wonder of it all. They asked Addison if he wanted to cut the cord. He looked as freaked out as I felt. "May I?" Diana asked, and she did.

They cleaned the little boy up and put him on my belly. I stared at the ceiling and fought the urge to look. The doctor said he had ten fingers and ten toes and was perfectly healthy.

*That's what you think.*

When the nurse asked if I wanted to hold him longer, I said I was too tired.

I missed him as soon as they took him away. I replayed the moments. The warm movement when they laid him on me. The way he stopped squirming when our skin made contact. The tiny creature that was swimming in my murky waters had surfaced and landed on the beach of my belly. There was that gasp for air, the gulping urge to take in life and announce his arrival. The way his small tummy moved in and out as his hands curled into half-fists, not sure if hands were for holding or hitting. And there was that faint creaking sound he made right before he screamed.

Those were the moments I could never drink away—no matter how hard I tried.

## Twenty-one

I couldn't see past the illuminated beams from the headlights. Like with most things, though, I did better if I didn't see too much. I thought of Andrew and the way he scratched his arms and the cool, even tone of his voice, never wavering or breaking, and how his eyes were still a little dead when he spoke.

*He's still using.*

I thought of him shooting up, shooting hoops, going to school, searching for his mother, seeing me, his half sister, for the first time, and suddenly I felt incredibly sad.

I clutched the wheel and leaned forward, pushing the car deeper into the rain.

I turned on the radio and there was that song, the one they played at the dance about how time could stand still, that a moment could fill a lifetime. The smell of Addison filled the car and summoned the feeling I had as we danced that night that he could stop the world.

The only sound I ever heard that day on the delivery bed was the sound of my son gasping for breath. His tiny voice cackled like the creak in the floorboard on the third step, and then his body shuddered as he let out a wail announcing he was alive and there was no turning back.

Only running away.

My head was swimming. I was becoming engulfed in a deeper

sense of drunkenness than I had when I got into the car. Memories flashed in and out of my mind as quickly as the wipers brushed away sheets of rain.

The marker for the highway was a clear sign from God. The overpass above me was well lit, and from the turnoff at the light where I sat, it seemed as if it were raining only where I was. I put on my turn signal to merge onto the interstate and thought of Addison's hands on my feet, washing them, and the way he still looked at me.

And the papers and the deed and the son.

The light changed. I drove past the turnoff for the highway out of town and headed across Main Street, over the railroad tracks, past the high school and the football field and Our Lady of Perpetual Sorrow, and made a left onto Elm.

The living room light was on and the blinds were open. Through the picture window I could see Addison sitting at the dining room table hunched over a stack of papers. For a moment I forgot I was driving and lost control of the steering wheel and swerved over the curb and onto Addison's front lawn.

I slammed on the brake and flew forward, smashing my head against the steering wheel, feeling the hard smack of the horn against my forehead, and hearing the blare wailing like a siren just as everything went black.

## Twenty-two

I STOLE THE MONEY from Diana's wallet when she and Addison
went to the nursery to see the baby. I had left Jared's money back
at the house. The nurse said I would be able to leave in the morning
and get on with being a mother. Addison said we would talk about
what to do next. Diana said she would get the spare room ready. I
wasn't sure how much more ready it could be; she had been deco-
rating it for months. Before she left, she took a picture of me and
smiled. "Just in case you forget what this day was like."

I called a Yellow Cab from the waiting area and asked them to
meet me in front of the convenience store across the street from the
hospital. I was sore and woozy but not too weak to stand. The
beatings had prepared me for this. It was two in the morning when
I slipped down the stairs and out the door with three hundred dollars and the maternity clothes I came in with. I got into the cab and
asked the driver to take me to the bus station.

I bought a six-pack of beer at the 7-Eleven and drank it as I
waited for the next bus out of Pittsburgh. It was going to Altoona.

It was the first of many stops I made on the road back to
Wilton.

## TWENTY-THREE

I OPENED MY EYES and saw a younger, male version of myself standing next to my bed tossing a baseball into a mitt.

"You snore," he said. I lifted my head off the pillow to confirm I was awake and realized this was exactly what I thought it was—my second encounter with my son. His hair was dark auburn and thick like mine, with a bold wave running through the middle of his head right above his ears. He wore it short with buzzed spikes sticking up off his forehead. His eyes were chocolate brown and big. The rest of his face dimmed in contrast to their boldness. Even his eyebrows arched naturally in the middle like mine. I looked better as a boy.

"I'm Alex," he said. "Who are you?" I fell back on the pillow. His name was Alex?

"Cat," I said. I wasn't quite ready to spring the news on him that he was exchanging pleasantries with his namesake.

"That's a strange name." He whipped the baseball into the mitt so hard it made me flinch. He laughed. "You're jumpy," he said.

"I need coffee and a . . ." I looked around the room for my purse while making a smoking gesture with my hand. As I sat up, I realized I was in my bra and underwear. I covered myself.

"Cigarette?" he asked. I nodded. "Your clothes are on the chair. Dad washed them for you. Purse is here." He pointed to the floor next to my side of the bed. "There's no smoking in the house. Besides, it's a bad habit, you should stop."

"Right." I couldn't take my eyes off him as he tossed the ball and circled the bed. His energy radiated everywhere. His smooth pale skin was unscarred and perfect. His demeanor suggested he was a happy boy. "How old are you?"

"Nine, almost ten. How old are you?"

"Twenty-seven, almost twenty-eight. Can you get me my clothes?"

He looked at the chair and paused. I wondered what he was thinking. If he saw the resemblance or if finding women in their underwear was something he was used to from having Addison for a father. He walked to the chair and used his mitt to scoop up the clothes and dropped them next to me. He was lean and wore his jeans loose and off his hips, like Addison.

The room was filled with granny antiques, big dark furniture that would dwarf anyone who stood next to it. The bed was a high four-poster style with fluffy pillows and a crocheted bedspread pushed down to the foot. It smelled like moth balls and the sweetness of old perfume. On the mirrored bureau was a framed photograph of a young woman holding a baby.

"That's my granny holding Dad when he was a baby. We look alike."

I wasn't sure if he meant he and I or he and his dad, so I didn't say anything. My forehead was throbbing. At first I thought it was from the drink. I touched it.

"You beaned it on the steering wheel," he said.

"Excuse me?"

"Beaned it. Hit it. You passed out after you turfed our lawn."

"I didn't do it on purpose."

He laughed. His eyes and mouth widened in an expression just short of pure joy. "Which part? Turfing our lawn or banging your head?"

I couldn't help myself; I laughed too. "Neither."

"Good, because I'd wonder about someone who'd do something that stupid."

I needed to put on my clothes but I did not want him to leave just yet. "Can you turn around so I can get dressed?"

"I can go," he mumbled, as he turned his flushed cheeks away. "I'm not even supposed to be in here. Dad said I shouldn't bother you."

I made a motion for him to spin around. "You're not, stay a minute." I reached for my blouse, holding the blanket to my chest, and dropped it when I knew I could slip the sleeves on and cover myself as quickly as possible. I swung my legs over the side and did the same with my pants. "All done." I was standing, feeling as shaky sober as I did drunk. Now I could see how tall he was. He came up to my shoulders. If he walked toward me and hugged me, his head would fit perfectly in the crook of my shoulder. I leaned back against the bed and touched my stomach in the same place where he had been both inside and then outside, resting and reaching for me as he gasped for life so long ago.

He turned around and looked me up and down with the same intensity that Addison did.

"You're weird," he said finally.

"Gee, thanks."

"I didn't mean you're weird like it was bad, just . . ."

"I know, weird."

"Yeah."

We sized each other up for a few more moments. His hands were thick and solid, like my father's, not at all like mine or Addison's, and upon closer inspection the line of his mouth was my dad's as well.

"Shoes?" I asked.

"Downstairs."

I reached for my purse and rifled through it for a cigarette. The papers and the deed fell out along with keys and empty cigarette packs. Alex came to help me. That's when I saw it: the kidney-shaped birthmark on his right hand in the small curve between his thumb and index finger. The light-brown mark that set my father's hand apart from all others.

I pulled away. I felt like I was going to faint. As I tried to focus on getting everything back in the bag, I could feel his eyes on me. I stopped and looked up at the wall in front of me. There was a dime-store painting of a doe-eyed girl swinging under a weeping willow in a white lacy party dress as a man and a woman stood by watching in their Victorian finest. Everyone was smiling and enjoying the day as a happy family.

"Cat?"

I turned to him. That face, open and wanting to be adored. Was mine like that at that age? "I'm . . ." Tears began to well.

"Weird?" he said, half-smiling.

"Yeah."

"I play baseball," he said.

"You any good?" I asked, throwing my purse on my shoulder and walking toward the door. The floor was cold on my bare feet. I hoped my socks were downstairs as well. This would hold me, this small encounter. I could go back now, back to New York or wherever, and forget all this.

"Yeah, I have a practice game this afternoon. Want to come?"

"It's February. Isn't it a little early for baseball?"

"I'm on a traveling team; we start the regular season at the end of March."

I opened the door as he followed, tossing the ball in the air.

"Alex, come have lunch before you go." Addison's voice came from downstairs. I followed the sound to the stairway. "And put your jersey on. Danny's mom is picking you up."

"Danny's my best friend." He went back down the hall past the room I was in and into his. I felt dizzy and gripped the stairwell as I slowly came down to face Addison.

The stairs ended in a small alcove joining the living and dining rooms. The front door was in front of me. I wondered if I could sneak out.

Addison was standing in the doorway of the kitchen facing me. The house was simply decorated with sturdy pine furniture and warmly painted walls. On the wall above the table was a large, framed black-and-white photograph of Diana holding a small baby in the air; both are laughing and looking at the camera. Alex was right: he and Addison looked alike as babies. They were beautiful.

*He isn't who you think he is. . . .*

"Hungry?" Addison asked.

"Not really." Actually, I was starving. "Sorry about the lawn."

"You need to eat. I'm making lunch." He ignored my apology and didn't seem at all surprised I was there or interested in whether or not I had just spoken to my son. He waved me into the kitchen.

Addison had set the small round table that sat by a picture window facing the yard. "Coffee?" he asked. I nodded. There were three plates on the table. He was expecting us to eat together.

"Would you mind if I went outside to smoke?" I asked.

"Use the sliding doors over there," he said, pointing to the dining room, which overlooked a large deck. "I built that myself."

"Impressive." I wasn't sure who it was that responded to him. It certainly wasn't the me I had been living with; this person was calmer, almost nice. She reminded me of how I was back before everything started, back when I was seven. I resisted the urge to tell Addison what had happened upstairs, about the deed and Andrew and the notes from my mother. I was full of contradictory impulses; I wanted to go and stay. I wanted to tell him everything and keep it all a secret.

I lit a cigarette and surveyed the yard. There was a swing set in the back that had no swings, only a slide that had gotten rusty. The sun was coming through the clouds and felt warm on my face as I exhaled. The smoke burned as it went down. I felt as light-headed as a teenager taking her first puff. My feet were bare and the deck boards were cold and rough. Still, warmer days were coming.

"Are you coming to my game?" Alex dropped my shoes next to me. "Dad said you forgot these. Your socks are in the dryer." I slipped them on.

"So it's just you and your dad here?"

"Pretty much." He went down the stairs to the yard and gathered up a bat and some balls. The snow had melted enough to leave a wide stretch of grass. Alex wore a baseball jersey that said "Dinizio's All Stars" on the back. "Sometimes Mrs. Daley comes to babysit, although I think I'm too old for one. Don't you?"

"I don't know. I don't know much about kids."

He tossed the ball high in the air and spun around to catch it. I got the feeling he was showing off for me.

"My mom's dead," he said.

I fell back against the screen door but caught myself before I went through it. Alex came up the stairs. "You okay?"

"Yeah, I think I need to eat."

"Wait!" He went down to the yard to gather his stuff.

"What did she die of?" I called to him.

"Cancer," he said. "There's a picture of her in the dining room holding me."

Diana was dead. Although there wasn't a day of my life I didn't think of her, I never allowed myself to imagine what had become of her. She raised Alex, that much I suspected; but when did she die? And was she a good mother to him? Did she and Addison raise him together?

"Soup's on," Addison shouted from the kitchen. Alex bounded back toward me as I put out my cigarette and followed him into the house. I excused myself to use the bathroom, thinking I could collect myself there. The pendulum of emotion had swung back to the leaving side. What made me think I could navigate these waters?

The bathroom was filled with framed photos of Alex through the years. Every picture was a different version of him. He was my father. He was me. He was Addison. I felt a pull in my abdomen, like a contraction. I had missed it all. Thank God. Right?

I needed a shower, clean clothes, a haircut, a different story. I needed somewhere else to go. I needed to read the rest of the papers my mother left, to ask Addison about the deed. I needed a drink, a coffee, some food.

I rinsed my mouth and tried to straighten my hair but that damn wave kept my left side from lying flat. I lifted my shirt and looked at the scars Alex left. The way my skin had stretched to accommodate him and the way it went back when he found his way out. But it didn't go back all the way; he had left his mark on me, like every other man did.

I came back to the kitchen and stood in front of my empty seat. "I should go, guys. I've got stuff to do and you've got baseball and . . ." I was motioning toward the door as I felt my voice crack. Addison and Alex sat at their seats like an old married couple, used to the day-to-day order of meals shared and time well spent. Here I was, a drunken loner infringing on their routine, their lives.

"Dad, help her," Alex said, looking at me and then at him.

Addison got up and slipped my purse off my shoulder and placed it on the floor. He pulled my seat out and eased me into it. "Stay for lunch; then you can go."

"Are you okay?" Alex asked.

I pulled the small paper napkin out from under the soup spoon and wiped the tears that had been streaming down my face. I hadn't realized I was crying until I saw the alarm in Alex's face.

"Fine. Just tired." I looked at the plate Addison had put in front of me. He squeezed my shoulder. I cried harder.

"This is my favorite lunch." Alex smiled as he crumbled saltines into his bowl of tomato soup and bit into a grilled cheese sandwich. "Do you like soup?"

His voice had the beginnings of Jared's deep rasp. There was that birthmark again. I watched it as he stirred in his crackers.

I nodded as I took a sip. It was Campbell's from a can, but it was hot and steamy, and it felt almost as good as a drink. I closed my eyes. "I haven't had tomato soup since I was little," I said.

"Where did you grow up?" Alex asked.

"Here, in Wilton." Alex looked at Addison. I wondered who he thought I was and didn't know how much more I should say.

"She's Mrs. Rucker's daughter," Addison said.

"Oh." Alex paused and took a sip of soup and thought about what to say next. "Sorry," Alex said.

"Thanks."

"So, did you know my dad when he was younger?"

I looked at Addison; he smiled, giving away nothing.

"Yup."

Outside a horn beeped. "Danny's mom, let's go." Addison stood up.

Alex shoved another bit of sandwich into his mouth, grabbed his equipment, and pulled on his baseball hat. "See you at the game," he said, and ran out the door, leaving us alone.

I continued to eat. The solidness of the food helped me feel more grounded. The room felt smaller without Alex.

"I didn't come here on purpose," I said, after Addison and I had eaten in silence for a few minutes. "I was leaving. I ended up here. I wanted . . ." I couldn't say it.

"You threw up on yourself. I washed your clothes." He didn't look at me. He took a bite and stared straight ahead. We sat for a while longer. His hands were weathered and freckled as he spooned soup into his thin lips. I pictured him at the dining room table, paying bills or doing whatever it was when I drove up on the lawn and fell against the horn. Did he come out alone or get Alex to help him? And when did I throw up? The only memory I had was of my head hitting something hard, and then the sound of the ball in the mitt and the sight of my son above me.

It was hard to know how they saw me, harder still to feel what it might be like to see me slowly disintegrating in front of their eyes. Part of me was glad they did, glad Alex thought I was weird; that would push his suspicions back further, if he had them. Addison, well, what did I care what he thought?

I felt tired again, like I could push my plate away and rest my head and sleep until I woke up as someone else. The urge to run had been replaced by a desire to get it over with, whatever it was I had been avoiding all these years.

Addison stayed focused on his lunch. I wanted to make contact with him, to thank him for doing what he did for Alex, but I didn't know what he did. I had been so busy with my own story, I forgot there were other ones that needed telling.

I took a deep breath as if I were preparing to swim underwater and exhaled. "I don't know how to start," I said, my voice breaking.

Addison made eye contact with me at last, in that devouring way his son had inherited. I returned his stare and felt something I hadn't in a long time, keenly, acutely, alive—it made me feel nauseous.

"He thinks of Diana as his mother. She raised him until he was four. I was in and out of his life. I don't know what I was thinking; I guess I was still trying to prove something, but Diana, she wasn't trying to do anything except love Alex."

"Alex," I said.

"We decided to name him after you. Especially after you left. Diana insisted on it. She said he needed to be connected to you. She always said you would come back. She told him that as well."

"He thinks of Diana as his mother," I said.

"Does that bother you?"

"No," I lied.

Addison took our plates. "This is hard, Alex. Part of me wants to throw you out of here and tell you to go to hell." He dropped them in the sink and put his hands on his hips. "Do you have any idea how long we looked for you?"

I gripped the table. Addison's anger actually felt better than his kindness; this I could understand. This would make it easier. Addison took a breath as if he had made a decision and turned the water on in the sink and threw me a dish towel. "You dry," he said, "then you're taking a shower and coming to Alex's game. We will make dinner and you will spend one evening with us. Then you decide what you tell him. He knows he had a birth mother who left him. He has some information about you."

I opened my mouth to say I didn't think I could do that just as he handed me a plate. I did as I was told.

## TWENTY-FOUR

"WHEN I WAS IN the hospital after my fall, I dreamed about a boy playing baseball. I thought it was me but I think I was dreaming of him before I even knew I was pregnant."

"He's good, isn't he?"

"Amazing," I said. You didn't need to know much about baseball to know Alex had a gift. He held the mitt as if it were an extension of his hand and rounded the bases and worked the field as if it were his natural habitat. Joy exuded out of him with every pitch he threw. "He's so . . ."

"Happy?"

"Yeah."

"I know."

The inning was over. Alex spotted us and waved. Addison lifted my hand. "He's waving at us," he said. His hand lingered. I felt a rush. How did he still have this effect on me?

I showed Addison the deed and the note from my mother during the game. He said my father had told him about the house a long time ago and had told him my mother was in love with his father.

"He wanted me to stay away from you," Addison said.

"If anyone should have stayed away, it was him," I said.

"Andrew is her son, isn't he?" Addison asked. I looked at him. "Come on, he looks like your mother and a little like me."

I nodded. "She still loved your dad. I think that's why she killed herself. She couldn't bear it anymore."

"I don't know. Knowing her grandson was without his mother seemed pretty rough on her. Maybe it was a little of both or maybe . . ."

I knew what he was going to say. He was right. "Maybe we'll never really know."

Back at the house I watched Addison and Alex move through their dinner prep like a comedy team. Alex would set up a story and Addison would finish it. Then Addison would tell me something about Alex and he would jump in with embellishments and details.

I wasn't sure how it was possible to be with them so easily, especially when it seemed there was more that needed to be said.

"So you knew my dad a long time ago?" Alex asked, as we ate our spaghetti. Addison had become a good cook.

Addison and I exchanged looks.

"I knew him back when he was a stud," I said. Addison flinched, surprised.

"Dad? A stud? Hardly." Alex laughed. "He never goes out with anyone. He says relationships are too complicated."

"You don't go out with anyone?" I laughed.

"I had my fun," he said. "What about you, Alex?"

I was about to answer when I heard Alex jump in; I forgot he didn't know my name.

"Dad, I'm almost ten; I don't think I need to date yet." He blushed, and when he did, he looked exactly like Addison.

"How about hitting the books? Cat and I will do the dishes, and then we'll have dessert."

"I just want to ask Cat one more question. Dad said you lived in New York. Is that true?"

I nodded.

"I want to live there. I want to be an artist."

"I thought you wanted to be a baseball player," I said.

"Both," Addison and Alex said in unison.

"New York is great. It's easy to get lost there."

"Do you still live there?"

I wiped my mouth with my napkin and stepped back into the immediate past, where I was the woman with the boxes in the backseat, the beat-up car, and a drinking habit. I wasn't this woman my son was imagining in his mind.

"I don't know," I answered. "I'm not sure where I'm living right now."

Alex went to do homework as Addison and I cleared the table.

"So you don't date? That seems so out of character for you," I said, as I scraped the leftovers into the garbage.

"Not really."

"But you used to be such a . . . a . . ."

"Player?"

I laughed. "Yeah."

"Having a child sobered me up. Not at first; I left right after you did. I managed to stick around for a week and then I slipped out in the night and left Alex with Diana. I wasn't ready for a baby, wasn't even ready for a relationship. Maybe if Diana hadn't been there I would have stepped up; I would like to think I would have. What about you?"

"What about me?"

"Would you have stayed with him if Diana hadn't been there?"

The real answer was "No, I wasn't going to raise that freak of nature," but I couldn't say that, especially now, when it was clear this boy was no freak. Even if he was, did that make him less deserving of love?

"It's hard to say."

"You panicked, didn't you?"

I wasn't ready to talk about this. Did he think I left because I couldn't handle the burden of a child? God, that made me sound so weak. How could anyone forgive me if that's what they thought? But that's all they could ever think, so it would have to be. No one would ever know I would have stayed if I knew Addison was his father.

"Yeah. It was complicated," I said.

"Weren't you curious?"

I dropped a plate and it smashed on the floor in front of my bare feet. Addison stepped forward and grabbed me by the waist to pull me away. "Watch yourself," he said, as we collided together in an embrace.

We were dancing again. At least that's what it felt like, his body pressed against mine as my hands reached for his shoulders to steady myself. He smelled so good.

"Alex," he whispered.

The elephants of the past were sleeping, but they would be awake soon and I would return to my job as keeper of the herd. Not yet, though. For a moment I was that girl in the apartment above the garage, the one who wanted him beyond anything I had let myself desire.

"I missed," I said, as I looked down, afraid of the power of my own words. He lifted my head and kissed me as we stood away from the broken glass.

"Cat!" Alex called from upstairs. Addison and I jumped apart. His shoes crunched on the shards of plate as I slammed my elbow against the counter and howled. We both laughed. "Cat!"

"Maybe now you understand why I don't date that much," he said.

"Yes?" I answered, following the sound to the stairs.

"Come see my room," he said.

I looked to Addison for approval. "That's big. He doesn't even let me in it."

I went upstairs and followed him down the hallway to his door. "It's a little messy." He let me in.

Pieces of paper were taped to every square inch of the room. There were sketches on them, comic-style, with frames and action and dialogue. Something was familiar about the drawings, the characters. I felt my heart beating rapidly, my pulse throbbing in my throat.

*This is not possible.*

"Dad gave me this book last year when he was cleaning out the garage. He said it belonged to a friend." He held up the black sketchbook I had left behind in my backpack. The red one he had given me was thrown across the ravine but this one had been saved. He handed it to me. My hands started to shake.

"I started to read it. I loved it so much I figured I'd draw some adventures of my own. These are my adventures of Kitty Kat." I looked at the drawings on the walls. He had captured the essence of Kitty Kat, but had added something different, a strength in her eyes that mine did not have, and the definition of line was sleeker, more skilled. He was drawing my story, making it up as he went. I felt the room spinning and needed to sit down.

"When you told me your name was Cat, I wondered if it was you."

I cleared off some space on his bed and sat down with the book. My drawings. I hadn't seen them for so long. His drawings, so vibrant and alive, I never imagined.

"It is me," I said, stroking the book. I didn't know where to look; my desire to see his work was as strong as the one to see mine.

I heard a phone ring and Addison walk to get it. I wanted to stay in the room filled with our drawings forever. I wanted to read his version of my life. I wanted to be the woman in his drawings.

Addison opened the door.

"It's Wendy. She needs to speak with you. Your father woke up."

## Twenty-five

I RAN AS FAST as I could. Through Alex's bedroom, down the hall,
where I slipped on a rug, and then bolted down the stairs, out
the door, across the lawn, and over the divot I put in the grass. I
tripped on the curb but caught myself and hit my stride in the middle of the street. I was running again, this time with no car or
money or purse. The air was cold, black, and razor sharp. Every
breath felt like I was inhaling shards of glass. I prayed for the sta-
mina to get me somewhere.

I ran from the sound of Wendy's voice saying the words "Dad
woke up. He wants to see you." I ran from Alex's drawings, so
close to mine and yet filled with more soul, more life, more of
everything. I ran from Wilton and the papers in my purse and the
deed and Andrew Reilly with that hunger to connect.

I ran because that is what I do. In all the years, the bus and train
stations, the seedy hotels where I holed up for days drinking and
lying on dirty sheets staring at water stains on ceilings, at all the
crappy jobs where I served drinks, fending off the pawing hands of
desperate drunks while gulping down their free cocktails, knowing
full well that you can never get something for nothing—all those
years, I knew I was running. I knew I wasn't living a life but avoiding one.

The ground beneath me was hard and every step I took shot a
splinter of pain through my bad ankle. Ahead of me was nothing

but blacktop leading to another street and another road I had to travel.

The hardest part of leaving isn't the looking back; it isn't the loss you feel for a place or people; it's the fear that what you intended to leave isn't ever going to go, and that what you really want, you're never going to get.

My hands clenched into fists as I tried to keep up the pace I had established as I tore out of Addison's house. I did not want to see my father—did not want to touch, know, or feel him. Which would be worse—if he was sorry or if he wasn't? And what is sorry anyway? What does remorse get you?

"He's not going to make it," Wendy had said on the phone. "This could be your last chance to say good-bye."

"Alex!"

Behind me was the sound of other footsteps and voices calling my name. I turned as I ran and saw Addison and Alex coming after me. Addison was ahead, closing in as he moved from darkness to light. His stride was sure and seemed more practiced than mine. Alex lingered behind, waving. His call was weaker, but I heard it. "Cat," he cried, "come back."

I kept going.

"Stay there!"

I turned. Addison was motioning for Alex to stay put as he held his hand out for me to stop. My body responded before my brain could process what was happening. I felt myself winding down, and although I was still moving, I knew I wasn't going anywhere.

Addison caught up to me and grabbed the back of my shirt and pulled me to a stop. I bent over and put my hands on my knees and struggled to get my breath back. He did the same as he balled the piece of my shirt into his fist and panted.

"Goddamn you," he huffed.

I tried to pry his hand loose but it wouldn't budge. I was so winded it wouldn't have surprised me if I started coughing blood.

"Let me go," I begged.

"Dad, are you okay?" Alex called. "Cat?"

"Go back to the house," Addison shouted. "We're fine."

Alex lingered in the street with his hands on his hips, hopping from foot to foot in worry.

"You should go back with him," I said.

Addison looked up and held his ribs. "You need to stop running."

"You don't know what I need," I said, as I wiped my mouth.

He tugged on my shirt in frustration, pulling me closer. I tried again to push his hand away but his grip was too strong, so I shoved him, hoping he would fall, and he did, taking me with him. We fell together like two fugitives handcuffed together. He did not loosen his hold on me.

"Let me go!" I shouted as we struggled to get up. "You want me to say I'm sorry? I'm sorry. You want me to jump into his life and be his mother? I can't do that. It's too late. You think I can stop running? How am I going to do that? Everywhere I look I remember that night. Every day for the last ten years I think of those hands reaching into me, taking parts of me he had no right to take. He destroyed me."

Addison let go and I fell over, not realizing that his grip was all that had been holding me up.

"No, you did that."

"Does it make you feel better to think I did this to myself?" I stood up and steadied myself against the rush of dizziness that came over me.

"This isn't about what makes me feel better," Addison said.

"Really? Was it easier for you to swoop down and save the day when Diana died, knowing I would always be more irresponsible than you? It must be great to have me to measure yourself against. As long as I'm the big fuckup, you can be the hero."

"This is how you do it, isn't it? This is how you justify your choices? Everyone else is to blame for your misery."

"So you're the model of responsibility? Please. You took advantage of my and Diana's feelings for you and then you left. You're no different than my father. You were a destroyer too. So you came back. So you did the right thing. You were the one who made the mess. It was yours to clean up. I was the one who was messed with. There's a difference."

"So you're a victim and that excuses you? Look at you, you're a drunk. You have no life, no friends, no connection to anything, including your son. Your father didn't do that, you did. You're a destroyer too, Alex. You have a son you neglected. Maybe you're more like your father than you know."

I looked up into the winter sky, so dark and bleak. February, the worst month of the year, short days, unbearable chill followed by enough warmth to make you think spring might come, though it's still so far away. I hated my life the most in the winter.

Addison was right. There was no defense. If my father had told me he had been beaten every day as a child, it still wouldn't excuse what he did to me. Even my mother's loneliness could not undo the pain of her choices. And rape did not excuse abandoning that baby.

It did not.

I looked away and began to cry.

Addison pulled me to him and wrapped his arms around me. I fell into his chest and smelled the orange musk of his body. I wanted to wrap my arms around him and hold on for life. I wanted it to be over, however it ended.

I pulled away.

Addison released me like he was pushing a boat away from a dock. I fell back on my heels and tried to find my footing.

"You want to go, go. This time make sure you get gone." He reached into his pocket and threw my car keys in the street next to my feet and walked away.

It was cold again—this time the chill came from the inside out. My mouth opened to say the words "Come back," but nothing came out.

I thought of those drawings, of the way Alex drew Kitty Kat, the sureness of her jaw, the righteous look in her eye, and of how he seemed to know her better than I did. How determined she had been to stop the Hand. To win her fight.

I thought of Diana holding Alex as a baby night after night as he cried, missing something but not knowing what. Over time he forgot about what was missing and reached toward what was there, someone who stayed, someone who loved him completely.

Down the street past the silhouette of Addison, in the doorway of their house, Alex stood and watched the scene of his father chasing his mother. Whether he knew it consciously or not, he would one day know that that was what he saw. How did it end? With his father not being able to hold her, with them not being enough for her to stay?

And who would know my story? Who would tell him the truth?

There were different ways to feel pain, and not even the physical beatings or the touching could match the shame I felt for leaving Alex. Even if he was my father's son, the very painful truth was, I was his mother.

I looked at the road ahead and at the ground I had covered since leaving, and, as always, I had not gone as far as I had thought. I picked up the keys and starting moving. This time I went back.

The door was closed when I got to the house. I knocked. My hands were shaking as I waited and hoped it was not too late. Addison opened the door, and after a moment of looking at me, he motioned for me to come in. I felt tears welling as I struggled to find the courage to speak.

"Will you come with me?"

"Let me see if I can get Mrs. Daley to watch Alex," he said without hesitating, as if he had been waiting for ten years for me to ask him.

# Twenty-six

M Y FATHER WAS moved out of intensive care and into the
same small room I was in ten years ago. The corridor
walls were still the blue-green color of bathroom cleaner and the
floors were scuffed and mopped to a finish a few years beyond a
shine.

Addison walked ahead of me, reading the signs and asking for
directions as I followed numbly. If there had been an empty
stretcher I would have lain on it and slept until I woke up or was
left for dead and rolled to the morgue.

On the drive over, the reality of what I was doing settled in.
Even if I forgot, my body had a memory of its own. The shooting
pain in the base of my pelvis reminded me of that.

"Are you okay?" Addison had asked in the car. My palms were
open and resting in my lap as if I were waiting for a heavy load to
drop from the sky.

For the first time Addison looked at me with something other
than pity. My choice to see my father had garnered a small amount
of respect from him. The tone of his voice was more familiar, like he
was with a friend rather than a crazy woman he was talking off a
ledge. Not many people treated me with regard. I was either too
young or too drunk. Diana was the only one. While I dismissed it
while it was happening, I recognized its absence when it was gone.

"It won't change anything," I said finally.

"Do you want it to?"

His skin still seemed so smooth. I imagined it would be warm to the touch if I reached across the armrest and traced the line of his jaw down to his Adam's apple, which bobbed when he laughed. I could travel the muscles of his arm as it gripped the gearshift and place my palm over his hand and wait for him to hold it. I could change it all by reaching out.

"I'd really like a drink."

"Yeah. I would too."

We sat in silence until he turned into the visitors' parking lot.

"Here we are," he said as he put the car in park and turned off the ignition. I reached for his arm and squeezed it. He took my hand and warmed it between his palms.

"What if he's not done with me?" I said.

"You said he destroyed you that night. You need to find out if that's true."

"Come on, Mr. Rucker, lift up. There, good boy."

A bag of bones lay in the bed struggling for breath as clear tubes tethered him to oxygen tanks against the wall. A nurse hovered, trying to get a pillow under his shoulders.

I stood in the doorway and surveyed what was left of my father. He was gray, from the ashen tone of his complexion to the silver strands of his hair to the beard struggling to hang on to his crumbling face. Where was the man who pounded the life out of me in a blinding rage?

"Are you family?" the nurse asked, as she wiped his mouth with a wet cloth.

"Sort of," I answered. "I'm his daughter."

"Alex?"

I nodded.

"He's been asking for you."

"How is he?" Addison asked as he stood behind me with his hand on my back, gently guiding me over the threshold.

"He's pretty alert now but he fades in and out. I'll be at the nurses' station if you need me."

In spite of the cold, the window was open, no doubt at my father's request in one of his lucid moments. My father needed cold like a vampire needs blood.

A pair of green striped pajamas hung over the back of one of the guest chairs. I had a vision of my mother bringing him clean things before she killed herself. Did she tell him what she was going to do as he lay in a coma? Was he finally forced to listen to her? And if so, what did she say?

*You ruined everything.*

That wouldn't cover it.

Watching my father labor for air, it was difficult to say which was harder, breathing in or breathing out. The effort required his full concentration as he stared at the ceiling.

"Dad," I said, my voice as hollow as it was the night I begged him to stop. My legs felt unsteady, as if the ground beneath me was moving. I gripped the railing at his side.

He turned his head toward the sound of my voice and locked his eyes on mine. The fire in his pupils was still there. The slow disintegration of his body could not extinguish it. I jumped back as if I had been shocked.

"You're too thin," he said in the voice that looped in my head my whole life.

I looked at Addison for permission to go. He urged me on with his hands.

"What do you want?" I said, as I remained a few steps away from the bed.

"I want our daughter," he said.

"We don't have a daughter."

*Oh, God, did he know about Alex?*

"We have three children," he said, trying to hold up three fingers.

"It's Alex."

"He's never going to be with you."

I walked to the edge of the bed so he could get a closer look at me.

"Dad, it's Alex, your daughter."

He turned toward the intravenous bag dripping into him. I wondered if it was morphine and imagined myself ripping it out of his arm and sticking it in mine. He closed his eyes and his mouth and his jaw slackened as if he were asleep.

I looked around the room searching for a sign to tell me what to do. This was useless. How could he be asking for me when he didn't even recognize me? I didn't feel anything close to what I imagined I would feel. This was annoying and frustrating. All the years I thought about him drinking in his chair with no one to sit next to him. The way he pushed what he did out of his mind, day after day, drink after drink, until he didn't have to think about whether or not it was right to touch me the way he did; all he knew was that it was necessary, like pissing.

He opened his eyes and looked right at me.

"You look old," he said. "Not as pretty."

"You look like you're about to die."

"Good," he said. He pointed to the cup of water on the nightstand next to a picture he had propped up against the reading light. It was a photo of me when I was five. I'm wearing a crown my mother had made for my birthday and leaning over a cake covered in strawberries with five candles flickering. My father, Jared, and Wendy are around me and we're all looking at my mother, who was crouching in front of the table taking the picture. My mother was shouting for us to say "Cheese," and for some reason I thought that was funny and was laughing as I tried to blow out my candles. My whole face was smiling, from my open mouth to the twinkle of my eyes. I was holding Jared's and Wendy's hands as Dad leaned closer to help me blow out my candles. The picture captured the moment right before the lights went out.

I placed the photo facedown and picked up the cup and brought it to his mouth. He could not get the straw in on the first attempt, and as hard as I tried, I could not force myself to touch him. He struggled as I steadied my aim.

"Hold still, for Christ sake," I snapped. His mouth made contact and he took a long pull on the straw. Water dribbled down his chin. Seeing him as helpless as he was almost made me wish for the stronger version of him.

Addison took the cup from my hand.

"You're still fucking him?" Dad said, when Addison removed the straw from his mouth.

"You and your mother can't keep your hands off those Watkins men."

Addison looked at me.

"You'd think you would have learned from your mother. I tried to teach you."

"How did you do that, Dad?"

"I never laid a hand on you or your sister." He lifted a bony index finger and pointed at me. His fingernails were yellow and long. "If it weren't for me your mother would be in a home somewhere. She is a disgrace."

"You treated her like garbage."

"She is lucky I forgave her."

"What part did you forgive her for, Dad, getting pregnant or not loving you?"

Before I could finish he reached out and grabbed my wrist and squeezed it tightly. "You're just like her. What did you do with his baby?" My father looked at Addison. "Like father, like son."

I pulled away but his grip was too tight. "Did he promise to take care of you? Did he give you the farm too? Did he ask his best friend to marry you so you wouldn't be alone? Did he help you find a family for the baby?" His voice made a gurgling sound as he spoke.

"Let go of me," I said. I was feeling the old rage again, the good kind that helped me get away more times than not. The kind that helped me crawl to a bush that night at the ravine. I reached down to pull his hand off me and saw the birthmark. The one I saw on Alex's hand.

The monitor above my father's bed began to beep rapidly as my father's grip tightened on me.

"Your mother is a whore," he said. "She still doesn't know for sure whose baby it was. I had her first, just like . . ." I grabbed my father's wrist and squeezed harder, forcing him to let go. He gasped for air.

A nurse's voice came over the intercom. "Mr. Rucker? Are you okay?" The beeping grew louder as my father's breathing became more labored.

"Like what, Dad? Go ahead and say it." I leaned in close and shouted in his face. I didn't care that Addison was there, I wanted him to say it. I wanted him to shout it from the rooftops to tell the world what he did to me. I wanted his last words to be the admission. I was tired of being the only one who knew the truth.

"Tell him what you did."

The nurse rushed in as Addison pried my hand off my father. "Alex, let go."

"Get her out of here!" the nurse said as she and Addison looked at me like I was the monster.

"He isn't who you think he is," I shouted as Addison pulled me out of the room.

## TWENTY-SEVEN

THE OFFICIAL CAUSE of death was heart failure.

I called Wendy and Jared and told them to get to the hospital as quickly as possible, as they were trying to revive him. He had used up his last reserve of energy to spew one final round of bile my way.

Wendy came and they let her spend a few moments alone with him before they took him away. She was distraught. "He only wanted you," she said as Willard consoled her.

Lucky me.

Addison drove me back to the house. We rode most of the way in silence. I felt pressure to pretend that an evil spell had been finally broken with his passing. Addison wanted me to feel better and that made me feel worse. My father's death did not kill the monster in my head.

"I'll stay if you want me to," he said as we pulled off the main road.

"I'll be okay," I said.

Jared was sitting at the kitchen table, resting his head in his hands. His white, starched shirtsleeves were rolled up, and his blue pinstriped suit jacket was resting on the back of the chair. There was coffee on the stove and an empty mug next to it.

"Is this for me?" I asked as I dropped my bag on the table.

He nodded.

The coffee pot holder was worn into the shape of the handle. On the counter it was misshapen and frayed, but in my hand it fit the curve of the percolator perfectly, keeping the heat at bay. The handle was still loose; it had been my whole life. I held the glass bulb of the lid and poured a steaming cup, just like my mother had all the years of her life.

I had her delicate fingers and his rough palms.

"I thought you'd be gone." Jared wiped tears from his eyes.

"So did I."

I took the photo out of my pocket and slid it across the table toward Jared. After they wheeled my father out and stripped the bed, I slipped back into his room and took it. On the back my father had written "My family," and in the spots where our heads appeared on the other side he had written our names and drawn a circle around mine and added rays to make it look like the sun.

"It was on his nightstand."

I got up and found what was left of a bottle under the sink and poured myself a tall one. "Want one?"

Jared studied the photo as if someone had told him there was a clue hidden somewhere in our faces. "He's really dead?" he said, as I quelled my shaking hands with a shot.

"Yup." I poured another.

"I'm glad," Jared said. I drank to that.

"I just wish the end had been more painful." I moved too quickly and lost my footing. "Oops."

Jared helped me to my chair.

We sat in silence and sipped our coffee. What if having them gone was worse, not better? Now all that was left was the past bearing down on all of us.

"Now that he's dead, do you feel better?" Jared asked. He had the same look he gave me that night in the motel, the trembling lip, the glassy stare, the naked plea for forgiveness. I grabbed Jared's tie and pulled him to me.

"Nothing helps. You should know that."

And just like that, we were back where our story had ended seven years ago, in the motel in Massachusetts.

## Twenty-eight

I T WAS FEBRUARY, and it was pouring. Large blankets of rain crackled like hot oil against the small picture window that overlooked the parking lot.

Jared had tracked me down outside of Boston after he called the bar where I was working. Tony, the owner, told him where he might find me.

He looked so different from the last time I had seen him, so grown up and altered. As if he came from a different family, a different place. His clothing was expensive and dry-cleaner-pressed. His manner was formal, as if he were administering charity to the lame and anxious to get back to the club for lunch.

I thought the knock on the door was Dan's Liquor Emporium or the Domino's Pizza guy. At first I didn't recognize him. Perhaps it was because I was coming off a three-day drinking binge that dulled my senses or maybe it was something more truthful. The person at the door was my real brother. The one I remembered was a figment of my imagination.

It was storming and he said he couldn't stay. His fiancée was waiting in the car. They were on their way to meet her parents in Cambridge.

"I need to tell you something." I was sitting on the bed trying to stay upright. As hard as I tried to push away from the intensity of seeing him, I couldn't manage it very well. I hadn't showered in days, nor had I changed out of the ratty T-shirt and torn sweat-pants I had been wearing when I checked in. This was my pattern. I'd work in a bar, save whatever cash I didn't drink, get into a fight with the manager, get fired, and drink until I was numb. I believed every binge would be my last. I wasn't praying for salvation, I was looking for peace. Peace never came, but the motel bill always did. When the money ran out, I took a shower, paid my bill, packed the car, and started over. Some stops were better than others, some jobs paid more, and some people tried to help, but the only thing that quieted the memories was amber, and it burned going down.

My love for Jared was something that had sustained me in those days and seemed to float above any feelings I had about anyone, except of course that baby gurgling on my belly. I wasn't sure that was love, though; it was more like something a notch beyond it, some emotion I was not equipped to access. But Jared, he was love for me. A man who did me no harm, who made me feel safe.

Jared took off his wet Penn State windbreaker and put it on the chair by the door. He turned away from me and looked out the window as he crossed his arms. His shoulders tensed. He still had the sturdy build of a football player, but the bulk had been replaced with an elegant sleekness. I wasn't sure if it was his body or the cut of his clothes that made him seem so tailored for a different life. I looked even worse next to him. I smelled.

"I was there that night. I was in the back of the truck." His voice boomed like thunder over the rush of rain. I could hear the trickle of a stream of water coming from somewhere close and wondered how long it would take before the storm would be inside.

"I don't think so," I said. I wished the liquor would get here. I looked through my duffel for a clean T-shirt.

"I came after you when Dad took you out of the dance."

I dropped the T-shirt and looked at him. I picked at the skin at the base of my right thumbnail. It was calloused after all the years of tearing. When the blood came, I sucked on it, seeking solace in the rusty iron flavor. I resisted anything that took me back to that night. I avoided trucks, dances, dresses, men, ravines, hope, love, sex. My leg started to twitch.

"I don't want to talk about this," I said.

"I was there the whole time." His measured tone was cracking. He moved closer, as if he were prepared to force the words into me if he had to. "I jumped in the back and rolled toward the cab so no one would see me. It was storming. I couldn't hear anything but I knew something bad was going to happen. I rode in the back to the ravine and I waited until he dragged you to the bridge."

"Stop it," I said, getting up and walking to the window, hoping to see a delivery truck. Maybe there was something left in a glass or bottle somewhere.

I remembered that thud in the back as we were pulling out of the parking lot. Dad pulled at me before I could look back to see what made the noise.

"I wanted to help you. That's why I went, but when I saw his face, I—"

"Enough," I said, searching the room. He didn't hear me.

"He was hitting you and shouting about how he wasn't going to let another Watkins man steal from him. You were trying to get away . . ."

I charged at him and pushed him back over the plastic table and chairs. We came crashing down onto the floor. I was straddling his hips and swinging my fists at his chest. "Shut up!" It was too late; I was on the bridge with the mud in my face and the weight of my father bearing down and crushing me. And now there was more to know.

"I wanted to do something, Cat. I wanted to save you but I . . . God, I don't know. I've played that scene out every day trying to understand why I froze. I guess I was afraid. I was afraid he would kill me."

I buried my head in the mildewed green carpet and wailed. He reached for me.

"Don't touch me," I growled, as I wiped snot from my nose with the back of my hand.

"I'm so sorry."

This was the whole point, wasn't it? I had learned there is always more to feel even when you think you have gotten to the bottom; it's just a resting place on the downward spiral.

There are all kinds of ways to hurt someone. The only thing worse than being hurt is the denial of it. In a way, forgiving Jared for watching my small life get destroyed felt like a betrayal of all that was left of me. If I couldn't have a brother who saved me, a father who protected me, a mother who nurtured me, and a sister who adored me, then I could have my rage.

"What is worse, Jared? Watching or doing?" I got up off the floor and went to the bathroom and got a glass of lukewarm tap water and drank it.

"I was nineteen, Cat."

"Did you see everything?"

"I saw him hitting you. I saw him tear your clothes." Now Jared was getting uncomfortable. If he saw it all, he wasn't going to say, and I wasn't going to make him. He must have known. He found me without underwear. He carried me and saw the bruises. And what about Addison? Had they speculated?

I would never know because I would never ask. There was more to protect than my pride; there was the baby. Who would love him if they knew the possibility?

I stayed in the room for another week and ended up in an emergency room for alcohol poisoning. Close but no cigar.

I didn't see Jared again until my mother died.

## TWENTY-NINE

I LET GO OF Jared's tie and went to the refrigerator and opened it, knowing there was nothing I wanted in there. My palms were sweaty and I felt a hard ball of panic in my stomach.

"I should have stopped him," Jared said, as if we were still having the conversation in the motel room.

"Should we order deli platters?"

I opened the freezer and surveyed the frozen parcels wrapped in white paper and marked by Mom with her black Sharpie pen. "Sunday Roast, 1/26," it said on a package that looked like a giant Tootsie Roll. The only way to banish my mother from this house would be to burn it down. Jared shifted in his chair and struggled for words. I could feel his stare. Finally, he sighed and summoned the words.

"Help me, please," he said. His voice sounded like Alex's. I turned around. Tears welled in his eyes as his left hand cupped his right fist as if one were a ball and the other a mitt. This was a nervous habit of Jared's, born from years of playing ball. I had missed it until that moment. I had felt it but could not name it. I had seen the birthmark, the eyelashes, the hair, the ease with people, even the sharp tongue, and had placed the genetic source, me, Addison, my mother, my father, but when I saw him run and the way Alex carried himself and the sureness of his gait, I did not know the source until I saw Jared at the table. My son was like his uncle. He could be like my father without being his child, couldn't he?

As hard as I tried to disengage, I couldn't. There was the openness of his gaze, the way his body relaxed when we made contact, the way his eyes anchored you to him; Alex had Jared in him too.

"Don't you need forgiveness?" Jared asked.

I pictured a portrait of the men who made my son: Addison's scoundrel father, my monster dad, my weak brother, and the man I hoped was his natural father, Addison. Each of them deeply, terminally flawed. And yet, they made that little boy who may be the best combination of all.

And if that is true of Alex, is that true of all of us? Of Jared, Wendy? Me? Are we the best of our relations?

"I would have stopped him if I could," he said.

Jared rested his head in his arms and began to weep. He appeared smaller in his sorrow, like a boy being punished in school. More like the brother I used to know. He clenched his right hand into a fist and pounded it into the table. I felt a stirring, an impulse to act. As Jared lifted his fist again I caught it and held it tightly with both of my hands and pulled it to my chest.

*He isn't who you think he is. . . .*

"I know," I said. And I meant it. The sad truth was, he couldn't; no one could. The words escaped from my mouth before I could take them back. After a moment, his hand relaxed, and we slowly wove our fingers together like we did as kids, lying in the grass watching the clouds.

I was as surprised by my tenderness as he was. I had been certain there was nothing good left to feel. I was sure the loving part of me had died on the bridge. I sought refuge in that certainty. I lived on one side of the hard line and everyone lived on the other, except the boy. He walked it.

Jared looked up. I smiled weakly, as if I were trying to remember how to do it.

He smiled back.

We sat like that until the headlights from Wendy's car illuminated the back wall of the kitchen.

Jared, Wendy, and I stood alone at the top of the hill and watched as my father's casket was lowered into the ground next to my mother's. The wind whipped across the long yawn of cemetery, rattling the leaves on the trees behind us. The sun stood high in the sky, teasing the day with the brightness of spring and its imminent arrival. As the minister said his last prayer, I imagined the world turned upside down, with the dead watching us and wondering if we were the lost souls.

Without the thread of my parents tying us together, Wendy, Jared, and I seemed like lonely strangers crashing an old man's funeral. Walking back to Jared's car, I wondered if we would have liked one another if we had met outside of Wilton. If there was something more between us than genetics and time poorly spent.

## THIRTY

WILLARD AND ADDISON were at the house setting up when we pulled into the driveway from the cemetery. Wendy was unusually quiet.

At breakfast Willard told me Wendy had lost another baby a few weeks before and had not rebounded like she usually did. Wendy had miscarried three times in the last three years. I couldn't imagine wanting anything that badly.

"Are you okay?" I asked as we walked from the car to the house. Wendy's dress hung on her like a shiny black pillowcase. Her eyes were sallow and bloodshot, and in spite of expertly applied makeup, she had no color. She shook her head and walked ahead. "What?" I said.

"I can't remember the last time you asked me how I was." Her legs wobbled on the gravel as she made her way to the back door. "Come to think of it, I'm not sure you ever did."

We were at the stoop and she continued up the stairs while I stayed back and felt my pockets for a cigarette. Wendy did not turn to see if she had stung me, nor did she hold the door. She stepped into the kitchen and took off her coat as if she were the mistress of the manor.

I sat on the step and lit up. She was right; I never asked. She never asked either.

"Andrew's on his way." Addison came out and sat close to me and took a long drag from my cigarette.

"Anyone tell you these will kill you?"

"Really? Liquor is quicker."

It was getting dark, although it was only four P.M. We were expecting a few people to stop by to pay their respects, but not many. No Bundt cakes for Dad, that's for sure.

"How are you doing?" Addison asked, nudging me with his shoulder. I took the cigarette back from him.

"Same."

"As what?"

"As before. I'm fine. No regrets."

"None?"

"Not with my father. Don't worry, I've got a pile over you and Alex."

"So now it's me and Alex?" He smiled and nudged me again.

"Don't flatter yourself. You know what I meant."

A car pulled into the driveway. Andrew got out. He was wearing an open trench coat and a dress shirt and tie that had been loosened. His hair was ruffled and framed his face. He looked like a cross between Addison and Jared, with my mother's eyes. I wondered if he was nervous. At Addison's urging, I had called Andrew and invited him to the wake. I had also promised him I would tell Wendy and Jared.

Addison got up and shook Andrew's hand. Although they had met at the park, this was the first time they had acknowledged their connection.

The kitchen smelled like strong black coffee. Willard had brought his espresso maker. He said that aside from Wendy, it was the only thing he could not live without. He wrapped my palm around a hot mug of it when I came back in, "You look better holding this," he said. Wendy and Jared were taking the deli platters out of the refrigerator. Addison went into the living room to set up folding chairs. Andrew hung up his coat.

I looked at the people around me and wondered who they were. What made us a family? Certainly not a common experience, as each of us had a different story, and although we shared characters, the villain in mine might be the hero in Wendy's. Was it DNA? That invisible thread that made Wendy and I have the same patch of spider veins above our knees? What was the bond and when, if ever, did I feel it?

The last time I felt their hands in mine, my left in my father's and my right in my mother's, I was five. They were swinging me back and forth in the front yard. It was summer and almost dusk. Sheets and towels hung from the clothesline and were gently lifted by the cool rush of evening air sneaking up behind us. We laughed as they lifted me higher while they walked toward the house. I was so filled with love for them, I thought I would bleed from it. I was theirs, they were mine. We were connected.

By the time I was seven, I was afraid of many things, including storms. I should have been asleep. It was dark and quiet between the smack of thunder and searing flash of lightning. I was whimpering into my pillow, afraid to make a sound. "Come to me," Wendy called from across the room. In the quick snap of lightning, I saw her lifting her covers, patting the warm spot next to her. "Run," she said and I did. I covered the space between us in three jumps and landed in her arms. Our laughter muted the thunder.

At seventeen Jared carried me. He lifted me from the bushes and tried not to slip on the mud. I couldn't see, my eyes were so swollen. I reached for his cheek. It was wet. He was crying and saying how sorry he was. I didn't want to hold on but he made me. He told me I was going to be okay. He told me he was sorry. He held on when I didn't want to.

Addison and Diana placed the baby on my eighteen-year-old belly. He was so warm and I was so cold. He was slippery and gurgling and reaching for me with that half-fist. He didn't roll off; he knew how to balance himself on me. "Hello," I whispered, hoping he didn't know that I was really saying good-bye.

———

"Jared and Wendy," I said. No one heard me. My chest felt like hot stones were resting on both lungs. Although the coffee was warm in my hands, my lips were cold and stiff, as if the words would freeze into slivers of ice before they came out. "Jared, Wendy," I said again, louder. "I need to tell you something."

Alex was asleep when Addison and I got back to their house. Although I was hoarse from talking, I had one more thing I needed to do.

"I think you should wait until morning," Addison said. "You can stay here."

I could have dropped where I was standing and slept for five days. We had left Jared, Wendy, and Andrew sitting together, picking at the otherwise untouched deli platters. No one but the Igbys and Burt the mailman had shown up to pay their respects. I shocked the Igbys by introducing Andrew as my brother. They didn't believe me until I asked them to look at Addison and Jared and compare. Andrew was what you got when you mixed our genes. You got Alex too, but the Igbys may have known that all along.

Jared and Wendy did.

"Isn't it funny," Wendy said, out on the porch as I took a cigarette break, "that what you were good at was getting pregnant."

I was glad to see her spunk had returned. I had suspected, or rather, I had always known, that what made Wendy feel best about herself was knowing I was worse off. She wasn't much of a sister, and something told me she wouldn't be much of a mother either. Just because you want a child doesn't mean you deserve one.

"And drinking. Don't forget how good I am at that," I said. She took the cigarette from my mouth and sucked it down like she had been having an affair with smoking for years. She crossed her arms and looked out into the long, dark blanket of land in front of us.

Jared would have to sort out the paperwork, just as Addison would have to introduce Andrew to his, or rather, their, father. Addison and Andrew had promised to try to get the farm turned over to all of us. I had extracted some promises of my own.

"He loves me." I looked at her, not sure whom she was talking about. "Willard." I nodded. Wendy didn't give me back the cigarette so I lit another. "What was it like to give birth?"

"It was a long time ago."

"You remember. Tell me."

And so I did. And while we worked our way down to the last inhale, I told the story of my son's birth.

"You want a cup of tea? Decaf?" Addison was turning off the lights in the dining room and running through the habitual checklist of duties a homeowner does before he goes to bed. He looked good in his life, his house. I was glad for Alex. Glad he had had Diana to love him at the beginning and glad Addison had stepped in and carried on.

"No, I'm okay." My voice quivered as I watched him moving around me. I felt like I was visiting a life I could have had but didn't choose.

Addison walked over to the small hutch in the dining room and opened a drawer. "I have something for you," he said. He handed me a brown velvet pouch. "I've been holding on to these for a while."

I felt it before I knew for sure. It was my mother's pearls. The ones I lost the night we were together. I spilled them into my hand and smelled them. The rush of my mother's scent brought tears to my eyes.

Addison took them and put them on me. "So beautiful," he said. He smiled. "You and your mother, so beautiful."

After ten years of running I had arrived back where I started. In that garage apartment with Addison, feeling the magnitude of my own attraction. I had lost everything but this; it was still as vivid and intense as it had been then.

I followed him up the stairs and into his room, and without saying a word, we undressed and climbed into bed and met each other in the middle as if we had been doing that all along.

# Thirty-one

I THREW ADDISON OFF me like a heavy blanket that was suffocating me. The cold air mapped a chill along the perimeter of my body. Addison rolled onto his back, taking care not to touch me. We lay next to each other but not together, like a continent split by a tidal wave of memory. I was an island again.

I never got used to the ways my body betrayed me. When it was beaten it healed, when it was touched it responded without consideration of the consequences, and when it was raped I feared it had made life. A body's job is to protect the heart, not expose it, not to lead it places it could not hide.

There was no use in covering myself; I was naked.

"It still hurts," I said. Tears trickled into my ears.

Addison rolled toward me and dammed his body against mine. He brushed the hair away from my face and took my hand.

*He isn't who you think he is. . . .*

The sun wasn't up yet and neither were Alex or Addison. I slipped on my clothes and carried my shoes out to the porch before I put them on. My car had been in the driveway since I had turfed the lawn.

It started easily. I felt a surge of panic as I pulled out of the driveway and thought I saw a shadow in the garage window but realized it was probably the morning light.

There was only one place left for me to go and then I would be done with Wilton.

The roads were empty. Except for the occasional delivery truck, I had the town to myself. I drove past the Elks Lodge, where the dance was, and followed the same path my father had taken in his truck. I had never driven to Rucker's Ravine, but I knew the way.

My hands were clammy as they gripped the steering wheel. I smelled like Addison, that mix of sweat and oranges. I told myself it would protect me. I could still feel him inside me. The way he eased himself in and moved with me, every wave erasing the boundary that separated us. I floated in and out of myself, not me and not him, but something safe in between.

The rope bridge was still there but frayed. Tire tracks were frozen in the ground, and although it was impossible, I imagined they were from my father's truck. The leaves had abandoned the trees in the small woods, making it seem more like a closet of skeletons than a place where I could have hidden.

I walked to the edge of the ravine and stood staring out over to the other side and took a deep breath. I prayed for the guts to make it over.

I was looking for the sketchbook my father had thrown across, hoping some of it had survived. If I was going to tell my son who I was, I needed him to see the good part too.

I was outside my body, floating high above the ravine. Just like I did that night. I saw myself at the edge reaching for the thick rope knot that connected the bridge to an old tree trunk.

I had no fear of falling anymore. The wooden planks strung between the two rope railings were sparse, and in order to get on the bridge I would have to take a long stride forward. I gripped the rope on both sides and willed my foot onto the first plank. The bridge swayed in the wind as a plank on the other side wiggled loose. I thought about the book flying in the air, the gilded edges twinkling through the storm and landing somewhere over there. Somewhere safe, I hoped.

I moved slowly and focused on each step. The cold air stung my chapped hands and cut across my cheeks, like the rain that night.

I had to jump at the other side to land, as the boards were too flimsy to risk. My foot slipped on the smooth slope that led up to the grassy landing. The same place I fell before. This time I caught myself.

There were frozen footprints on the path to the meadow and, like the tire tracks, I wondered if the last two people who had been here were my father and me.

I searched the brittle grass, which had grown waist-high and flourished in spite of a winter filled with storms. As I trudged through half-frozen, muddy puddles and tried to imagine where the book might have landed, I began to realize how foolish it was to think it had survived.

Still I kept looking, hoping something remained. Although I had not sketched anything beyond a doodle since that night, I continued to experience my life in frames. I drew in my head, mapping out story lines and adventures. Drinking occupied my hands now. I couldn't do both.

Drinking. God, I wanted to be alone in a bed with a remote in one hand and a bottle in the other, holed up for the duration of the cold weather.

"Cat!" I heard a voice coming from the bridge. "Help!"

I turned toward the sound, wondering if I had imagined it. "Help!" It was clear and loud and very real. It sounded like a child. I started running.

Alex was halfway across the bridge, gripping the rope with both hands and struggling to stay still. His bike was turned over near the entrance on the other side as if he had jumped off and run across the bridge. He had been the shadow in the garage. He had followed me.

"I can't move," he yelled. His face was pale and open, as if he were frozen in place.

"Are you stuck?"

He shook his head.

"Hurt?"

"I'm going to fall. Oh, God, I'm going to fall."

My knees started shaking as I moved as close as I could to the bridge. I wiped my hands on my jeans and reached out to him. "No, you're not. Look at me."

He looked down.

"Alex, look at me." I was pointing at my eyes. He focused on me. I nodded. "Good. Now think about taking a step toward me."

"I can't. Oh, God, Dad is going to kill me." He turned toward his bike as if Addison were standing there.

"Alex, me." He looked back.

"You have to come for me. I'm scared."

The bridge swayed. Alex screamed. My legs buckled as if I were the one on the bridge struggling to stay still, as if I were Alex and he were me or we were the same. I did not feel my feet, only my pulse beating in my throat, as I leaped to the first plank and made my way toward him.

"Stay still," I said. "I'm coming."

He was whimpering but holding steady with his eyes locked on mine as I worked my way toward him inch by inch. The bridge was rocking wildly. The ropes were creaking as they grew taut from our weight. I looked down.

"Me!" Alex said.

Our eyes connected as I moved more swiftly. When I reached him, he let go of the ropes and wrapped his arms around my waist. I felt the bridge give way, or was I imagining it? I gripped the ropes and tried to maneuver myself into a more steady position. "Thank you," he said into my belly, his head resting between my breasts.

"Don't thank me yet; we have to get back."

I talked him across. When his foot almost slipped through a plank, I told him to put his feet on top of mine and I walked us to solid ground.

"Okay. We're good now," I said, trying to pry him off. He

wouldn't let go. He hugged me tightly and cried. I could feel him breathing against me. He smelled like oranges and talcum powder. I stroked his hair and said, "Shhh," like Addison had done for me the night before.

"I don't want you to go," he said.

I thought about saying I wasn't going anywhere, but that was a lie and there had been too many of those. I pushed him away from me and wiped the tears off his cheeks with my shirtsleeve.

"You okay?"

He nodded.

"Good. That was a bad idea."

"I followed you."

"I figured."

"You're leaving, aren't you?"

"Yeah. For a while."

I picked up his bike and pushed it to my car as we walked. I opened the back door, and with his help we got it in the backseat. We got in and I started the car and put the heat on high. We sat together, watching the bridge twist in the wind. I turned the heat down. Alex and I were both sitting with our palms open and resting on our knees with our index fingers curled slightly.

"I'm your mother," I said finally.

He nodded.

"Something bad happened to me here. That's why I left."

"Was it me?" he asked.

I finally knew the answer.

"No," I said, as I began to cry. "It had nothing to do with you."

He reached for my hand. I looked down and rubbed my thumb against his coffee-colored birthmark.

"I miss Diana," he said.

"Me too."

## THIRTY-TWO

IT WAS THE AFTERNOON of my son's eleventh birthday. I was leaning against the Grover Cleveland statue and waiting for school to
let out. It was one of those luscious spring days when the sun's light
makes everything appear crisper, more focused.

I had been sober for one year, twelve days, and eighteen hours.
The waistband on my jeans was cutting a ridge in my once flat, and
now rounder, stomach. Without alcohol I needed something, so
food comforted me. Double Stuf Oreos took the edge off. I carried
a dozen or so around with me in a ziplock bag in my purse next to a
copy of my mother's note—her message in a bottle cast from an island of regret.

*He isn't who you think he is. . . .*

My palms were sweaty, and I had that odd, new feeling of not
quite fitting in my own skin. One of the downsides to being sober is
you get to feel uncomfortable most of the time.

I'd been gone for ten years.

I knew I would leave Wilton and Alex again. What I didn't know
is if I would ever come back. Addison was right; if I was to go I
needed to get gone, and if I were to stay? I wasn't sure how to do that.

Alex and I sat in the car for hours that day at Rucker's Ravine and
talked about his life. He told me he missed me, even though he
never knew me. "Does that sound stupid?" he asked.

"No," I said.

We went to breakfast at the Omega diner and discovered our mutual love for onion rings and chocolate milkshakes. I began to feel woefully incapable of sustaining a presence in his life. I wanted to drink more than I wanted to be with him.

I called Addison from the pay phone by the restroom and asked him to come get us. I didn't tell him he was only taking Alex until he got there.

Addison wasn't surprised. He acted as if he had known all along that this was how it would go. Instead of feeling relieved, I was disappointed. Perhaps I had hoped he would fight for me to stay. Alex wasn't as accommodating, and insisted on understanding why I had to go.

"I'm not a good person," I said, as he turned away to hide his tears.

"How can you say that? You're my mother," he said. I didn't understand that in his mind, if I was not a good person, then neither was he. It wouldn't have mattered to explain that I was sure he had more of Addison in him than me and more of me than my father.

"That's not what she means," Addison said. "She means she doesn't feel good. She needs to get better."

Alex looked at me as if I had a big tumor coming out of my head that he hadn't noticed before.

"I haven't been myself for a long time," I said, as I brushed my hand through Alex's flannel-soft hair. It would have been easy to love a boy with hair that smooth.

In the end, Addison and Alex let me go. Alex made me promise to come back as soon as I felt better. "There are worse things than leaving," Addison said, as he walked me to the car. I wondered what he meant. The only thing worse than leaving is coming back?

Alex stood rigidly by Addison's truck like a good soldier and watched me leave for the second time in his short life.

I drove through the night and found myself in Pittsburgh just as the sun was coming up. I found my way to Diana's old house and fell asleep in my car. A neighbor told me where she was buried and made me a hot cup of coffee to go.

I told Diana everything that day. I started standing up, and as I got deeper into the story, I sat on her grave and leaned against her headstone and talked until I was hoarse. I found words to describe what had happened that night. Words I had never spoken to a living soul. Words I could only say to the woman who had mothered my child and who tried to mother me. I needed her to know there was a reason I did what I did.

I got halfway back to the car before I realized I had not said the one thing I needed to say. I went back and kneeled next to her headstone and got close to the earth and whispered, "Thank you." Maybe it was the wind, or the way the branch of the oak tree that stood guard beside her grave gave way, or maybe it was the ground beneath me releasing the cold, but I felt a shift, a slow turning.

I checked into the Viking Motel out by the airport with a case of bourbon and a phone number for Domino's Pizza. I stripped down to a T-shirt and panties and crawled into bed with the remote and a bottle. This was how I treated myself. It was my reward.

My purse was filled with my mother's papers. There was more to know. Questions that needed answers; children who needed to know their parents—Andrew, Alex, and possibly all of us. There was nothing to run from anymore except who I became, and that was nothing.

I lost count of days and bottles. I drifted in and out of a boozy haze, with my dreams and the TV blending into a hyperreality. I rolled over onto the remote and let the world click by. I didn't want to be alone, but I didn't care what kept me company.

I woke up in a small bed in Mercy Hospital with a pudgy-faced nun holding my hand and smiling as if I were the baby Jesus.

"You came back to us," she said.

My throat was sore from having my stomach pumped. I had

been asleep for three days. I had no memory of leaving the motel or of anything else.

"Do you know who you are?" she said, as she brought a cup of water to my lips. The sun beamed through the window, bathing her in a halo of amber light. I was in a white nightgown, lying on crisp linen sheets. The air smelled sweet, like blueberry muffins baking in a kitchen down the hall. Everything felt focused, sharp, and unreal. I was too alive to not be dead.

"Do you know who you are?" the nun asked again, after I sipped cool water.

My thoughts scrambled in search of the best way to answer. I am alone. I am Alex Rucker. I am a drunk. I am a daughter who was raped by her father. I am a sister. I am a half sister. I am my mother's daughter. I am a woman. My mind scrolled the list, trying to find the one that defined me the most. The nun lifted me by the shoulders and put a pillow under my back so I could sit up. She waited patiently.

I began to cry. She took my hand.

"I am a mother," I said.

Sister Anna helped me find a red gilded sketchbook just like the one Addison got for me so many years ago. I bought two.

I started drawing again as I went through rehab. I became as dependent on the pen as I had been on booze. I drew the adventures of Kitty Kat from memory and picked up her story where I thought it had ended in a soggy pit on the bad side of Rucker's Ravine. I got her away from the Hand and into a whole new set of adventures with a nemesis called Jack D.

During the day I rested, went to meetings, and stayed with Sister Anna in her small house behind railroad tracks that led nowhere. I ate what she cooked and got back my taste for food. At night, I sat on the cot in her attic, where I slept and filled the book with the images in my head, and slowly drew myself back to life.

Anna insisted I stay with her until I knew where I was going. I told her I might never know; she said I was closer than I thought. I wrote Addison a letter to let him know I was okay and to thank him for being the father of my son. The days of doubting were coming to an end for me.

We went to visit Diana again when I made ninety days without a drink. I told Anna what happened as we planted white petunias in front of Diana's headstone. Anna listened with ease and lack of judgment. When I was done, she put her small garden shovel down and embraced me. "You poor child," she whispered. "You needed a mother's love."

What I heard was, "Your poor child needs a mother's love."

When I told her that later in the car she laughed. "That's God's way," she said.

I rolled my eyes and asked her if we could stop for pizza. There's only so much healing and God shit I could take in a day.

When I hit a year sober, Anna loaned me the money to go back to Wilton. I had saved some money from the part-time job Anna got me at the hospital helping patients with their paperwork, but it wasn't enough. She took me shopping for new clothes, as my old ones were too small. We also picked out paper and ribbon for the other gilded book. On my last night she taught me how to wrap a gift.

I packed the clothes and few possessions I had collected over the year into a small duffel bag I bought at the hospital thrift store. I was wearing my mother's pearls, as I had every day since Addison gave them back to me. Checking the dresser one last time, I found the ziplock bag of documents I had gotten from my mother's safe-deposit box. In the frenzy, I had stopped at the deed, never looking at what was underneath. I was carrying them in my purse when I was found in the hotel. I remembered them in the hospital and Anna assured me they were in safekeeping at her house. I had thought of the documents a few times during my recovery but had not followed up. Roger, one of my recovery counselors, always said, "It's not the answer to your problems you are looking for, it's the courage to face them."

My mother's note was on the top—I pulled it out and smelled it, trying one more time to make some part of her come alive so I could ask her myself what she meant.

*He isn't who you think he is. . . .*

A year later, it could still mean so many things. Andrew, my father, Addison; but I believed then as I do now that she meant my son. She was right, he was so much more.

*I am not who I thought I was.*

I sorted through the papers; most of them were the legal documents: her Social Security card, the family's birth certificates, and a few photos—all of them of her children, including one of Andrew as a baby. At the bottom of the pile was an unopened manila envelope addressed to me from Diana, postmarked around the time of her death.

Anna called up to me to see if I wanted a cup of tea. My voice broke when I said yes, as I felt a rush of unexpected emotion. Another letter from the grave; what was up with these women?

Downstairs Anna rustled around as I unclasped the envelope and broke through the seal of tape around the edge. I pulled out a set of papers with a note clipped to the top. It was her round, loopy handwriting. I remembered it from the to-do lists she used to leave me, written on her notepads that had "Diana McKenzie" printed in bold, plain letters at the top.

*Sweetie—*
*Thought you might want to know this at some point.*
*I figured you would get home eventually, so I sent it there.*
*Consider this my offering for a happy life.*
*Love you always,*
*Diana*

I had a flash of memory reading the last line: Diana swabbing my mouth while I was in labor. I unclipped the note from the documents.

At first glance I thought she was sending me Alex's medical

records. The heading on the front page confirmed what kind of record it was. Diana had done a paternity test.

The letter from the lab confirmed that the "alleged father, Addison James Watkins, cannot be excluded" as the biological father of Alexander McKenzie Watkins. Farther down it indicated that there was a 99.99 percent probability.

The report was dated a few weeks after Alex was born. She had swabbed Addison as well.

A photograph dropped out between the sheets of paper. It was the one she took of me and Alex the day of his arrival. I look so young and so . . . I started to cry.

The next morning, I got up before dawn to avoid saying goodbye, but Anna was waiting by the door with a packed lunch and a Bible. She held my hand as we walked to the car and I let her.

Before I drove off she thanked me for telling her my story. "It helps," she said. It was then I realized I had never asked her about her life. I hadn't even cared. She must have sensed this small recognition, and before I could ask she said, "He's in jail and the baby is in heaven." She made the sign of the cross and wished me well.

I found Jared in an apartment complex in a small suburb of Columbus. His wife gave me the directions. "We aren't together anymore," she said. She didn't seem that sad about it. The carved oak door she held open dwarfed her. When she spoke, her voice echoed in the cavernous entrance hall. She was blond and fair and thin, and had the air of someone who used to be pretty and was waiting for it to come back.

"Tell him he's late with the check," she called to me as I made my way down the brick path that led away from a house that looked like the giant's castle from *Jack and the Beanstalk*.

I found Jared floating on a raft in the indoor pool that was one of the amenities of his condo complex. His eyes were closed and his hands were resting at his sides, like my mother's were the day Andrew unzipped her bag. Jared's body was softer, less chiseled.

"You're late with the check," I said.

He fell off his raft and went under. I laughed and handed him a towel.

"Holy crap, Cat," he said as he lifted himself out. "You scared the shit out of me."

"That's my job."

Jared rubbed the towel through his hair like he did as a teenager coming out of the bathroom trailing steam behind him.

"You look different."

"I colored my hair," I said, as I sat on the end of a chaise and watched him dry off. He put on a terry robe and slid on flip-flops. Jared's eyes took an inventory of me.

"No, it's something else," he said.

"I'm fatter."

"Yeah, who isn't?" He pinched an inch of flab on his belly. "What the hell are you doing here? Is someone else dead?"

"No. I was passing through and thought I'd . . ."

Before I could finish, Jared took me in his arms and hugged me so hard he lifted me off the ground.

"I don't care why, just that you're here." Jared held on long after I landed. His arms pulled me close to his chest, which was damp and smelled like chlorine mixed with ginger. His skin was cool and the color of white peaches. I fit in Jared's arms the way Alex fit in mine, like human puzzle pieces.

I stayed with Jared in his bachelor apartment in Columbus for a few days on my way to Wilton. I showed him the letters and we talked a little about the past. He told me he had kept in touch with Wendy and Andrew and Addison. He was in the process of getting a divorce; he said losing Mom and Dad had made his marriage seem pointless. "Ever feel like you're running and you're not sure if it's away from or toward something?"

I nodded. "The thing is, there is always something to get away from. If you keep looking back you can't see what you might be heading toward."

"Something good?" he said, as if I knew.

"I don't know. I think we get to decide that for ourselves," I said.

Wendy moved back to the farm with Willard to live with Andrew as they prepared for their daughter to arrive. Andrew had convinced them to adopt and to come back to Wilton. Andrew had gone to California to meet his father, and while he did not get a fairy tale reunion, Jared Watkins acknowledged Andrew as his son. Jared showed Andrew a letter my mother had sent to him the day she killed herself, asking Jared to turn the farm over to her children. Jared respected her wishes and turned the farm over to us. My mother's death had righted a good deal of wrongs after all. Andrew had found his father at last, and although on some level I'm sure he was a disappointment, at least he knew where he came from.

The school bell rang and the doors burst open with screaming middle schoolers. I shifted the shopping bag with his birthday present to my other hand as I scanned the crowd for my son. I thought about the years I spent wondering if I would be able to pick him out of a crowd, if I would know him easily. The better question would have been, would he have known me?

His backpack appeared taller than he was as I saw him bounding out the door with a dark-haired girl. She was trying to ignore him, but, like his father, he was hard to resist. She smiled before she pushed him away. He laughed.

I waved and he saw me. I was afraid he might run in the other direction or flip me the bird or turn away, but he was not me. He came toward me instead and smiled shyly.

"Dad said you were coming back," he said. "Are you better?"

"I'm getting there. Happy birthday," I said, handing him the bag.

"You remembered? How did you know?"

"I was there when you were born," I said.

"Oh, yeah." We laughed. "Can I open it?"

"Wait for Dad. He's coming." Addison had been waiting by his car at my request. We had agreed I would do this on my own.

"Dad's here too?" he said, as if he could not imagine a universe where such things could happen.

I pointed behind him as Addison rushed up and snatched him in his arms. "Happy birthday. You like your present?"

"Dad!" Alex hit him in embarrassment. "You promised you wouldn't say anything."

"Say what?" I asked.

"Alex asked for you for his birthday."

I felt a rush of something flood my chest. This was the old sign that it was time for a drink, but I had learned a new trick in rehab that I was still practicing. I learned how to breathe. I took a deep one as I felt my chest open up to a strange emotion I suspected was close to joy.

"Are you sure you wouldn't have preferred a new mitt?" I said, joking.

He laughed. "Well, I do need one."

Addison looked at me and smiled and I felt that flood again. This time when I breathed, I felt the urge to touch him. I held back; there were still mountains to climb before I got there.

Alex opened the present and loved the book and set of pens.

"Your dad gave me a book exactly like this when we first met."

"This is cool."

"I started it for you," I said. "Open it."

On the first two pages I had sketched out the story of his birth and included drawings of Addison and Diana. I put in as much detail as I could.

As we walked to the car he looked at the captions and laughed at the exaggerated way I had Addison's eyes popping out of his head when he came out. "Dad, see how funny you look," he said.

"That's pretty accurate. I was freaked out," Addison said, ruffling Alex's hair.

"Were you?" Alex said to me.

"For about ten years," I said.

"But you're not anymore, right?"

"I'm working on it, kid," I said, and without thinking, I put my arms around him and hugged him. He fit perfectly in my arms.

Alex looked back at the book and got to the end of the second page and turned it to a blank one. "Ahh . . . tell me how it ends," he said, as Addison opened the car door for me.

"I can't. It's your story now."

## ACKNOWLEDGMENTS

Writing this book has been one of the great adventures of my life. I am truly grateful to everyone who helped me along the way, including those cited here and others I am sure to forget. Thanks to my agent, Jean Naggar, and everyone on her team at the Jean V. Naggar Literary Agency, Inc. In addition to believing in Cat and helping this story find a home, she has been a gentle and encouraging guide into the world of publishing. Thanks to my editors, Jane von Mehren and Porscha Burke, who brought great passion and care to the story and helped me find its final shape, and to everyone at Random House who has worked hard to bring this story to you. Special thanks to all the readers over the years, including those in writing groups and workshops, and to Ivone DeOliveira for her proofreading help. Thanks to Christie Cox for dropping everything and helping me with copyedits, and for believing so fiercely in the book; to Lester and Harvey Pyle, who showed me life on a farm; to Gwyn Cready, for always believing my stories (even the one about being cloned); to my brother Patrick, who took a chance and read an American author; to Beth, Sara, Caroline, and Emily Coyne and Sophia and Giuseppe Scorcia, for their love and support; to Gina, Marc, Christopher, and Matthew Mehalakes for sharing their lives with me and giving me a beautiful place to write. Thanks to my sister, Tami, for her unwavering and unconditional faith in me; to Donna Alleluia for her friendship; to Catherine Racette for listening; to Frank Polistena for his support; and to Laura Josephs for her guidance.

Finally, a special thanks to the women survivors who gifted me with their stories. I am in awe of their courage and fortitude.

# THE LAST BRIDGE

Teri Coyne

A Reader's Guide

# A CONVERSATION WITH TERI COYNE

Random House Reader's Circle had the chance to sit down with Teri Coyne to speak with her about her novel, her love of literature, and her intense, vibrant characters.

**Random House Reader's Circle:** When you wrote this novel, did you expect people to connect with your characters so strongly?

**Teri Coyne:** I hoped readers would connect with the characters, especially with Cat, but I didn't expect the reaction I have gotten. I have heard from women and men of different ages and backgrounds that relate to her struggles. Some have even told me their experiences were similar to hers. The response has been really strong.

**RHRC:** Who were the first characters you worked on for this novel? Where did you start telling this story?

**TC:** Everything started with Cat; her voice told me the story and as details emerged in the writing, so did additional characters. The characters that came to life quickly were Addison, the mother and father, and little Alex. The story started with the mother's suicide; although the book went through many revisions, the opening of the novel never changed.

**RHRC:** What was your inspiration for *The Last Bridge*? Where did you come up with the idea for the story?

**TC:** The story came to me as an image of a woman taping garbage bags to the walls of a farmhouse kitchen and then a voice that said,

"Two days after my father had a stroke my mother shot herself in the head." I don't know where the image or the line came from, but it was powerful. I thought it might be the beginning of a short story, but it soon became clear I was in the grip of a novel. Looking back, I think the story was a way for me to explore the idea of choice over experience and the impact of abuse on individuals and families.

**RHRC:** How long did it take for you to complete the novel? How did you know where it ended?

**TC:** I worked on the novel for over ten years. Once I knew I was writing a novel I realized I had no idea how to do it! I took a lot of workshops and found a few mentors to help me shape the story. I also had moments of doubt and felt overwhelmed by the power of the story and had to work through all that. As for the ending, I always knew it would address one of the central questions of the book—are we the product of our experiences or of our choices? I knew Cat would make a choice, and I knew the book would end on a hopeful note.

**RHRC:** And then what? Did you know that you had something special here? How did you go about getting *The Last Bridge* published?

**TC:** I knew I had a story that needed to be told, and I believed I would find an audience for it and have it published, *but* I also understood that the book had to be the absolute best it could be before I tried to get it published—that's another reason why it took so long to finish. Just as I knew I had to learn how to write a novel, I knew I needed to learn about the business of being published. These are two different things, and I try to keep them separate. I was prepared for the process to take a while, as I needed to find an agent first. I made a list of agents I thought would represent me well and started at the beginning. I figured it would take me at least a year.

The first agent I queried wanted to represent me, and soon after, I sold the book. So the whole process took about six months—from getting an agent to selling the book. Wait, ten years and six months!

**RHRC:** How did you find the editorial process? What was that like for you as a first-time author?

**TC:** After working on many drafts of *The Last Bridge* and being in workshops and getting an enormous amount of feedback, I was ready for the editorial process and was relieved I had the skills to go through the changes. The most important thing I learned through the process was to stay open to feedback and trust your vision of the story. You also have to trust your editors. If they believe in your story, they are trying to make it better.

**RHRC:** Were there any parts of the story that you were surprised to receive edits on? Was there anything you found yourself having to fight for?

**TC:** The best part of the experience was knowing from the start what the issues were with the manuscript. I had a conference call with my editors before we accepted the offer, and every issue was discussed, so my eyes were wide open. The biggest issue was the handling of the ending and the importance of revealing a key piece of information. This was the most difficult part of the editorial process, as—while I understood the need to do it—I was not sure how I was going to handle it. Once I was clear what was needed, I was given the freedom to address it as I wanted, and I have to admit, I think all the editorial changes made the book stronger. Editors are editors for a reason! I appreciated the help.

**RHRC:** How would you describe *The Last Bridge*? Do you think it's a love story? A tragedy? A mystery?

**TC:** I'm not sure I could ever write a book that wasn't a love story of some kind, as the nature of love is at the core of what I want to explore as a writer.

One of my readers sent me a note that said what they related to most about Cat was how she was surrounded by love but could not see it for most of the story. Everyone in the story is wounded in a critical way; love is the power that heals some of them.

**RHRC:** Which other writers inspire you? Are there any books you would recommend to readers who enjoyed this work?

**TC:** Oh gosh, this is always a hard question, as there are so many writers I admire. I really like Lionel Shriver and would recommend *We Need To Talk About Kevin* if you want to dig into another dark exploration of what makes someone a parent. I also love Sarah Waters for the way she structures stories and manages to surprise me all the time; *Fingersmith* is one of my favorites. I loved *Olive Kitteridge* by Elizabeth Strout, a great example of how the impact of the story can sneak up on you. I have to stop or else I will fill pages. . . .

**RHRC:** Cat's story has so many themes: family secrets, the nature of love, what makes a woman a mother, running away from the past, battling addictions. Was it challenging to determine which of these things you wanted to explore and which characters would express them?

**TC:** Yes. I guess that's too short of an answer! It was very challenging but extremely important for me to weave all those themes together. People's lives are complicated, women's lives even more so. There is no addiction without trauma (at least in my experience), no present without the influence of the past, and absolutely no perfect family. Everyone has a secret—in fact, most of us have many. Whether they are experiences or feelings, we hide more than we re-

veal, but being silent does not mean we are not ruled by those secrets.

As a writer, I want to know what those secrets are, I want to
peel away the layers and say what is not said. At the beginning of
the story it appears that being an alcoholic is the biggest problem
Cat has, but slowly as the past reveals itself we see it is more an expression of a deeper trauma and a way to numb her pain.

RHRC: Can you tell us a bit about which characters were the hardest for you to write, and why? And the easiest?

TC: The hardest character to write was the father, and the hardest
scene was the one on the bridge. While it would have been easier to
make him completely despicable, I didn't want him to be one di-
mensional. I wanted to show how he, too, was a product of his experiences, even if we don't know what all of them were. Still, he has
violent and damaging compulsions, and it was hard to bring that to
life.

I loved Ruth Igby—I know she is a minor character, but she is
so real to me and so annoying in a great, neighborlike way. One of
my favorite scenes was the one where Cat goes to dinner at the
Igbys'.

RHRC: And in closing, what are you looking forward to the most
now that the book is finished?

TC: I am really looking forward to getting the paperback version of
*The Last Bridge* into the hands of more readers and book clubs. I
love connecting with readers and hearing their reactions and stories. I am also looking forward to finishing my second novel, which
is almost done.

# READING GROUP
# QUESTIONS AND TOPICS FOR DISCUSSION

1. Who is the "he" in Cat's mother's note, *"He isn't who you think he is . . ."*? What do you think Maureen Rucker meant to tell her daughter in her note?

2. Why do you think Cat's mother committed suicide when she did?

3. After watching their father beat Cat at the dining room table, Wendy says to her, "Cat, if he says no dessert just say no" (62). Do you think Wendy always took their father's side? How much do you think Wendy knew about her father's abusing Cat? Do you think she was also abused?

4. Upon introducing Willard to Cat, Wendy says, "Be nice. . . . He's hard of hearing. . . . Not circumcised either" (18). Why do you think Wendy is with Willard? What role do you think he plays in her life?

5. Addison, expressing his disappointment and anger at his own father's betrayal, says to Cat, "Your dad isn't like my dad. . . . At least your dad stayed with the family. At least he takes care of you guys. He loves you" (96). What similarities do you see between Addison's and Cat's feelings about their fathers? How do you think those similarities impact their closeness to each other?

6. How do you define the word "parent" and the role a parent is supposed to play in his or her children's lives? What makes a person a parent?

7. Why do you think Andrew chose to tell Cat who he was, but did not reach out to Jared or Wendy—the seemingly more stable siblings—with his revelation?

8. What do you think Cat's father really thought of her? Do you think he ever spoke to anyone else about her or anyone else in his family? What types of things do you think he would say?

9. Cat is a talented artist, as is her son. What role does her art play in her life? In her son's life? Throughout the novel? What do you think her art is meant to reflect? How do you express yourself or find clarity during times of stress or hardship?

10. When Sister Anna asks Cat if she knows who she is (218), Cat runs through a list of roles: "I am Alex Rucker. I am a drunk. I am a daughter who was raped by her father. I am a sister. I am a half sister. I am my mother's daughter. I am a woman." She finally lands on the one that defines her most, saying, "I am a mother." Why does this role define her the most? Why do you think she was able to admit that? What role defines you most in your life? Has it changed over the years, and if so, why?

11. What do you think happens between Cat, Addison, and Alex after the story ends?

12. What instances of love do you see throughout this novel? What characters do you think demonstrate their love for each other most clearly? Who experiences the most trouble in this area?

13. Alex carries her entire life around in her purse. What types of things do you carry with you every day, things you can't live without or items you would take with you if you were fleeing a fire?

14. Alex spends ten years drinking heavily and running from her tormenting thoughts and memories. Are you comfortable with the thoughts that creep into your head in the still moments of your life?

15. One of the Ruckers' biggest secrets was Mr. Rucker's horrific abuse, and the possibly tragic consequences of his actions. What other secrets did members of the family keep from one another, or from their neighbors? Are you or someone in your family harboring a secret? What would the impact be if it ever came out?

16. In this novel, Cat is forced to go back to her childhood home and face the most horrific elements of her past—from her parents' home to walking the plank—in order to even have a chance at a healthy future. If you had to go back and face an incident from your past, what would it be? What are your greatest fears about it?

PHOTO: © MICHAEL J. RICHTER

TERI COYNE is an alumna of New York University. In addition to writing fiction, Teri wrote and performed stand-up comedy for many years. *The Last Bridge* is her first novel. She divides her time between New York City and the North Fork of Long Island. Visit her website at www.tericoyne.com.

# Join the Random House Reader's Circle to enhance your book club or personal reading experience.

## Our FREE monthly e-newsletter gives you:

- Sneak-peek excerpts from our newest titles

- Exclusive interviews with your favorite authors

- Special offers and promotions giving you access to advance copies of books, our free "Book Club Companion" quarterly magazine, and much more

- Fun ideas to spice up your book club meetings: creative activities, outings, and discussion topics

- Opportunities to invite an author to your next book club meeting

- Anecdotes and pearls of wisdom from other book group members . . . and the opportunity to share your own!

To sign up, visit our website at
**www.randomhousereaderscircle.com**

**When you see this seal on the outside, there's a great book club read inside.**